CURIOSITY AND
THE CAT

CURIOSITY AND THE CAT

Martin Treanor

Fire Hornet Codex

FIRE HORNET CODEX - a **DRPZ Publishing** imprint

FireHornetCodex.com

Come hither hence, hark heed me tell,

O' feral folk, in shadows dwell,

'Mid twisted thorn, and buckled branch,

Bide they who yen the merry dance.

PROLOGUE – Concerning a girl

Like many an unsettling tale told by a hearth fire or in a dark wood, this one begins with a curious child. A peculiar, precocious young girl whom I had the pleasant good fortune to observe on a couple of occasions before that day. The first, as she attempted to loop a plastic ring over a wooden peg. One eye clenched shut. Her tongue poking from the side of her mouth. Her forehead creased so tightly her freckles all but merged into one.

It might be said that, from the Jolly Roger pendulum ride to Richie Rabbit's Rockin' Ring-toss, the amusements of London's Notting Hill Summer Fair held the power to rouse the desires of any excitable seven-year-old. Yet, this curious child seemed to burst with extra eagerness. It was as though the sun above enhanced her zeal; seven hundred million tonnes of unbridled power, exploding every second to be absorbed by this imp of a girl. It radiated from her skin. It energised the space around her. In those few seconds, she had the capacity to change all, to be anything she wanted to be. And yet, imbued with the ability to achieve the greatest of things, this bundle of brightness seemed to settle for the simplest of dreams: to loop a plastic ring over a peg. To achieve this one, precise, and finite task.

Now, who could fail but be captivated by such dedication?

I encountered her again, a month later to the day but the child a whole digit older in years. She danced among the garden bluebells; her yellow dress glowing in the sunshine. Her copper-coloured hair flowing on the breeze. A smile stretching from one ear to the other, as though nothing could dent her enthusiasm. This sunburst gleamed, as she had one month earlier at the summer fair. Her zest for life manifested in the rosiness of her cheeks, as she spun like a dancer on a stage, caught in the spotlight of her ambition, concentrating on the specific details of each and every step.

Again, I thought to myself, only the hardest heart could ignore such commitment.

Then I saw her this time, soaked wet and sitting in a muddy puddle beneath a boarded-up window. Her arms slumped by her sides. Her palms facing upwards. She appeared a dejected soul, clad in a soggy white ballet tutu. Blood-splattered. Messed with grime. And two gossamer fairy wings drooping from either shoulder, the wire supports warped out of shape where she leaned back against the ivy and crumbling brick.

Her once vibrant freckles appeared marred and, in some ways, debased by the vacant look in her eyes. Her stare fixed upon some imaginary spot below the rain-soaked pavement. People passed. Most turned their heads in alarm. Some good sorts even stopped to enquire about her wellbeing, sympathetic to the bedraggled figure with eyes gazing out from beneath pendulous ropes of sodden hair.

Overhead, the grey late evening clouds became one.

A thunderclap shook the sky and drizzle became a downpour.

The onlookers gave up their pursuits, of gawking, of concern, and scurried away into doorways and sheltered corners, clinging to their umbrellas, pressing their chins to their chests.

For her part, as the deluge crashed down, the girl just stared at her spot on the ground.

Her thoughts entranced by a vision of a distant realm that only she could see; brought to existence by the blood dripping from her fingertips.

ONE – Concerning a cat and Curiosity

Sometimes, Curiosity Portland loathed her life. Her most descriptive words being: *boring, repetitive. Feeling alone.* And yet, she also adored the buzz of being so young. *The possibility. The wonder. The excitement of discovering new things.*

And today was her eighth birthday.

Her mother took her on a shopping trip to Westbourne Grove. Not to get something birthday-worthy and nice, though. They went to buy her new shoes. Just that. New shoes. And, as her mother dragged her past *Candy Canes*, Curiosity fantasised over the delights within. Because *Candy Canes* had sweets. It had floor to ceiling sweets. They came in tall, cylindrical, glass jars. They came in tubes and packets. They came in large, crinkly, paper bags called *Lucky Bags*. Curiosity adored Lucky Bags. Most of the time, they also contained a toy to build: a little house, or a red car with funny-face stickers, or maybe a puzzle, where silver balls had to be rolled into the clown's eyes. On the rare occasions that Mummy bought her one, she liked to postpone opening it until she got home. She wanted to savour the expectation, to defer the delight of unveiling the unknown.

At the mere sight of a Lucky Bag, a smile burst upon

her face, because the sweets might sate her tooth, but the toys taxed her mind. If truth be told, the whole of Westbourne Grove taxed Curiosity's mind with too many things to ponder: from the ornate buildings with carvings above their doors to the lure of dark basements.

She was infatuated. She was enlivened.

Birthday or not, however, there would be no Lucky Bag today.

There never was when Mummy was in one of her disorganised states.

Two doors down from *Elegant Mobiles* – where her mother had just upgraded her phone – *Fancy Fruits* made the coolest and the absolute coldest smoothies on the planet. Even Curiosity's daddy conceded their *awesomeness* (her word) and he was a serious person, taught serious stuff to students at a university. Archaeology. She also assumed his seriousness was one of the reasons why he didn't live with her and Mummy anymore.

Well, that and *his obsession with his latest female acquisition* (Mummy's words).

On scorching July days such as this day, a Coconut-milk Chill helped the summer holidays taste like heaven. Or what Curiosity reckoned heaven might taste like if there was one, and smoothies were on the menu.

But Curiosity reckoned there would be no smoothie today either.

There never was when Mummy was in one of her disorganised states.

Back out on the street, seemingly unsatisfied with

whatever route they had taken, Mummy made an about turn and walked – *marched* – them both back past *Elegant Mobiles* and into *Bright as Buttons*. She seemed agitated. As if the decision to come into the shop had caused her a degree of stress. There was a slight tremble in her hands and the smell of stale wine on her breath. Then, she smiled. It looked strange on her face.

'Because it's your birthday,' she said, 'I thought we could pop in here for five minutes before we go to the shoe shop. But only five minutes.'

Curiosity replied with a curt, 'Okay,' before dashing to a familiar corner.

Bright as Buttons sold ribbons and needlecraft things, along with fabric to make blouses and dresses. Not as if anyone in Curiosity's home ever made blouses or dresses. Making clothes was for working people to do, and her mummy didn't even wear those types of clothes anyway. She wore slim, mummy skirts, silk blouses, and Chanel jackets, white with blue trim, sometimes blue with white trim. As for Curiosity; she wouldn't be seen dead in the dainty dress. Normal girls wore dainty dresses.

'Why won't you wear a nice dress?' her mother might snap. So often Curiosity found it tiresome. 'It's ladylike to wear a dress. The girls in our family are cursed with unsightly freckles. And this god-awful, unfashionably, curly, auburn hair. So, we must work all the harder to achieve the perfect look.'

'I like jeans,' Curiosity might sometimes reply, if she

saw any point in answering and her words got through her mother's mulishness.

On the odd occasion they did get through, and her mother would answer with, 'Jeans are for tidying your bedroom. They're not for when we're out in public. We can't do much about your freckles, as yet. You are a little too young for cosmetics. We could clip your hair. But you always create such a stink.'

Curiosity usually backed away from her mother at this point, setting a protective hand on her head. *Get off,* she would snap, within her mind. *There's no way you're touching my hair. I like it long. And it's not auburn. It's red.*

'Why do you have to be so damned awkward?' her mother would drone on. Each new diatribe diverging little to the last. 'Wearing a tasteful dress is what nice girls do. As ladies, we must always present ourselves.' Mummy tended to illustrate this point by running her hands over her super-slim midriff and waist. She would then take a quick squint in any opportune shop window to check her makeup, before patting down her hair, always tied into a tidy bun.

Curiosity also thought it a bit hypocritical how her mother's *present ourselves* didn't apply to her breath stinking of last night's wine.

Anyway, regardless of what Mummy thought or wished; Curiosity Portland wore jeans. She wore black jeans in the cold weather, and knee length, black shorts on hot summer days such as today, along with washed-out, charity-shop t-shirts – like the skull emblazoned one she was wearing at present – which her mother hated and, therefore, Curiosity loved to bits.

She would spew her guts up before anything pink saw its way onto her body.

She did like flowers, though. And anything that grew.

As well as material and accessories, *Bright as Buttons* sold buttons. The hint came with the name. Some of them were tiny charm bells and, if Mummy deemed the occasion convenient, she conceded to letting Curiosity rummage through the boxes to find additional ones for her collection.

Curiosity owned two hundred and twenty-two charm bells, of many sizes, colours, shapes, and sparkles. She didn't choose any old bell. When laid out upon her bed, even after two hundred and twenty-two, each one had to fit and contribute something to the others.

Five minutes later to the second, while Curiosity rummaged through an old shoe-box, her mother said, 'Finish that. We have to go.'

'Coming,' Curiosity replied, but hardly registered saying it.

Mummy snatched her by the hand and rushed them both out through the door and across the pedestrian crossing to a shop called *Freaky Feet*. The tug hurt and Curiosity wasn't happy about being dragged away from her box of buttons.

Freaky Feet sold shoes.

It had cool shoes, and not so cool shoes with big, shiny buckles which were Mummy's preferred type. Having just turned eight-years-old, however, Curiosity felt nothing like a kid anymore and wanted, much to her mother's disapproval, a very grown-up pair of red baseball boots.

'Ugh! They're hideous,' Mummy said. 'Why can't you be like other girls?'

Curiosity didn't reply. *What would be the point?* And the process didn't take long either. The shop-person checked Curiosity's feet on the *foot-size-thingy*. Mummy made her do a couple of mock walks up and down the shop, and took a quick look in the floor mirror. She uttered her umpteenth displeasure with her daughter's choice. Curiosity, however, didn't care and instructed her mother she would wear her new boots home. Mummy scoffed. Rolled her eyes but didn't protest or forbid. They went to the till. The man put Curiosity's old shoes into a paper bag and handed it to Mummy, who paid with her platinum credit card, said, 'thank you' in her usual snooty dismissive tone and marched them both back out to the pedestrian crossing.

She stopped abruptly at the kerb. 'Well that all went much quicker than expected. I thought we would be in there for an eternity. You have the oddest feet.'

The lights at the pedestrian crossing turned green and they stepped out onto the road.

An oncoming car stopped too late. Its bumper just centimetres from hitting Mummy's legs.

She threw the driver – a girl, with blonde, pineapple tuft hair and orange make-up – a disdainful glare and, when they reached the other side, as if nothing at all had happened, took up where she had left off:

'As I was saying, I have them too. *Clumpy clodhoppers,* Aunt Lily used to call them. It's why I agreed to your awful choice. What's the point in getting handmade shoes when you will be grown out of them in a matter of weeks? Your feet really are the oddest. If they were webbed, you could swim the channel.' She laughed.

Curiosity didn't. She'd heard it too many times before.

They turned towards the corner with Bingham Crescent. A woman, about Mummy's age, was hugging a little girl, about Curiosity's age. The girl laughed. Hugged the woman tighter. They seemed happy.

Mummy appeared to have noticed them too. A slight smile creasing the corners of her mouth. 'What do you say to a Coconut-milk Chill?' she said. 'Seeing how it's still your birthday?'

The offer stumped Curiosity. Allowing her to look for charm bells was one thing, *but a second treat? Well, that was something that had never happened before.* With a combination of shock, disbelief, and justifiable wariness, Curiosity processed the proposal for hidden pitfalls. Her mother looked down and smiled again. It seemed genuine, and Curiosity's heartbeat skipped so loud in her chest she heard it above the noise of the traffic. When she spotted the tall, slim, Prada-clad frame of her mummy's best friend, Faithe Henning, exiting the doorway of *Elegant Mobiles*, however, those feet came down to earth quicker than pop turns to pee.

'Rosina,' Faithe said . . . screeched. Faithe always screeched. She came from the USA, the Upper East Side, Manhattan, New York, where – Curiosity reckoned – everyone screeched when saying hello to each other.

'Faithe,' Mummy replied, also a bit screechy, 'I didn't expect to see you here so early?'

'I had business to attend to. And you look fabulous.'

'You too,' Rosina (Mummy) said. She planted two air-kisses a good ten centimetres away from both of Faithe's cheeks. 'Do you know, I was in the very same shop not but a half hour ago, buying a new phone . . . problems?'

'Isn't there always?' They both laughed. Faithe reciprocated the two air-kisses and led Mummy and Curiosity closer to the corner with Bingham Crescent. 'Let's move away from all the busy shoppers.'

Mummy said, 'So, how have you been?'

As if she didn't know already, Curiosity thought. *Given they had been together, drinking until late the night before.*

Faithe replied with, 'Good, good.' She looked down at Curiosity. 'Happy birthday, Cupcake. Love the new boots. They're awesome. I hope you are enjoying your special day.' She winked. 'Eight is an extraordinary age. It's always marks the start of something new and wondrous.'

Curiosity nodded. Smiled. It was good manners. After that, she zoned out.

She didn't get grown-ups and their feigned happiness and need to gossip.

It was better to ignore them.

They stood for more minutes than Curiosity cared to count. Mummy and Faithe gabbing the world to rights and Curiosity drifting away in her thoughts. To her, life should be a whirlwind. It should be about desire, exploration, and the consumption of all things new and exciting. History engaged her. Space intrigued her. Tales of fantasy and invention captivated her imagination to the level of addiction. Standing still on Westbourne Grove, while her mummy schmoozed with Faithe Henning, felt the greatest torture.

To entertain herself, she watched the people ranging in and out of shops.

They reminded her of the wildebeest she had seen in a documentary. They seemed as disconnected from each other as she did to her mummy most of the time. Cars beeped their horns. Many stressed looking faces rushed by. Other, more composed people, sat serene and carefree outside cafés, drinking coffees, eating cakes and ornately crafted sandwiches.

Nearly all of them wore hats and sunglasses. As if sunshine was something to be shunned.

Two daddy-longlegs swooped close to her head. They flew, one behind the other, down the street, followed by a bunch of others. Big ones. Bigger than her fingers. Followed by a tall, thin man, in a shabby black suit and white bowtie. He smelled like dry leaves. Or maybe earth. Smiled at her, before stopping at the corner where Westbourne Grove met Bingham Crescent. The daddy-longlegs swarmed around his head but he seemed unbothered.

Mummy still gabbed with her friend.

Faithe glanced down at Curiosity. She winked and nodded in the direction of the corner. The man and daddy-longlegs had gone, but a scrawny black tomcat, with a dirty white patch on its chest, was lying, belly up to the sun, stretched across a shop doorway.

Curiosity, however, didn't recognise this shop.

From the smoothies in *Fancy Fruits*, to the charm bells in *Bright as Buttons*, she was certain she knew all of the stores along this stretch of the street. She felt bothered that one might have escaped her attention, but also fascinated.

A bright beam of sunshine, dappled with a multitude of tiny, flickering lights, picked out a large bowed window, made up of many smaller windows, curving the whole length of the shop-front to a doorway that was so narrow, if she hadn't noticed the cat, she might have missed it all together. The whole building was thick with ivy. It reached up the walls and over the roof like a fairy-house from one of her story-books. Above the bowed window, and below two others on the first and only upper floor, a red and white striped awning extended out across the pavement. It cast a shadow over the tomcat that, seemingly unhappy with the arrangement, leaped to its feet and glanced her way, before sauntering off around the corner into Bingham Crescent.

As to the contents of the shop window, she could only speculate.

She was standing too far away to see them with any detail. And yet, to an inquisitive soul like Curiosity, it seemed as though every other outlet along the road had disappeared.

Only this shop shone out.

TWO – Concerning temptation and providence

Taking a few tentative steps to the side, Curiosity moved closer to the shop. She checked to see if her mother had noticed. She hadn't or, if she had, not enough to interrupt her conversation with Faithe Henning.

They were talking about Daddy again.

They talked about him a lot, and never in a good way.

The words she picked out most being: *gold-digger* and *total loser*, said with a sneer by Faithe Henning and punctuated with a dismissive wave of her hand.

Taking Mummy's lack of attentiveness as approval to explore, Curiosity walked up to the shop window. Bathed in a mote-dappled ray of sunshine, beneath the awning and framed by ivy and written in gold letters on a red background, a sign said, *The Grotto Toy Shop*. The colours were vibrant. The words appeared to ripple. The window panes also seemed to ripple, like water on a lake, and they grew brighter. Whiter. The glare blinding. But it didn't hurt her eyes, nor did it make her look away.

To her right, the light blazed out through the narrow doorway, which appeared to have widened, revealing a checkerboard doorstep of red and white tiles. It reminded her of the queen's court in her illustrated edition of *Alice's Adventures in*

Wonderland. A book she read most nights before sleep, losing herself to a world where anything might be possible.

She moved closer to the door. Hidden within the ivy, the doorposts were made of shiny, green marble, and decorated with leaves and flowers: bluebells, foxgloves, and primroses. Flowers she knew from the back garden and sometimes wore in her hair. The ivy coiled around and through these marble flowers, as though living plant and stone had become one. There were cap-shaped mushrooms, also made of stone. Dozens of them. From behind which tiny, marmoreal faces peered out, with sniped noses, pointed ears, and upturned foxgloves on their heads. Impish. Like pixies. Their almond shaped eyes cut from glistening black glass.

The bizarre faces were unnerving. Their eyes staring straight out. Their faces smiling, with a peculiar leer that seemed to be only for her.

Yet she kind of liked it too; the attention.

It made her feel special.

Through the window she saw shelves stacked with dolls. They didn't interest her, though. Dolls weren't her thing. Sure, she possessed a few, at Mummy's insistence, for when she arranged for Arabella Heffington Jeffries to come to play. But, in general, Curiosity preferred action toys, spaceship stuff and things to build with nuts and bolts. Toys that taxed her brain and made her feel different.

A little way inside the open doorway, hooked to the back of the glossy black door, she saw dressing up clothes and frilly parasols. There were sparkling *Little Princess* tiaras, two toy prams, and the constituent parts of a *Tiny People Kitchen.*

Curiosity, however, reckoned the better, cooler stuff lay farther inside.

She took a cautionary peek back at her mother, who was still chatting with Faithe and seemingly unaware she had gone. Faithe, however, glanced her way and winked again, before looking back to Mummy. It felt like encouragement. Permission. So, stepping past the black and white tomcat that also seemed agreeable to her choice, Curiosity went inside.

The shop had changed. Now, as well as the dolls and tiaras, rows of clear, plastic bags hung from hooks along the walls. So many she found it hard to make out any brick-work underneath. Some of the bags contained little green dinosaurs. Others had cowboys on horses, marbles, *Super-Agent* spy kits with sucker guns, miniature plastic cars, and garlands of toys that enticed her to explore deeper. And she did so. Noticing that she was walking down an aisle, flanked on each side by high shelves that reached from floor to ceiling. They were constructed from rough-cut, gnarly, brown wood. They looked very old, but not worn. And the room smelled of freshly mown grass. The sunlight shining through the window dappling the shelves, picking out certain toys: electric racing-car sets, remote control 4x4s, aeroplanes, helicopters, space-rockets, and models that required gluing together. Curiosity also noticed how, the farther in she went, the less dolly-like the toys had become. It was as if the shop had thought to test her at first then, having worked out her preference of playthings, had stocked the shelves to match her desires.

She took her steps slowly.

She wanted to take it all in and examine everything.

As she neared the end of the aisle, the sunshine dimmed, casting shadows across the floor-tiles as if, somewhere behind her, leaves fluttered on a breeze. The air became cooler. There was a whispered chattering sound, close by her ears, constant and quite intense. Perhaps the sound of insects, droning on the air, which she searched for and, finding none, determined to be somewhere else in the shop, or up among the ornate cornices of the ceiling.

Most children might feel scared in such circumstances.

Curiosity Portland, however, was made of hardier stuff, more speculative stuff. The whispering was merely nature doing its thing. The chill was a consequence of being inside. The fading light held intrigue and an invitation to investigate further. If she had a whole week to spend here, she felt sure there wouldn't be enough time to take it all in.

And, it was such thoughts that caused her to disregard the bizarreness of the place.

The shop appeared to be empty. No other children scoured the shelves. No shopkeeper enquired how they might be of assistance. She felt fully alone in this curious but marvellous place. With only the whispered drone she couldn't quite identify to keep her company.

She moved on.

A bulky wooden counter stood centre-place of the back wall. An old, brass cash register sat atop it, alongside a small plaster figurine that was about ten centimetres tall and, apart from the cash register, the only object upon the counter-top which, on her way down the aisle, she hadn't even noticed as being there. It seemed to have just arrived, occupying pride of place, set against the backdrop of a floor to ceiling curtain, covering the whole wall behind the counter and depicting branches and leaves that looked so natural she found it hard to discern whether they were fake or actual growing things.

A single spike of dusty sunlight, tinged with green, picked out the figurine in an altogether diverse way from the other sunbeams shining through the window. As if it had been created (at least to Curiosity's eyes and imagination) for this specific purpose. She felt enchanted by the green light. Even more so by the figurine. That all of the other items in the shop lost their appeal.

She wanted to get nearer.

She needed to be nearer.

Only to inspect, mind you, and see it up close.

To her sides, the wooden shelves seemed to shimmer at her decision. The droning sound grew louder. Still imperceptible as anything other than buzzing insects, but acute, urgent even. It was as though the whole shop was urging her onward, if not with words, then with emotion, and encouragement . . . or approval.

'How strangely strange,' Curiosity said aloud and, with a few rapid steps, darted forward, snatched the figurine from the counter-top and whisked it behind her back.

The sunbeams brightened. As blindingly as those she saw outside. Then, they dimmed.

She looked around, expecting to hear chastisement.

None came, so she brought the statuette around into the light.

It was a ballerina – stood upon a circular, black slate base – with angular features; sharp yet, to Curiosity's eyes, beautiful.

She had almond-shaped eyes, small pointed ears peeking through her hair and a nose that was no more than a bump in the centre of the face. Poised upon one ballet-slippered toe, the figure stood with the other leg jutting forward from beneath a tattered green tutu, her head cradled in the arc of an upstretched arm. On her back, four dragonfly-like wings flared, as if caught in mid-flutter. Her skin possessed no sheen. The finish being the plaster from which the statuette had been cast. She wore a bodice, coloured green like the tutu and decorated with Celtic knots. Her head bore a green and gold headdress, the only other colouring being a mild blushing to her alabaster cheeks and an application of scarlet making her lips appear almost real. All of this paled, however, beneath the representation of her copper-coloured hair that flowed away from her head as though caught in the eddy of an imaginary pirouette.

It was long. It was wild. It was bright.

It was like Curiosity's own hair.

Thinking the slightest pressure might cause it to shatter, she handled the figurine with the gentlest care. Yet also sensing it might be stronger than first assumed. Not to mention pleasant to touch. She found herself stroking the edges and contours as she might a small, furry animal. Furry animals being yet another of Curiosity's many preoccupations. In particular a friendly tabby cat she had found cold and cowering out among the garden flowerbeds.

She called her Blinky. Fed her scraps from the table. She even, on the often occasions when Mummy got herself too drunk to know otherwise, sneaked her up to the warmth of her bed, where the cat slept, curled into the space between Curiosity's waist and arm.

Blinky snored. Sometimes, she dribbled.

And broke Curiosity's heart when she died last winter.

Curiosity buried her only true friend, by way of a proper ceremony, in the same flowerbed where she had found her. The spot marked with a shiny pebble gravestone. Painted with bright colours and rainbows to signify how her beloved cat had made her feel. Not at all like the mangy bedraggled looking one she'd seen on the way into the shop, but happy, content. At peace, when all around her was only resentment and negativity. And, as she stroked the ballerina figurine, her mind drifted to memories of sunny days, sitting cross-legged in the back garden, nestled among the wildflowers. In her recollection, she felt the grass cooling her skin and the warmth and weight of Blinky sitting on her lap. The cat was purring and blinking up at her. Summer's fragrances saturating the air. Curiosity's thoughts wandering through the story-worlds of her books. Magical places where little girls went on amazing adventures and discovered wonderland realms. She held this daydream for quite a few moments before it was replaced by an overpowering urge to possess the figurine. Which was strange, given how it depicted a ballerina, and that ballet dancing could never be deemed something Curiosity felt excited about. And yet, she found herself checking her pocket for money, knowing full well from the beginning of the venture that she would come up empty. But such was her hope. That desire might outstrip logic. The reality of which was a barren pocket and crushed heart. And still, enhanced by the glowing green light, the ballerina seemed to call to her. It felt snug and at home in her tightening grip. As if it was meant to be there, belonged only to her, and why not?

Today was her birthday after all?

Why couldn't she have it?

If she somehow found the resolve to return it to the counter, *what was there to stop some other child from wandering in? A child who had the means to make it their own . . . to whom it should never belong?*

Curiosity glanced around for a shopkeeper.

She saw none.

At which point, the buzzing became more intense, like tiny wings peppering the air around her ears. They sounded like voices now, combined and speaking in unison. They were whispering, urging her to do the forbidden, to take the figurine. They wanted her to have what was rightfully hers.

At first, she shuddered at the thought of doing something so underhand.

But the green-tinged sunbeam throbbed. Her heart beat faster and her thoughts returned to the back garden, to the wildflowers and cool grass.

A sudden, stern voice made her jump:

'Come out of there,' it shouted.

Clutching the figurine to her chest, she spun around. A silhouette stood in the doorway, a curtain of dust motes barring its way, as though many tiny insects had congregated to stop this person from entering.

The voice spoke again: 'Come out of there right now.'

It was a voice Curiosity recognised and, shading her eyes beneath her free hand, confirmed it to be her mother's. She glanced down at the figurine. For a short, confused moment, she opted to set the little ballerina back on the counter. She even took a half step to do so. In another short but less confused moment, her hand dropped to her side, her fingertips finding the edge of her pocket, whereinto the figurine slipped, with the ease of always having belonged there.

Without looking back, Curiosity dashed to the doorway, out to the street and into sunlight, expecting to hear the usual catalogue of reprimands from her mother, for having walked off, for being rebellious. She braced for the almighty harangue. But no such chastisements came. Her mother seemed preoccupied. Was peering up to the first-floor windows above the awning. She did so only for a few moments, but long enough for Curiosity to notice her discomfort at being here.

Then, the customary look of disapproval returned.

She said no more and hauled Curiosity over to where Faithe Henning stood farther along Bingham Crescent.

'Have you been exploring, Cupcake?' Faithe asked.

'She's always up to something,' Mummy replied and huffed. 'She's not content unless she's being difficult.'

Faithe smiled and ruffled Curiosity's hair. 'Never mind,' she said. 'It's good to explore. Especially when you have such a special birthday.'

They carried on down Bingham Crescent towards home. The two women gabbing again. Curiosity thinking only about the figurine in her pocket. They walked a good hundred metres before she plucked up the courage to look behind and, expecting to see an irate shopkeeper burst out – fists shaking – from *The Grotto Toy Shop*, she braced for what might come next but, apart from the scrawny black and white tomcat lying with one leg bolt upright, licking its behind, the shop doorway was empty.

Feeling somewhat triumphant, her hand found its way into her pocket. Her fingertips rediscovering the little figurine. And yet, as the reality of what she had done set in, just as the fabulous toy shop disappeared beneath the glare of the sun, so did Curiosity's feeling of triumph, replaced with the heart-pounding panic of guilt.

THREE – Concerning old bricks and bad memories

A white-haired man with an arthritic limp trundled his shopping-trolley up to the corner of Westbourne Grove and Bingham Crescent.

Having recognised her from a distance, Brendan Cassidy had hoped to catch up with Rosina Portland, to remind her that he would be coming by her house around eight o'clock tomorrow morning. The lawn needed mowing and, with his advanced years and weary muscles, the bigger jobs took longer. He wanted to get an early start. If she wanted to, she could call it *overtime*, or *under-time*. He didn't care which, just as long as she let him get on with it.

Rosina called him *Cassidy*; no first name, just *Cassidy*.

As did most people since he first worked for her aunt Lily all those years before.

He liked it that way. He didn't do mixing with clients. Mixing brought familiarity, sometimes friendship, which led to heartache.

Slowed by the weight of the groceries in his trolley, by the time he had reached the corner, she had gone too far ahead to call after her without drawing attention. The wealthy types who lived around here didn't take too kindly to grizzled old Irishmen hollering out and interrupting their midday mille-feuilles and macchiatos. Go back a few decades, and just being Irish at all was cause enough to raise suspicion. Brendan had long ago learned to keep his accent tempered and his business to himself.

He gave up on the idea of catching up to Rosina Portland.

If, tomorrow morning, he woke her while cranking up the lawnmower, then so be it.

She slept too long on Saturdays anyway.

He turned to walk back down Westbourne Grove and noticed a scraggy black tomcat, with a mucky, white patch on its chest, stretched out and sunning itself across the threshold of a rundown shop doorway. Its eyes were fixed, staring up as though warning him not to come any closer. This creature one twentieth his size intimidated him. Its glare seemed to hold a genuine threat; as though a scratch or bite were but the opening weapons in its arsenal.

Only an eejit of a man would invite such wrath.

In the rural farmlands where Brendan came from, apart from a useful helper in a grain store overrun with rats, a cat could also harbour more malign traits. To those inclined to superstition, it might be a familiar, a shape-shifting demon. Maybe even one of nature's more furtive folk, warned of in erstwhile poems and hearthside tales of misfortune. Blather, to be sure, but blather to be heeded if a person was predisposed to that way of thinking. So, not being one to trifle with the genius of the great wordsmiths, or indeed centuries of folklore, Brendan Cassidy did as bid. He gave the cat a wide berth and, as he walked past, noticed the shop door lying ajar, which seemed strange because, in the many times he had passed this corner, he had never once seen the door other than firmly shut. And it was a shabby affair too; all but hidden beneath the tentacles of the ivy that swathed the whole building. Maculate with fungus. Black paint peeling away in soppy strips. Yet, Brendan reckoned at one time this might have been a labour of love and craftsmanship. A sight to behold if the years had seen fit to deal it a more favourable, less tragic hand.

He stopped. A shiver rippling down his spine and cold sweat percolating on the back of his neck. Much as always happened when he ventured too close to the old toy shop. The place terrified him. There were memories here, of sad and painful events that, in turn, had led to his broken heart.

At his feet, the cat glared.

Brendan ignored it, wiped the sweat from his neck and then, setting sad memories aside, took a step towards the door. His curiosity had won out over caution.

The tomcat shrieked and sprang up.

Brendan jumped back, his knee cracking and pain like the strike of a hammer shooting through his leg. With its body arched and hair spiked, the cat seemed to have lost its scrawniness and looked much larger than he had first reckoned; about the size of a bull terrier, with similar bulk and muscular tone. It snarled. Its mouth armed with an intimidating array of teeth, long and sharp enough to inflict a nasty bite to any shin that didn't draw back quickly enough. It mewled; a desolate dirge squeezed out past its nest of jagged fangs and raised a paw. Claws emerged. Tiny knives, unsheathed in readiness to strike. Brendan's first thought was to set his boot to the mangy mog and send it flying, claws and all down Bingham Crescent.

He decided, however, to leave well alone. His knee hurt like hellfire and, as his mother had always taught him, superstition had a nasty way of catching up with those who ignored its cautions.

And besides:

'There was probably nothing worth shite in the old shop anyway,' he mumbled inwardly, 'nothing but a burned-out pile of old bricks and bad memories.'

FOUR – Concerning the tale and teller

Now, at this point in the tale, it might be construed remiss – perhaps even rude – of me not to take a moment or two to introduce myself. Or at least give some explanation as to my stake in this piece. Well, when I say my stake, I mean where my influence lies. Not just the declaration of my intent, or indeed of my name.

I prefer to believe we are more than mere names. Just as I consider all the creatures of this good earth to be much more than their outward appearances. All too often, what the world sees becomes a means to pigeonhole a person or creature into some arbitrary identifiable but faceless subcategory: Curiosity Portland; child and daughter, Rosina Portland; mother and ex-wife, or even Faithe Henning; friend and confidante to said mother.

All things, however, have infinite potential.

All things are clay. Works in progress longing for a deft hand to set them to purpose.

And so, with a strong anathema for such conventions, I present myself (the real me) as both the moulder and teller of the tale.

I am the whisperer.

The quiet voice at your ear.

The observer, who took up a hinder position and, with a keen eye, bore witness to the events as they unfolded, so I might speculate, manipulate, spin my dreams because, as with the great Oberon, the world of dreams is where I hold my power and from wherein, I weave the story so all might hear, and perhaps – should a person take heed – learn.

And tale-telling is not something to belittle either.

It is a very important part of . . . well, of all things. Perhaps the most important. And an undertaking I have been tasked to perform for many generations now.

When functioning correctly, a tale possesses the art – for, indeed, it is an art – to bridge the past, present, and future. It is the custodian of historic events. Curator of the current. Foreteller of things to come. It – and, therefore, by extraction my good self – can deliver the light of knowledge. Think Aesop, Charles Perrault, the great James Stephens, perhaps a brother Grimm, or even the wondrous occurrences at Cottingley in England. A time and events I remember with immense fondness. The supposed fictions of two young girls offering hope in the last, wretched days of humankind's first Great War and from which basis I ask you now:

'Who has the right to decide what is and isn't fiction?'

'Who can truly define fable or fact?'

It is to this end, whether it is in the common interest or not, that I have taken up the mantle to enlighten those who would listen, because I believe people – such as your good selves – have the right to know of the clandestine forces with which you share this earth.

As truly as I believe you might want to know too.

Even if this proves the most dangerous of exploits.

For, to know is to be liberated. And, as most natural philosophers will attest, such liberation can therein expose the wonders of nature to investigation and scrutiny.

You see nature doesn't take too well to scrutiny.

Sure, all things desire attention, but only by their own will.

And, like an impudent child prodding a stick into a hornet's nest, young Curiosity Portland, by pilfering something not her own, had agitated powers beyond the cognition of one so young and impressionable. You see, the forces at work at the fringes of this world tend to be phlegmatic and unforgiving. They follow esoteric laws that are governed by ancient and finite mechanisms. They don't question and can never be manipulated by excuse or good argument. These hidden forces of creation are set. They can however possess a sense of humour. A wicked streak seeking to play with those with a fondness for adventure. They place temptations before those inclined to risk, setting forth a chain of events that can, in turn, lead the unwitting traveller to misfortune. They devise deceptions, to enchant, cajole, and ensnare those with unhappy hearts.

They actively seek out those discontented children who yearn for something wondrous.

Because – as I leave you to peer through her eyes and mind – you will see that...

FIVE – Concerning the unhappy heart

. . . Curiosity Portland yearned for something wondrous to happen. So it had been for most of her short life. But now, by succumbing to a spontaneous desire, she discovered that the best wonders – those with greatest attraction – also came with a heavy price.

Half an hour after returning from the old toy shop, she sat cross-legged and barefoot on the back garden lawn, in the sunshine, not far from where Mummy reclined on a patio lounger, drinking cocktails and gossiping with her friend Faithe. Arriving home, Curiosity had dashed to her bedroom and dumped her illicit prize into the drawer of her desk. She then took her *Alice's Adventures in Wonderland* picture-book to the garden, hoping to hide in the story and find a distraction from the guilt twisting like worms in her mind.

Usually Curiosity found distraction in all manner of books: fairy tales, nature, and even her knowledge of the house she was born into, because it offered a glimpse of how the countryside might have looked when only fields and woods surrounded its red brick walls. All of her major memories came from living here with her mother, Rosina and, for the first years of her life, with her father, Jeremy. To Curiosity, the oldness of the place held beguiling mystery, coupled with a sense of secrecy. Ominous. Scary. It had nooks and crannies. A sweeping staircase. And, on the upper floor, a landing that went all the way from her bedroom to the dark, windowless, farthest end of a long corridor.

Her father said the house was Jacobean. That it looked out of place among the spotless, white plastered, terraced homes built around it. For starters, it was detached and, although a big house, it spanned only two storeys instead of their four. It didn't have terracing to the first floor, and there was no portico revealing a grand entrance, just a *witch's hat roof* (as Curiosity called it) that rose up above a central, solid oak front door.

The main roof also looked out of place against the walls that towered to either side. It was made of rough-hewn, grey slate, and inclined upwards to a row of decorative ridge tiles. Every third of which was shaped into a dragonfly. At either end, two lofty chimney-stacks stood a good metre high, topped with clay chimney pots, and a high brick wall wrapped the front garden and drive, which also served to separate the house from the street and its neighbours.

To the rear, the back part of the house was marked by a single, central turret, which contained just one, small, oval window.

It was Curiosity's only outlook from her bedroom.

Through this window, sometimes with an unhappy heart because Mummy and Daddy were arguing downstairs, she would peer out over the expansive garden that rolled over cropped lawn and cottage-garden borders, steering her gaze past two tall yew hedges, via clumps of wildflowers, onward to a thick grove of ivy-clad birch, rowan, and blackthorn that grew dense enough to obscure the houses and city beyond. As though in mirror image to the grandness of the house itself and dominating the edge of the grove, a great and timeworn oak commanded centre station, with its trunk the breadth of a room and knotted boughs striking out like a giant weight-lifter in search of Olympic glory. The wooded area lapped at the roots of the great oak, as though caressing the great-great-grandfather of a vast family, stretching out to both sides in a palisade of limbs and shadows where, on occasion, inexplicable noises caught Curiosity's attention, and also her unease.

She often felt uneasy when contemplating the trees and bushes that her mother called her *dell*, and did so now again, as she sat reading her book. The pictures on the pages seemed bland and the words lacked their usual attraction. She found no comfort in the story, nothing to distract her remorse and, all the while, the dell loomed darkly. Although she fought against it, her gaze drifted in its direction. Her body spasming with a sudden jolt when a bush rustled in the breeze, or a crow landed on a branch to pick at some poor caterpillar destined to become its lunch. It was the same jitteriness she always felt when straying a few metres too close to the trees. Or when a ball ran off and went trundling down the lawn to come to a stop by the roots of the great oak.

Even though Curiosity considered herself to be unafraid of most things, in such circumstances the ball always stayed where it lay, yet strangely found its way back to the patio, at rest upon the flagstones by morning of the next day.

Maybe a fox had happened upon it and saw opportunity to pursue a game?

Perhaps it was the black and white tomcat that occasionally wandered in?

A cat so mangy that, at any other time, she would be kind to such a pitiful looking thing. But something about the tomcat both unnerved and attracted her, enough to draw her attention while out shopping with Mummy on Westbourne Grove, and again now, as it wandered back and forth across the borderline where the cultivated lawn met the ragged bushes of the dell.

It looked in her direction. Mewled before disappearing into the undergrowth.

Although intrigued, Curiosity stayed where she was, at the upper end of garden, on the cool soft grass, bathed in the scent of the wildflowers, where nature seemed kinder, and not so thorny or sinister.

SIX – Concerning Rosina's dell

A few metres from her daughter, Rosina Portland sat, semi-reclined on a patio lounger with a glass in her hand.

'I've always loved this garden,' she said to Faithe, who was lying on the other lounger. Her eyes closed. 'It's like being cut out of the world.'

'It sure is. A true oasis. Why do you think I call so often?'

'So, it's not for my irresistible company then?'

'Oh, here you go again with your *Little Miss Martyr* act,' Faithe replied. 'Don't you think you're too old and sensible for that.'

'Hey! Less of the old.'

'Well, you are.'

'We both are.'

'Speak for yourself. I might have more than a decade on you, but I'm much *much* younger in spirit.'

'Yeah, if the spirit is vodka.'

'Yes, that too. It's all part of the irresistible tapestry of life. And you're no stranger to the booze yourself. Remember, these afternoon drinks were your idea in the first place.'

'They help me cope.' She sipped her Black Russian. 'Having you here helps me cope.'

'Well, I don't need to cope. There's nothing important enough that I care about.'

'And, you think that's the right way to be?'

'Abso-defin-lutely. Thankfully, I went straight through my serious phase of life, and into the more comfortable couldn't give a flying fart about anything chapter. As for you, you're old before your time. When a woman – well, most women apart from me – enters her thirties, they think they have some kind of sacred duty to become more sensible. Down to earth. Logical. Miserable. Until they get close to forty, that is. Then they wise up. Drop all the *I must be seen as serious.*'

'I'm not overly serious, am I?'

Faithe scoffed. 'Yeah, right.' She sat upright, took a swig from her glass and lay back again. 'Maybe not all the time, though. But most of it. Except for this.' She held up her glass. 'I mean, cocktails on a weekday afternoon is a brilliant idea. One of your best. Decadent. Devilish. Wild even.'

Rosina smiled, and sipped from her own glass.

Staring down the garden, her gaze was drawn to the great oak and thick patch of tress that looked so out of place amid the looming concrete of the city. Indeed, at one time no house stood here at all. Being knowledgeable about such things, Jeremy had said that Aunt Lily's, and now her own red brick home was probably the first man-made object to occupy the woodland. Local archaeological digs determining that, to the ancient Catuvellauni, the area had been a place for worship. A forest of now gone oaks concealing sacred pools, wherein these superstitious Celts cast precious offerings to appease the unpredictable nature spirits they held to be their gods of chance or misfortune. One and a half millennia later, it seemed, even the good and Christian bishops, whilst laying claim to the natural order in the name of their one true god, also lacked courage enough to take spade to this small secluded space. No monasteries. No cathedrals. Not even a church. And, as farm, village, town, and eventually metropolis closed in – levelling the forest of oaks bar this one small thicket – even those who professed the protection of the divine feared the lore whispered about this last remaining cluster of bushes and trees. They called it *Devil's Dell.* A place steeped in superstition. Now no more than a part of Rosina's garden. Projecting her mind back in time, she reckoned many probably balked to venture near, and occasionally uttered a prayer they might be spared a dark, rainy night, stranded by way of an ill-shod horse or a wheel-spoke shattered without explanation.

Rosina felt their reticence too – but also the draw of the place.

'Have I ever walked you down to the dell?' she asked.

'No. And, if a wander through the thorny bushes is what you have in mind for this afternoon, I am quite comfortable right here.'

'Actually, I have very little in mind. Except for what we're doing right now that is: lounging on the patio, ice cold drinks in hand, taking in the rays.'

'The goddamned sensible option. The best, in fact. And why are you so obsessed with that dell anyway. Being you, I'm surprised that you didn't flatten it the moment you moved in. You could have built a tennis court, or a swimming pool, perhaps both. It would be way more in keeping with how you must have everything so orderly. Cocktails by the pool. Now that speaks to me.'

'Because it looks like something from a fairy tale.'

'What are you . . . five?'

'No. But I don't think I could ever spoil it. It reminds me of Aunt Lily. Her ghost would probably haunt me to oblivion if I even thought about doing anything to it.' She chuckled but it sounded flat, even to her own ears. 'I have vague memories of playing there when I was a girl. It was my own fantasy world, and I was queen of everything. Well, I think they're memories.'

'Oo! Juicy. What deeds have you got up to among those bushes, dear girl?'

'None. Nothing like that.' Rosina said. A shameful memory flashed but she pushed it aside. 'Anyway, is that all you ever think about?'

'It's the spice of life. And, anyway, what Dayton doesn't know won't hurt him. He has his golf and stuffy board meetings, I have . . . well I have my own little pastimes. I'll be forty-three, next birthday. It's only fair I get my enjoyments where I can. Especially when Nicholas comes by to work in the garden.' She laughed.

'Really? The gardener? You're a walking cliché. Aren't you afraid you'll get caught? Dayton isn't stupid you know?'

'Perhaps not, but what can he do? If we divorce, I get half of his estate, we move on, no harm done. Well, at least not to me.' She smiled while sipping at her glass. 'It's the American way. To aspire to anything less would be unpatriotic. Dayton is too obsessed with that company of his to give a damn what

I get up to in my spare time. A win, win situation, I would say. Anyway, I have it on good authority, he's hooking up on a regular basis with that leggy finance manager at his firm. It's amazing what ten grand and a private detective can dig out of the dirt.'

'Oh my god, you hired a private investigator?'

'Well, a girl has to protect her assets. Let's say I have a few handy photos and one video to call on should things turn messy.' She took a long, thin, pink cigarette out from a silver box. She offered the open box to Rosina.

'No thank you,' Rosina said, but waited for Faithe to light her cigarette before continuing. 'Well, I believe marriage should be a meeting of minds. And I think you're poking a lion there. As I said, Dayton isn't a fool. The sad thing is I can tell you enjoy it.' Faithe grinned. 'You don't see me hooking up, as you so delicately put it, with anyone and everyone, do you?'

'And why not, Rosina? We women have it hard enough as it is. To survive, we have to stay ahead of the game, and claim what is rightfully ours. You're a free woman. With cash to burn. You can do as you please.'

'I choose not to. Call it propriety if you like. I leave such behaviour to Jeremy. Let's change the topic now.'

'Yes, well, for a stylish, good-looking woman like you, company should amount to more than that of her daughter. Yes, these days you are pretty much skin and bones, anorexic even . . . but, putting your many issues aside, you're not a bad-looking woman. And it's a verifiable fact that everyone deserves attention now and again.'

Rosina rolled her eyes.

Faithe scoffed. 'You're such a prig sometimes.'

'Am I a *prig* or tasteful?'

'I'd say *prig*.'

'And you just like to belittle people.'

Faithe smiled. 'It's what I do.'

'Bully,' Rosina said, heightening her tone for playful effect but, joking aside, all this talk of adultery was making her uncomfortable. It churned up thoughts of the night Jeremy walked out, of the spiteful remarks, of feeling unworthy and insignificant. She finished off the last dregs of her Black Russian and asked, 'Refill?'

'Now you're talking.' Faithe downed the last of her drink in a single gulp and took a deep draw on her cigarette, a broad smile stretching across her face.

Getting up from the lounger, Rosina collected her friend's glass.

'Also, that whole ruckus with Jeremy might've gone a mite smoother if you'd hired a detective.' Faithe continued. 'You never know what might've come out in the wash.'

'It wasn't all Jeremy's fault. I was as much to blame.'

'That's horseshit, Rosina. And you know it. He was a conman from day one. He knew that you were set to inherit this house and he sucked you in like a black hole.'

'He could be very charming.'

'Hitler could be very charming, but decent people didn't go around marrying him now did they? Jeremy treated you like a doormat from the get go, but you were too soppy love-sick to see it. He had a . . . *has* a tremendous bod, I'll give him that, but he's also an asshole. You married far too quickly.

Why you stayed with him after he got with that hotel wait-ress I'll never know. And, to stay with that douche-bag for more than seven years. You would have been better back on the drugs.'

'Please don't say that. It's not funny. We were a couple. We were a family.'

'You were unhappy. Hell, girl, you were mentally abused.'

'Jeremy was . . . *is* a *Portland*. Remove but a smattering of direct in-line cousins, and he's as practically royalty.'

'No damned money though.'

'Portland is a great surname for Curiosity. As a family we looked magnificent. We still could, if Jeremy came back and Curiosity stopped being so damned contrary. Getting her to be a lady is like herding cats. Did I tell you, she's vegan now?'

'It's a phase. Kids have them,' Faithe said, waving her cigarette in dismissal. 'And, anyway, so am I.'

'What? You? Vegan?'

'Yup. A full-on veggie-head. A bone fide child of nature.'

'Rubbish.'

'No. Truth.'

'Well, I never knew that. Then again, we've never shared a meal, just drinks.'

'Some vodkas are made from vegetables. Potatoes actually.'

'Didn't know that either.'

'Well, there you go. Every day's a learning day. You should read more. About the world you live in. Curiosity does. She always has her nose in a book. So, who cares if she's vegan?'

'I do. Not because she is one, but because she does these things to spite me.'

'Oh, for Chris-sake grow up. She's eight years old and finding her place in the world. And I'll tell you this, as young as she is, she'll find it quicker than either of us. All this living in luxury has made us lazy. Complacent and indulgent. Good on her. Let her do her own thing. A child needs to find their own values. It's how they develop their creativity. Your emotional baggage, however, is way more permanent.'

'Permanent? I think not. It takes a long time to adjust to a marriage breakdown.'

'But it took you no time to marry the loser in the first place. Your stupidest decision ever.'

'Why are you always so nasty? You give me the same old spiel every time we have drink. The way you keep trawling through my mistakes, sometimes I don't know if you are being supportive or just trying to bring me down.'

'Don't be melodramatic. Of course, I've got your back. You're too sensitive, which makes you bossy. Not to me, but to that child of yours. It's why you crave other people's approval.'

'At least I'm not back on the Diazepam.'

'That's true. But it's like this, Rosina, you have much to give. And, as for Curiosity, what's your problem? She's an absolute dream of a child. She has all the right qualities. She is quiet and keeps to herself. What more could any mother ask for? Anyway, I'm more worried about this damn foolish take back Jeremy Portland idea of yours.'

'It would solve a lot of issues,' Rosina said, paused then added, 'anyway . . . those drinks.'

'Please. Bring me alcohol. I need something to smother the bull coming from your mouth.' Faithe paused, sat back, and peered down the garden towards the grove of trees. 'You know what, though,' she said aloud. 'You're probably right about that dell. There's something intoxicating about it. It's just a pity Jeremy Portland didn't go and get himself lost in there.' She puffed at her cigarette.

Setting both glasses on the kitchen's granite worktop, Rosina followed Faithe's gaze to the dell.

'Yes. It is intoxicating,' she said. 'I can't quite put my finger on it, and I know it's completely at odds with what I wanted for the rest of the property, but I find it enchanting. Daunting, but enchanting.'

She opened the freezer door, popped some ice-cubes into each glass, before topping them up from the pitcher of Black Russian she had pre-prepared. She walked back out to join her friend on the patio and stood, glasses in hand, gazing towards the bottom of the garden:

'I suppose it's all about memories. Everyone thought Aunt Lily was crazy, living alone with all those cats about the place. But I knew her as a wise woman.' She handed one of the glasses to Faithe, who said nothing more. And neither did Rosina. Gazing down the garden towards the dell and the mist that hadn't lifted since morning, she felt transfixed, her thoughts coalescing with the vapour swirling about the bushes, deeming it curious yet captivating how something usually so fleeting had hung around for much of the day.

Watching the wisps play upon the air, her emotions drifted from her unhappy, status obsessed adulthood back to a blurry recollection of a time when short dresses and ankle socks held no match for the sharp briars and thorns. A memory, or a daydream, of pushing through the undergrowth behind the big oak, oblivious to the scrapes, onward into the clearing she called her *enchanted pool*, where her creative mind had fashioned a refuge from the world . . . terrifying, and yet the only place she felt not alone.

SEVEN – Concerning the dread of a magnificent dream

For the rest of the afternoon, while Mummy and Faithe got drunker on cocktails, Curiosity stayed on the lawn, annoyed that Alice's adventures hadn't freed her from the guilt of stealing the figurine. On such a weird and distressing day, however, no end of wondrous stories about mad tea parties or talking rabbits could dispel her gloom.

Even as just a child, she possessed the wisdom to know that guilt weighed heavier than any distraction. She also caught herself glancing more frequently at the dell. Something she tried to resist but, as these glances became more frequent, her curiosity grew, a desire to seek out the unexplored places beyond the old oak tree. It was as though her despondency and the dell were connected. In there, she would find solace. A strange sense of belonging.

Later, at evening dinner, when Faithe had left on a drunken, taxi journey home, she sat at the kitchen counter, in silence, swirling reheated spaghetti on the tip of her fork.

Her mother was sitting next to her. 'Don't play with your food,' she barked, before eating a small forkful, her gaze fixed on an article about *The Independent Mother* in an old glamour magazine Faithe had given her before she left.

Curiosity didn't reply.

She felt no need to.

She didn't care what her mother wanted her to do, or not to do for that matter. She had more important things to consider. How her inquisitiveness had led to her stealing the figurine.

Sitting here, tracing patterns in her spaghetti dinner, with the knowledge that the stolen figurine sat tucked away in her desk drawer, her shame seemed too much to bear. Not so much that her soul might be destined for an eternity of damnation – as there was general agreement that is what happens if you steal things – but that, on the spur of the moment, she had given in, without thinking, and without weighing up the consequences.

And yet, she also felt the bittersweet joy of hearing the source of this guilt calling to her from her desk drawer. It was as though a voice spoke to her, not with words as such, but with sounds, like insect wings beating the air, or maybe a breeze squeezing through a small gap in the door to her bedroom.

She glanced from the kitchen, across the open *circulation space* – as Mummy called the area from the kitchen to the front door – and over to the stairs. When she did so, the sounds became louder, and intense, as though provoking her to come upstairs and fully embrace the deceiver she had inadvertently become when she had stumbled into the weird old toy shop.

She peered up at her mother.

Mummy was still reading the magazine and, apart from the sound of her flicking the pages, nothing else in the kitchen, or outside in the garden moved. Curiosity therefore deduced the sounds were in her head, a consequence of her actions that both confused and terrified her most.

Were head-voices what happens to everyone who steals?

Was this worthy punishment for her crime?

She wanted to do was to go back; back before the toy shop, before inquisitiveness, before temptation, before guilt . . . before these consequences.

'Eat up,' her mother snapped again.

Curiosity, however, didn't have the headspace for one of Mummy's moods right now. With much display, she rammed a too-big forkful into her mouth and chewed loudly, spaghetti sauce dribbling down her chin.

'Stop that,' her mother barked. 'It's unbecoming. And why do you have to be so damned impudent. I have a good mind to send you to boarding school. Get you out of my hair.'

'Do it then,' Curiosity snapped back. 'Anywhere is better than here.'

'You ungrateful child. I gave you everything. You'd have nothing, if it wasn't for me.'

'Yeah, well, you said the same about Daddy. And he left you.'

'Go to your room!'

Curiosity resisted.

'Right now!'

Wiping the sauce from her chin with the back of her hand and cleaning it on her shorts, Curiosity remained sitting, defiant.

'I said, go to your room. I've had enough of your insolence.'

'What? You're going to throw me out now, too?'

'If I get anymore cheek, yes.'

'Good. Do it. See if I care.'

'Go!' her mother shrieked. High-pitched. Manic.

It took a second or two to register then, leaping from her seat, Curiosity dashed up the stairs and plonked down, arms folded, on the top step. Her mother didn't say another word. She simply returned to her magazine, as if her total flip-out had been something normal. Expected even, given her having to endure such a wilful, backchatting daughter. For her part, Curiosity sat and seethed, too angry to go back down and too afraid to approach her bedroom. It took many hours of staring downstairs, out through the kitchen to the garden before she plucked up the courage to go to bed. If Mummy hadn't been laying it on thick and making a no-no of being anywhere near her right now, Curiosity might have quite happily never gone near her room ever again.

With slow, reluctant half-steps she moved along the landing corridor.

Upon reaching her bedroom, she stopped and took a deep breath before opening the door. She was met by an explosion of sunlight surging through the oval window. The brilliant twilight lustre illuminating every detail of the walls and furniture. It bathed her wardrobe in amber, setting fire to her shabby chic dresser, her tallboy, her cuddly toy (a ginger kitten from the *Home for Cats Foundation*) that lay resting on her pillow, the animal welfare posters covering Mummy's choice of hideous paisley patterned wallpaper, and the full-length mirror that blazed as bright as the sun it reflected.

The whole room had come alive. And the whispering had grown louder. Now nothing like insect wings at all, but hushed voices, hissing and speaking in an unintelligible language close to Curiosity's ears.

Before fully entering the room, she took a second to shout downstairs:

'Night, night, Mummy.'

It was the first time in years she had done so. She had hoped that the effort might soften the tense mood, and also close the mental gap between the merely unpleasant down there and an increasingly downright scary up here, where voices might be whispering inside her head or, then again, might not.

No answer came. There was nothing unusual about that and she didn't really expect one anyway. Before plucking up the courage to approach her room, she had seen her mother lying on one of the circulation space sofas, with a glass of red wine in her hand, engrossed in her glamour magazine article as if the words on the page held the answer to all of life's problems. Drinking wine was pretty much all she had done since Daddy left. Apart from when Faithe called and they drank cocktails too, getting drunker than usual.

Curiosity carried on into her room.

She peered across to her desk drawer. A thought popping into her head that the little figurine might suddenly come alive and leap out. Might grab her. Take her somewhere cold and uncaring, where stealing and guilt were as normal as playing with toys. This troubling thought was quickly followed by another, as if glossing over the first, a deduction that surely something so delicate and beautiful could never do anything vindictive or cruel.

The drone of whispered voices ceased.

Having heard them to some extent since entering the toy shop earlier that day, the silence felt strange, and she missed them. Yet it wasn't pure silence, more of a pause, an anticipation of sorts. By no conscious will of her own, her legs walked her across to her desk. Of course, she had made her legs do so. It would be crazy to believe otherwise. But she couldn't remember thinking it. Or wanting to. Only that she had and, either way, here she stood, wishing with all her heart to open the drawer, to touch and feel the figurine again, while logic cautioned against it, her guilt weighing heavily.

In answer to this dilemma, and with a flash of inspiration unparalleled in her short life, she determined she would return the figurine to the toy shop. She would place it back on the counter where she had found it. No harm done. No one any the wiser. In a single major move, her guilt would be gone. And the decision made her feel much better. So much so, given she would be returning the figurine anyway; she reckoned that there might also be no harm in holding it one more time.

Just to hold, mind you.

Not to keep.

She pulled the curtains on the oval window. Not that anyone could see in on the first floor, but to shut out the twilight and provide a sense of secrecy. She opened the drawer to her desk and felt elated when her fingers touched the edges of the figurine. With joy surging in her heart, she took it out and clutched to her chest; the sinful child with her shameful booty.

She sat on the edge of her bed, her fingertips caressing the chalky plaster, taking in every relief and cleft: the protruding limbs in graceful pose, the elegant features of the fairy lady's face. Once again, she found her thoughts drifting. Her eyes were open but, in her daydream, she visualised sunny days amid the garden wildflowers, the cool grass stroking her skin, summer scents and storybook realms filling her thoughts.

The sound of wings and whispered voices returned again. Only, this time they were gentler and alluring. Not at all pleasing. Yet, not unpleasant either. As she listened, the day-dream became more tangible. It began to form before her eyes. The bedroom walls blurred, as did the wardrobe, her desk, the dresser, the full-length mirror, her bed, and the cuddly-toy cat propped upon the pillow. The whole room turned opaque, as if composed of green mist. The walls dis-integrated and collapsed inwards like morning fog disappearing into the earth. From within this fog, small plant-shoots began to pop up; one here, another there, followed by all corners of the room.

The shoots grew rapidly, curling up through emerging grass, spattering the floor of her bedroom in a carpet of green. As they grew higher, their leaves unfurled in a tableau of brilliant, multi-coloured buds, followed by flowers opening to an invisible sun. Before her eyes a whole wildflower meadow was revealed. The furniture and the bed beneath her became knolls and hollows, dotted with yellow butter-cups, blue cornflowers, and bright red poppies. She felt the cool grass against her skin and smelled the sweet fragrances of the garden.

At the boundaries of her room, the walls shook.

Thick roots burst through the floor like nails through wood, shattering the planks to shards, which turned to dust and then to dirt. Clumps of birch erupted upwards, followed by rowan and blackthorn, creating a wooded grove from where the original walls of the room had been. From within the grove, thorny briars struck out from the shadows. They moved like snakes, coiling around the trunks of the trees, as though some unseen creator was weaving a replica of the garden dell here in Curiosity's bedroom.

With excited eyes and mind, she watched this miracle unfold and also envisioned what might come next. She imagined click beetles and hairy caterpillars, which immediately appeared, crawling and wriggling over the leaves of the plants and trees. She thought of ladybirds and butterflies, and they too appeared, fluttering down from the blue, cloudless sky that was once the ceiling, to settle on the flowers. She thought of pretty, turquoise dragonflies hovering upon the air, and they came too, their drone matching the whispering voices.

At this point, Curiosity realised that her own imagination had caused all of these things to exist. Whatever she thought became reality. Like a painter adding details to a great artwork, she was creating the scene.

She laughed out loud, dumbfounded yet overjoyed by the talent she possessed.

She imagined a crop of bluebells, which came into being in the farthest corner of the room. At first no more than sprouts, then stalks, leaves, and finally in a display of vivid colour. She followed the bluebells with milkwort, painting the opposite corner yellow. She pictured foxgloves, poppies, cowslip, harebell, primroses, and then a hedgehog, which came skittering out from among the wildflowers, glancing once in her direction and twitching its nose, before disappearing into the undergrowth where her wardrobe used to be. By her own invention, and as solid as any sight she might encounter in the real world, her spectacle of creation squirmed and grew, crowned with the tiny bird (a chaffinch) sitting upon a branch of a blackthorn tree, chirping a merry song, by the command of nothing other than Curiosity's wish for it to do so.

Ordinarily, a child might be frightened by such impossible occurrences but, being made of sterner stuff, of more speculative stuff, Curiosity saw only wonder. And, while she forged her daydream world, the figurine vibrated in her hands. It felt warm to the touch. Its beat matching her pulse, as though setting time or a background rhythm to her heartbeat. Awed by her creation, however, she hardly noticed. Not until the figurine grew warmer. The voices grew louder and harsher. They did indeed become unpleasant. Thunderous clouds gathered overhead. They cast shadows upon the bright summer scene and, with a suddenness that shocked her; the kingdom of her imagination went hazy and lost its wonder. An instant later, the grey clouds descended and turned to fog. It moved across the wildflower meadow. It enveloped the grassy knoll beneath her and, where there had been flower-strewn mounds and hollows, now only the fog prevailed. The trees and bushes were gone, turned to mist and reforming into her bedroom, complete with furniture and her mother's hideous paisley wallpaper.

With heartfelt loss, she watched her wondrous world

ebb away. The whispers ceased. The vibrations calmed. And, although she had borne witness to something fantastical and awesome, when her room solidified to plainness and normalcy, so did her rational mind, doubting the logic and likelihood of everything she had seen.

She questioned her sanity. In the real world, only insane people believed they held the power to manifest their fantasies and, if this was the case, then she surely must be going mad.

The thought scared her, as did the lifeless thing in her hands.

For its part, the figurine remained exactly that: a figurine.

In her guilt and emerging fear, however, Curiosity thought it to be so much more.

Jumping to her feet, she cast the offensive thing into the wastepaper bin beneath her desk, darted across, smothered it with crumpled-up scraps of old homework and dashed back to bed again, hoping that, by this gesture, the insanity might end. Still fully clothed, including her boots, she got underneath her duvet, pulled it over her head and waited.

Nothing happened.

It took her hours to find sleep.

Before tiredness finally took her, all she could do was worry about the craziness of her daydream, made stronger by her first real venture into inquisitiveness, temptation, and guilt. Like clouds before a storm, these thoughts kept her awake, because they were inexplicable, and inexplicable things can be terrifying to a child as imaginative as Curiosity.

Especially on such a weird and distressing day.

And Curiosity didn't sleep for long, either. As the night progressed, still disturbed by the events of the day, she woke often, snapping out of a recurring dream where woodland creatures cried out to her from deep within a vast forest. On the last such occasion, half-awake or dreaming, she heard tiny feet skittering across the floor. They scurried over her desk and along the headboard above her pillow. Peeking from beneath her duvet, she was sure she caught sight of shadows moving across the ceiling. They were long and thin, like the silhouettes of many tiny, skeletal people scampering from one place to another.

In response, she pulled the duvet back over her head and took to muttering, 'There's nothing there. There's nothing there.'

When she found the courage to look out again, she saw only her furniture and curtain-strained moonlight reflected in her full-length mirror.

The scampering had stopped. The silhouettes were gone.

Curiosity was unconvinced.

She sensed they were still there, peering at her from the dark corners.

EIGHT – Concerning the lure of sheltering trees

The next morning, Curiosity woke to a shard of sunlight breaching a crack in the curtains. Exhausted by her fitful night, she had fallen into a deep sleep sometime before dawn, but woke with a start and ran downstairs to the kitchen, still dressed in the clothes she had worn throughout the night.

It wasn't quite eight o'clock.

She was tired, but didn't want to stay a moment longer than was necessary in her room.

The figurine was there. And so, the things that cast the silhouettes might be there too.

She reached a bowl down from the cupboard and filled it with her mother's expensive designer granola, soaking it in oat milk. Much to Mummy's dissatisfaction, Curiosity had eaten little of her dinner the evening before. She'd had no appetite for spaghetti, or tomato sauce, or any food for that matter.

Now her hunger gnawed. Suppressing, if only for a moment or two, even her worries.

She fetched a spoon and swallowed a mouthful. It felt lumpy going down but good in her empty stomach. At the other end of the counter, Aurelija was standing by the ironing-board. A large pile of laundered clothing heaped in a plastic basket at her side. As one of her two, weekly *duty days*, Aurelija came on Saturdays, and Curiosity often watched the young, Lithuanian woman while she worked. In this case, ironing one of Mummy's slim-line skirts.

With her celebrity-shapely body and ability to go about her tasks with quiet diligence, Curiosity viewed Aurelija as the ideal woman. Her hair was black and long. Her posture rigid and always upright, as though nothing of this world could sway her self-confidence.

When he had lived with them, Daddy had also found much to admire about Aurelija too.

More than once, Curiosity had noticed his fixation with her chest which, hearing how Mummy talked about him, she also reckoned had little to do with the pretty, silver crucifix Aurelija wore on a chain around her neck.

She lifted the bowl from the counter and said, 'Hi Aurelija.'

Aurelija looked up from her task and responded with a nod and a smile.

She seldom said much, and Curiosity accepted this to be the extent of familiarity the woman wished to pursue. She also fully understood why she might wish to remain detached. Mummy could be very overbearing and, when in such a mood, avoidance of attracting her attention was always the best approach.

It lessened the likelihood of arguments.

Slurping down another spoonful of granola, Curiosity returned the smile.

Behind Aurelija, on the other side of the open patio-doors, her mother – wearing sunglasses, white blouse and slim-fit black trousers – lay on one of the loungers. Mummy never did anything, not even lounging, without being *properly attired*.

In one hand, she gripped a mug, which Curiosity reckoned, given the strong smell lingering in the kitchen, to be coffee. A thin, pastel blue cigarette drooping from the fingers of her other hand as though it weighed a full kilogram. Coffee and cigarettes were normal choice for Mummy's breakfast. Most likely due to the jug of Black Russians and glasses of wine she often shared with Faithe Henning most evenings since Daddy left.

It was, however, unusual to see her up this early.

Normally, apart from the days Aurelija came, Curiosity had most of the morning to herself.

Farther down the garden, dressed in his normal attire of blue overalls and heavy boots, Cassidy was standing by the open door of the wooden storage shed, hunched over, pouring petrol from a red, plastic container into a tractor style lawnmower.

When she went outside to the patio, Curiosity waved to the old gardener.

He nodded back.

Cassidy seldom smiled. Always too busy. But it didn't mean he wasn't nice.

He was often nice.

He taught her the names of insects, trees, and the wildflowers that grew in the garden. He told her tales about the time before people, when strange magical creatures populated the Earth. Some of which could change into anything or anyone they wished. One was a crow. Another was a horse. One was a cat. Of course, Mummy insisted that his stories were *poppycock*. But she often belittled anything Cassidy or Aurelija had to say. Especially if it involved discussing wages. Curiosity, however, liked his stories and was beginning to wonder if the strange black and white tomcat might be the one he'd mentioned in his tales.

Which would be poppycock.

But poppycock seemed to be the order of the day since discovering the old toy shop.

She sat down on one of the loungers and shuffled back to prop herself upright. The lounger creaked. She glanced up to the oval window of her bedroom, but looked away again when she heard her mother groan:

'Why do you have to be so noisy?' she snapped. There was real bite in her tone. She was peering over her sunglasses with a scowl, her eyes no more than slits, as though the sunlight caused her pain and the greatest inconvenience. 'All I could hear all night was you tossing, turning, and bumbling about in your room. What on Earth were you doing? You kept me awake with all your scrabbling around. I came down here for some peace and quiet. And what have you got there?'

'Breakfast.'

'What kind of breakfast?'

'Granola.'

'I hope you're not eating *my* granola? It's a mix that I have specially prepared by my health advisor. The run of the mill stuff from the supermarket is yours.' She drank some coffee and took a draw on her cigarette, before stubbing it out with numerous more butts in a brass bucket filled with sand. She sat back, closed her eyes, and moved her sunglasses higher on her nose.

'Don't worry. It is the run of the mill supermarket stuff,' Curiosity replied and lied. 'I don't like yours anyway.'

A loud rumble rose up from Cassidy's lawnmower.

Mummy bolted upright. 'Really, Cassidy? On a Saturday? I swear that Curiosity and you are in league to completely destroy any chance of me getting any rest.'

'Saturday is my day,' Cassidy replied, his growly brogue making the words sound assertive. 'In summer, Saturday is always my day. That's the way of it.'

'Well can you make next Saturday your day for that? There must be plenty of other chores you could be doing.'

Cassidy turned off then dismounted the lawnmower. He ran the fingers of one hand through his shaggy white hair and a string of words came mumbling from his lips. Although they were hard to make out with his accent, by the pucker on his face, Curiosity assumed them to be some of the Irish swear-words he liked to mutter when Mummy irritated him. He pushed the lawnmower back into the shed and, still grumbling, came back out with a hoe and began working on the weeds in the flowerbeds.

'That's better,' her mother said, and added, 'I had quite the afternoon yesterday,' as if the statement might surprise Curiosity. 'Faithe leads me totally astray sometimes. So, please be quiet. Mummy is having one of her relax days, and little girls making a racket are not conducive with a relax day.' She lay back down and sighed.

Curiosity continued eating her granola, clattering her spoon hard against the ceramic.

'And, do you really have to eat that out here? The kitchen is the place for eating breakfast.'

'Nope,' Curiosity replied, but didn't budge.

'So, why don't you take it inside then, and leave me to rest here alone? I'm feeling a tad sensitive today.'

A tad? Curiosity thought. By the bloodshot capillaries she had noticed in her mother's eyes, she reckoned *a tad* to be more than a mere understatement.

She got up, moved a few metres out onto the lawn, and sat cross-legged on the grass to continue with her breakfast. The action brought her closer to the dell. She shimmied back away from it then stopped. She shivered. Her life had gotten weird.

Wondrous to say the least, but weird.

She recalled that she had decided to return the figurine to the toy shop. To do so, she would have to convince Mummy to take her back to Westbourne Grove, and she thought of suggesting a visit to *Bright as Buttons*, perhaps under the guise of finding additions for her collection. Given her mother's present state, however, that approach appeared unlikely to happen. And anyway, since her daydream the night before, Curiosity had lost her enthusiasm for her charm bell collection. She had lost enthusiasm for most things except the figurine. It truly was a magnificent thing. And, as with all magnificent things, it was something that a girl with imagination found difficult to give up.

She glanced up at the oval window again.

A faint green light throbbed inside her bedroom and the whispering voices returned.

She got up and went into the kitchen, blowing a cheeky but quiet raspberry towards her mother on the way. She chuckled, placed her bowl and spoon into the dishwasher – a strict Mummy rule, and one of many when it came to living in her mother's house – went to her bedroom, retrieved the figurine from the wastepaper basket and returned to the garden.

In the time it took to eat her last spoonful of granola, she had decided to keep the figurine; *her* figurine.

It was nothing more than plaster and paint, but had sparked something wondrous: the power to create daydream worlds. So, she spent the rest of the morning sitting on the lawn a good distance away from where Mummy sat snoozing and who only woke on occasion to drink water, or coffee, or to read her magazine and smoke a cigarette. Curiosity settled in a pretty spot a few metres from the dell. A day earlier, she wouldn't have been caught dead this close to the under-growth, but it attracted her, nestled as she was among the untamed wildflowers, in a part of the garden normally only seen by Cassidy when he came down to clip back some of the scraggier bushes.

With his stories and knowledge of nature, she reckoned Cassidy knew everything about everything, even about her feeding Blinky, and definitely about what lay beyond among the wild brush and trees. Because, when his tasks took him too close to the bushes, he appeared tense. He became more alert than usual, seemed agitated, and quite often crossed himself a number of times in the way that catholic people seemed to do when they were worried about something or other.

And he had also looked worried when she walked closer to the lower end of the garden.

It was nothing definite, but he appeared to be keeping one eye on her while he worked.

Curiosity stayed where she was. She took off her boots. The copse of trees might threaten, but it also captivated. It aroused an urge for discovery. Charmed her adventurous mind. As she sat, bare-foot and cross-legged on the cool grass, studying the reliefs and features of *her* figurine, her fear dissipated. Evaporating as sure as her bedroom had become the knolls and hollows of her daydream the evening before.

The dell became more intriguing.

It became a place of wonder . . . a place to explore.

For now, however, she just lay back, clutching her beloved figurine to her chest, letting its warmth and soft throbs take her thoughts wherever they may.

The sun blazed down. Warming her skin.

Sweat broke out on her brow but she didn't flinch. Because, occasionally, when the heat became too much, a cooling shadow reached from within the trees and, like a sheltering hand, stretched out to shield her.

NINE – Concerning a cat and familiarity

Rosina felt *like hell's-own crap*, as Faithe might say.

The lounger was made of needles. Her head thumped. Her stomach rolling somersaults. Her body ached like she had tumbled the full length of the black ski-run at Château-Ville-Vieille, and no amount of painkillers, water, cigarettes, or coffee brought any relief. The whole world had become the greatest imposition. She was annoyed with everything but, most of all, she felt drained.

She slept a lot that morning, all the way into the afternoon. Woken only when a dog barked somewhere in a neighbour's garden, or a bird squawked, or her phone rang with a call from Jeremy, and another from a telesales man offering to take her claim for the car accident that didn't happen.

At least Curiosity stayed quiet, taking off to the bottom end of the garden, which was good for both of them, seeing how her disregard for best behaviour might test the will of any mother with a volatile temper.

Rosina told the telesales man to *bugger off*.

She closed the phone call with a huff, leaned back, and shut her eyes.

She drifted into slumber, dreaming of trees: birch, rowan,

oak, and blackthorn, draped in a canopy of leaves and crowned with a shroud of silver moonlight.

Dozens of tiny creatures stood on the branches of the trees. They had grey gangly bodies, and ovoid heads, with pointed ears and black slit-like eyes. Their teeth were jagged. They were whispering in unison, with words she couldn't quite make out but that frightened her, more so when they leaped and swung from the branches towards her.

She fled, running deeper into the forest.

They chased, raining down from the trees onto her body. They clambered over her head and onto her shoulders, and she smelled the stench of their skin, feeling their claws rake into her face and neck as if they were real, corporeal things.

She stumbled into a clearing, where the creatures disappeared, replaced by five girls with charred flesh, who burst from the ground around her feet: hideous grotesques with scorched scalps, their mouths caught in a scream, perhaps from terror, perhaps in accusation.

They gripped her legs and pulled her down.

Rosina woke with a start, to something brushing against the calf of her leg.

Alongside her lounger, a scruffy, black tomcat, with a grubby, white patch on its chest was sitting, licking its front paw and staring right at her. She got up and moved back towards the patio-doors and the kitchen.

Even though Aunt Lily had thirteen of them, Rosina disliked cats. And this one was coming on far too familiar.

'Shoo,' she said, swishing outwards with her hand. 'Off with you. You don't belong here.'

Her efforts didn't work. The cat stayed put. It mewled,

rubbed its body along the supports of the lounger, before moving towards her.

She jumped away and ran into the house. Behind her, Aurelija, the Lithuanian housemaid hurried off into the circulation space. She crossed herself and kissed the crucifix she wore around her neck.

For a good five minutes, the cat sat looking at Rosina from the patio before it took one last body rub against the lounger and sidled off down the garden. As it walked past the gardener, he stared and blessed himself, his gaze following its approach to the dell, before it stopped and glanced across the lawn at Curiosity.

She was lying on the grass, seemingly lost to the world.

The cat then glared back up the garden at Rosina.

It mewled and disappeared into the tree line, its short but menacing stay having churned up a sense of familiarity, a tear in the paper-thin barrier Rosina had constructed around a repressed memory . . . and a shameful deed.

While her mother looked down from the patio, Curiosity lay on the grass, with her eyes closed, clutching her figurine to her chest, oblivious to the tomcat taking interest in her, and immersed in a vision of a dancing lady: a ballerina, who was twirling upon her tip-toes, with her arms arched over her head, and her face the picture of grace and composure.

Given how, but two days earlier, she would have considered such thoughts as downright puke-inducing; it didn't strike her as strange that such a normal-girl fantasy might be perceived as out of character.

Now she only wanted to see the lady sissonne and

soubresaut, to watch her spin en-dedans, plié, pointe, and pirouette, words and steps Curiosity had never heard before, yet came to her as sure as if she had known them all her life.

TEN – Concerning the busy mother ... who makes the daughter

Rosina rang Faithe:

'Are you busy? Can you come?'

'Why?'

'Because I need you. The dreams are back.'

For a few seconds, Faithe didn't reply. 'It's inconvenient. I have Nicholas calling round.'

'Please,' Rosina pleaded. She needed company. She needed her friend. 'I dreamt about the tiny creatures again. And there was a cat, only it was real. I think it might be still here, down in the dell.'

'You dreamt about a cat?'

'No, not a dream it was real. It scared me. Please come. I need you.'

On the other end of the phone, Faithe huffed.

'All right,' she said. 'But you owe me. In more ways than one. I was looking forward to Nick's visit today.'

'I promise I'll make it up to you.'

'You'd better.'

After an anxious half hour pacing the kitchen, Faithe arrived and *parked her butt,* as she termed it, on one of the patio loungers.

She was smoking a lilac-coloured cigarette.

Rosina fetched her friend a cup of coffee, which she viewed with disdain, swilling it around as though Rosina had handed her a container filled with dirty dishwater:

'Don't you think this is a mite basic for such a sunny afternoon,' she said. 'You must have something that can Irish it up a bit?'

Rosina was sitting opposite to Faithe, sipping cold water. 'Not for me, thank you. My head has been thumping like a kettledrum all day.'

'I wasn't talking about you. It is a totally self-centred request, and anyway, girls like us can never enjoy themselves too much.' She chuckled, while taking a draw of her cigarette.

'Thanks for coming. I am worried. And Curiosity hasn't been the slightest help either, clattering around with her breakfast things all morning.'

'She's a kid. And you are stuck up your own ass. You limeys take things way too seriously, especially when it comes to your children. Anyway, it's Saturday, isn't this one of Jeremy's days? Why isn't she with him?'

'He rang. He said that he's running late, which is nothing new. He's probably too busy with his girlfriend. You would approve. You and Jeremy have much in common. You haven't . . . ?'

'Don't be puerile.' Faithe stubbed her cigarette out in the sand-bucket. 'He has a great ass. It looks great in those chinos he always wears. But he's still too much stiff shirt and no shazam for me. He's your type. You know, stuck up.'

'There's no need to be nasty.'

'I'm being truthful, Sugarplum.' She drank a mouthful of coffee and gazed at the cup with a sneer. 'What about the Kahlúa?'

'It's in the drinks cabinet.'

'What's it doing there? It should be in my cup.'

'I didn't want to repeat of yesterday. My nerves couldn't take it.'

'Jesus, Rosina, just get the booze would you.'

Rosina huffed. She went through to the kitchen and into the circulation space. On the way through she passed Aurelija, who looked up for a few seconds from vacuuming. Rosina said nothing. She did smile, though, with approval more than friendliness.

She fetched the bottle of Kahlúa from the drink's cabinet, returned to the patio, and poured a splash into Faithe's coffee cup.

Faithe glared until she poured some more.

Rosina then handed her the bottle which, by the mollified expression on Faithe's face, was what she wanted all along.

Faithe downed a good mouthful. She said, 'That's better,' leaned back in her lounger, smacked her lips, and asked, 'now, what's all this about scary dreams and cats?'

Rosina thought for a second before she spoke. 'Do you know, when you put it like that, it does sound foolish.'

'It sounds deluded. If you're regressing, that's the last thing we need. But you called, so here I am – always the friend indeed.'

She took another swig of her *coffee*. Which Rosina reckoned had stopped being coffee with the last, hefty dash of Kahlúa.

'Jeez, that's sweet,' she said, grinned and added, 'are you sure you won't join me?'

'Maybe later,' Rosina said. 'When I clear my head. The dream was so damned frightening. It was like I was actually there, lost in a forest, with these – these ugly, skinny, little things chasing after me. They were clambering all over my body. Ghastly, grey things, with jagged teeth and pointed ears. They stank like Cassidy's compost heap. It gives me the jitters just thinking about it. And the hands. Horrible burned hands were pulling me down into the dirt. I woke up to something rubbing against my leg. It was a cat. A mangy, horrid looking thing, with yucky bare patches all over its fur.' She shivered. 'It went into the dell down there.'

'It's probably just something to do with the fire,' Faithe said but sounded unconcerned. 'You've had more than one or two scary dreams in your time.'

'What fire? Oh that – maybe. Oh, I don't know. I hope not. This one seemed so real, though. And I just know that tomcat had something to do with it.'

'Can you hear yourself? You really think that some stray cat had something to do with some dreams you had decades ago? You sound like a nut-job. Oh, yeah, I forgot . . . you are a nut-job.' She laughed and took another large swig from her coffee cup.

'That's not funny. It's harsh, and hurtful.'

Faithe scoffed, and gave a dismissive wave of her hand. 'You're too sensitive. Always were.'

'I felt genuinely frightened. And Curiosity was no help at all; mooning around at the bottom of the garden like some lost soul. That girl gets stranger by the day.'

'What's she doing down there?'

'I'm not sure. Sleeping, I think. I've never seen her go so far down the garden before. She truly is one strange child, not at all what I expected, or needed. Sometimes, it seems like she is not mine at all.'

'Well, that can't be true. I was there when the little critter popped out. I had to be, seeing that Mister Jeremy, I'm-way-too-important, Portland was too busy to attend the birth of his own damned daughter.'

'The joys of going into labour early.'

'What gets me,' Faithe continued, 'is why any woman would put herself through that torture in the first place. And for what? Icky-sticky fingers. Boogers. Poop-splattered diapers. And all topped with knowing that your stretch marks are forever, your tits are heading south, and your ass is as big as a float in the *Macy's Thanksgiving Day Parade*. No way José. That's not for me. Give me a cigarette, a tall cocktail and lounger to stretch out on any day. And I like sleeping in. A lot. Anything before nine o'clock in the morning is just unnatural.'

'You think my breasts are heading south?'

'You said it, Sister.'

'I think they look just fine.'

'You keep telling yourself that. You're getting saggy. And

it's safe to say that your best years are well and truly behind you.'

'You're being a real bully today. More so than usual.'

'Just telling you what you need to hear.' She sniggered. 'Tough love, Sugarplum. It's what got you off the antidepressants. And remember, it was you who called me.'

'I needed you here. I was scared.'

'Yeah, well. You could do worse than copy your daughter. She knows how to take life easy.'

'She's obstinate.'

'She's a charm.'

'She refuses to assimilate.'

Faithe rolled her eyes. 'Jesus, Rosina, having a child was supposed to be good for you. It was meant to give you purpose. I didn't expect you to treat her like your own personal dress-up doll. You're too heavy on her. Not that I'm against disciplining children, quite the contrary. But she is special, and you're stifling her. You've read the headline, being an *Independent Mother* isn't about control. It's about letting both parent and child do their own thing. She sure doesn't need you breathing down her neck all the time.'

Rosina recalled the article in the magazine. Her mood softened, and so did her concern about the dream.

'It's not even as though she's a bad child,' she continued. 'I don't think she's ever talked back once. But she just has to be wilful to the point of frustration. Look at her now, lying down there with not a care in the world? It's not good. Not if she wants to move in the right circles.'

'You're delusional, and way too obsessed with that goddamned Ladies' Forum. I'd swear that most of your neuroses stem from trying to impress those jerks. And, as for that stuck-up shapeshifter, Ophelia Heffington Jeffries, she completely gets my goat. The only thing she ever did with any confidence was get with that hairy-nosed husband of hers.'

'Good lord, Faithe, bitter much.'

'I detest pretention. It's the refuge of the unimaginative.' She peered into at her cup, and then shook it at Rosina. 'Can you get me some ice for this coffee?'

Rosina sighed and went into the kitchen. She returned with a few ice-cubes in her hand and plopped them into Faithe's cup.

They splashed.

Faithe glared.

Rosina smirked and sat down again. 'Ophelia does a lot for charity.'

Faithe took a long drink. 'For Chis-sake, Rosina,' she said. 'The woman is a gold-plated snob, pure and simple. You can save Curiosity from all that. She's a delight. She's unique.'

'What is wrong with helping Curiosity to assimilate?'

'She's not like other kids. She's not a brainless zombie. She can be anything she wants to be. The girl has zing. Just look at her now?'

They both peered down the garden.

Curiosity was spinning on her tip-toes, cradling her head in the arc of her upward stretched arms. Her hair flowed on the breeze. A smile lit up her face.

'Good lord,' Rosina said. 'Is she doing ballet?'

'Looks like it to me,' Faithe replied, drank a mouthful

from her cup, and picked out two violet-coloured cigarettes from the pack on her lap.

She offered one to Rosina, who took it, albeit with a distracted acceptance.

Faithe produced a lighter from her bag, lit both cigarettes and took a draw. 'Do you know?' she continued. 'If I was ever forced to have a kid – even though the chances of such a tragedy is absolutely zilch – I suppose I could do worse than have one like your Curiosity. Where you've got your messed-up dreams and mental health issues, that girl's got spirit. You would do yourself a favour to remember that.'

Rosina didn't reply, nor did she smoke her cigarette. Instead, she sat forward on her lounger, gazing with astonishment at her usually less than feminine daughter spin and skip across the lawn at the end of the garden.

Sunshine gleamed off Curiosity's hair. Her upper body surrounded by what appeared from a distance to be a swarm of daddy-longlegs. They looked larger than normal insects, swirling around her like smoke caught in the tailwind of a speeding vehicle.

Rosina watched intensely. Although Curiosity's dancing appeared clumsy and unrefined, she liked this new development in her daughter. And the steps seemed familiar to her which, in turn, made her feel uneasy.

Why?

She hadn't the faintest idea. And she didn't get time to speculate either because, before she had a chance to think about it, a horn blared, a number of times, at the front of the house.

'Sounds like your asshole ex-husband making popular with the neighbours again,' Faithe said.

Rosina looked around into the kitchen, waiting for Jeremy's imminent and showy arrival. She always kept the front door unlatched on Jeremy's days. It saved having to get up to let him in.

His feignedly apologetic entrances annoyed her.

His mere presence annoyed her.

Aurelija was standing by the patio doors with one hand clasped around her crucifix.

Rosina followed the direction of her stare. It went past the gardener, who had stopped working and, like Aurelija, was gazing at the dell.

Curiosity wasn't dancing anymore.

She stood a few steps into the undergrowth, somewhat concealed by the bushes and dwarfed by the huge trunk of the oak tree. The daddy-longlegs still swarmed about her head and, in contrast to the sunny garden, the oak tree towered over her casting a cloak of black. It wrapped her in its shadows, spilling out across the brush. And, within it, Curiosity held her arms outstretched, as though waiting for an invitation to go farther, or expecting the imminent embrace of a friend.

ELEVEN – Concerning Jeremy

The argument began the way it always did:

Jeremy said, 'Sorry I'm a bit late,' and smiled.

Rosina countered with, 'You're always late.' She was glowering as usual.

'I was busy,' he continued. 'It's that time of year for the faculty. There's first semester prep. Late marking. I have papers to edit. And there is a big conference coming up. Are you ready to go, Spud?' he shouted down to Curiosity, who was standing among the bushes at the end of the garden.

She ignored him.

'It's always *that time of year for the faculty*,' Rosina said. 'You always have *a big conference coming up*. What you are really saying is that you just don't care about us. Only about yourself and your floozy.'

Jeremy rolled his eyes. 'You're like a broken record,' he said. 'Don't you ever let up? And don't call Lauren a floozy. She is a nice person. Come on Curiosity, get up here now.'

She ignored him again.

'She's got a nice body more like.'

'Jesus, Rosina. It never ends Why do you think I couldn't stand living with you? You just prattle on. Nagging. About your depression. About how the whole world is out to get you and how nobody likes you.'

'Piss off, Jeremy.'

'You piss off, Rosina.' He grinned, and shouted to Curiosity. 'Would you bloody well get up here.'

'That's nice,' Rosina said, 'swearing at your daughter. How very mature of you. You are such a good parent.'

'What like you?' He sniggered. 'You can't even get through the morning without pouring a bottle of wine down your neck. Look, Rosina, I'm not getting into this again. Just let me take the kid and I'll get out of your hair.'

'Good,' Rosina said. 'You do that.'

Jeremy stepped out onto the lawn. 'Why is she down there anyway? I thought you didn't like people mucking around in your precious dell.'

'I don't know why she's down there. And it's none of your business anyway.'

'So, she's only my business when it suits you.'

'If you like.'

'Christ. You're such a control freak, smothering her, protecting this house and that damned dell. If I had my way, I would've dug the whole thing up the moment we moved in. There could be a Saxon horde in there, Celtic, maybe even Roman.' He breathed in a long sigh. 'But we'll never know now, will we? And all because it reminds you of your batty, old aunt.'

'Well, the dell isn't yours. And neither am I. But Curiosity is your daughter. So, try to be a father and pick her up when you're supposed to.'

He ignored her. 'Curiosity, I won't tell you again, come up here now.'

She didn't budge.

He moved another few steps down the garden. 'Jesus, Curiosity. Will you come on!'

Jeremy then looked once at Rosina, who was wearing a smug grin, and marched down the lawn towards his daughter.

As he neared the dell, an unsettling sense of wariness moved through him.

He went there once, when they had just moved in and Rosina was otherwise engaged with decorating the house. He wanted to look over the place, access the area for further exploration and maybe even a possible dig. He would swear blind the bushes had moved. And not in a normal, blowing in the breeze way, but really moved, as if they had meant to, even though to think they might be nonsense of the highest order.

If he was honest, the dell gave him the creeps.

And it did so again now.

As he approached the trees they darkened, as if a light had been turned off somewhere within and, when he reached the line of the bushes, the briars struck out towards him like a cracked whip, the surrounding ferns thickening, their fronds spreading wider. It was as before. The plants seemed to be moving. He licked his finger and raised it up to check for wind. There wasn't any. Not even a breeze.

Perhaps air was blowing out from farther inside, but he didn't feel it on his skin.

Curiosity was standing a few metres into the dell waist high in the bushes.

'What is up with you today?' he said. 'Come on. We need to go. I have important things to do.'

Curiosity either hadn't heard him or was ignoring him, because she didn't stir nor glance in his direction.

'This is ridiculous.' Jeremy took a step towards her. The bracken tightened, the briars whipped out, and the bushes shook as if a single large or many small things were scuttling towards him.

He recoiled and stepped back up the garden.

The scuttling stopped and Curiosity stayed as she was.

'Curiosity,' he shouted. 'Come here now.'

She didn't move, nor look around.

'I've had enough of this,' he then snapped and dashed into the bushes. Their branches contracted. Or at least they seemed to, as if intentionally closing around him, pressing in so tightly it felt like wading through mud. They blocked his way, the roots at his feet restricting his steps, but he made it far enough to reach out and grab Curiosity by the shoulder.

She spun around and, as if breaking from a trance, glared at him. There was rage there too, and a hint of something feral. A second later, she stomped out from the bushes and ran up the garden into the kitchen.

Jeremy followed her onto the lawn. He did so with ease. The bushes and bracken slacker now, not as restraining, and the briars returning to as they had been, stationary, hanging limp and unthreatening.

He shrugged, walked up the garden and, without looking

in their direction, went past Rosina and her American friend, through the patio doors, and into the kitchen.

Curiosity was standing on the other side of the circulation space by the front door,

'Get your stuff.' He shouted across to her.

She didn't move, only glared at him.

'Fair enough then,' he said and turned to face Rosina. 'I'll let you get back to . . .' he looked over at Faithe, '. . . your liquid lunch with your best pal here.'

'I haven't been drinking today, I'll have you know.'

Faithe just grinned and raised her coffee cup in a gesture of 'cheers'.

Jeremy scoffed. 'Whatever you say.'

'Get out.'

'I'll bring her back later.'

'Get out. I have things to do.'

'Of course, you do. You have to get drunk again.' He made off briskly across the kitchen and circulation space, half expecting a coffee cup to come cracking against the back of his head.

When he joined Curiosity by the front door, he glanced back through the kitchen, out the patio doors, and down the garden at the dell. With a sudden, violent swish, every tree and every bush, bramble, briar, and patch of bracken swayed to one side before they came to rest again.

Jeremy snatched Curiosity's hand and left.

He slammed the door so hard behind him the walls rattled.

'He really is an asshole,' Faithe said.

'He is,' Rosina replied. 'The world's biggest. But he is also

Curiosity's father, and I only wish he would realise that. If he returned home like any other normal . . .'

'Oh, for Cris'sake,' Faithe interrupted. 'Not this again. Look, he is a lying, cheating, scheming creep. You are on your own. Better get used to it.'

'But we were a family.'

'You were a mess. You still are.'

Rosina sat down on one of the loungers. 'No need to be rude about it.'

'There is every need. You have to wake up. People are simple creatures, searching for the same old worn-out patterns. Even you. Especially you. They crave familiar situations, and are little more than a bag of hormones. Fight, flight, fornicate. The sum of most human behaviour in three succinct words. Get a job. Attract a mate. Have a kid. Buy a house to hide in. And find an enemy to hate. Basic survival. Nothing more. No beauty. No spirit. No appreciation. And, when the whole thing goes tits up, begin the whole sick ride all over again. There are a rare few who manage to break the cycle but sadly, Sugarplum, you're not one of those.'

'You are saying I'm shallow?'

'You're not shallow, as such. You are just one of the herd. Moooo!' She sniggered and lit a cigarette.

Rosina huffed.

'This thing with Jeremy has left you floundering in dead space,' Faithe continued with smoke drifting out of her mouth and nostrils. 'You are looking for something or someone to latch on to. Someone who will make all the bad stuff disappear so you can start over again. And you think it's Jeremy, because he is test-driven. Familiar. With him, you know what to expect, and will put up with anything as long as you can keep your house, manipulate your kid and, no doubt, find some other poor schmuck to hate. Well, it's not like that. Life is crap and then more crap happens. That's the way of it. That's how things are. No order. Just delightful chaos. Your only saving grace is you have me to watch over you. To latch on to.' She took a draw on her cigarette and smiled. It looked more like a leer.

Rosina didn't reply and, from that point, they sat in silence. She felt angry, hurt, and worried.

She gazed into the distance, not fully aware of the world going on around her, seething about her argument with her ex-husband, sulking over Faithe's harsh words, and mulling over how her daughter had been acting out of character: venturing close to the dell, ballet dancing, or at least something as close as to be equated to ballet dancing.

Actually – thinking about it – the girl had hardly said boo to a goose since coming home from their shopping trip the day before, and all this from a child who usually came across as obstinate as to be a right royal nuisance. For anyone with the eyes to see it, Curiosity's demeanour had become more standoffish than usual, cold even.

She had changed.

She seemed happier but not quite with it, like crazy people. Throw in the Lithuanian woman's fearful stare, and Rosina felt a chill move through her, a sense of foreboding, coupled with the re-emergence of obscure memories she had suppressed because, to recall them, might prove too frightening to contemplate.

As for Curiosity, she was none too happy about being wrenched away from her daydreams. Her parents should have left her alone. They did most other times. Leaving her alone was what they did best. They should have left her to explore and follow the hissing voices into the dell; voices that sounded unpleasant and scary, but also so very alluring.

TWELVE – Concerning the power of magic

The faux leather car seat squeaked and felt hot against the back of her legs. Even with the top down, the passing air did little to cool the heat rising from the upholstery. Her bum was sweating, her back sticky, and the thought of sitting on the skin of a dead animal made her flesh crawl and stomach turn.

Daddy had come alone, and Curiosity didn't bother to inquire if Lauren would be at his flat. Most times, when they arrived there, she would be lying on the couch, dressed in just a satin nightie, tapping at her phone like a crazy person or engrossed in one of her celebrity magazines that, even at eight years old, Curiosity knew paid no more contribution to society than to rot brain cells to porridge. Actually, Curiosity couldn't care less what her father and his latest girlfriend got up to.

And she had no doubts what they *got up to* as well.

She wasn't stupid about that kind of thing.

Daddy had always played around.

'It's what he does best,' Mummy said, more times than could be counted, and usually before she burst into tears and stared at Curiosity as though it was her fault.

As for Lauren, she stank like the perfume aisle at Fortnum and Mason. She wore too much makeup and was rude, especially when, by merely asking to sit on the couch, Curiosity interrupted her 'reading'.

But Curiosity didn't give a damn about any of them.

All she wanted to do right now was to go back home, get out of this hot car, and return to the bottom of the garden. She wanted to spin and reel across the grass, to mimic the figurine she held in her hands, caressing it with her fingertips as though it was a real, live, tiny creature; *her* real, live, tiny, creature, who granted the magic to create dream-worlds and the passion to be a ballerina.

She was so engrossed that they had driven all the way to Marble Arch and onto Park Lane before she noticed that Daddy had detoured from the usual route to his apartment. But she cared little about this too. Her only focus was the figurine.

He spoke first.

He seemed calmer, as if the frequent arguments with Mummy were only incidental interruptions to his day.

'I need to pick up some papers at my office,' he said. 'There is a conference next week and I need my research data. Afterwards we can get some *Happy Burgers*. What do you say?'

'I don't eat burgers,' Curiosity said, without looking up from her figurine.

'Since when?'

'Since three weeks ago. Including last week when you wanted to feed me burgers and I told you I don't eat burgers.'

'Oh yeah, I remember now. And it still bemuses me why. But it's a nice sunny day. After I finish up at the university, we could get some supermarket food and sit out in Greenwich Park for a half-hour or so. How does that sound?'

'I take it I won't be staying at your flat tonight then?'

'You know I would love you to stay, Spud. But I have . . .' He hit the brakes. 'Get out of the bloody way,' he shouted at a lad eating an ice lolly, who seemed unaware of where the footpath ended and the road began, probably due to the phone he was holding pressed against his ear. The lad carried on regardless. When he passed, Daddy snorted and shook his head. He revved the engine and sped off, hooking a left around Hyde Park Corner and wittering on about 'the witless numbskull'.

Curiosity chuckled.

When Daddy calmed, he continued, 'As I was saying, I can't have you over tonight because I have booked tickets to Tosca. I'm trying to broaden Lauren's grasp of things cultural.'

That'll take a stretch, Curiosity thought, reckoning Lauren's flirtation with her father was more to do with securing a better final grade than her need to broaden her grasp of *things cultural.*

She had become accustomed to his excuses, and his relationships. She had also become acclimatised to his patchy parenting skills, made evident by his inclination to feed her a diet of burgers, fries, and fizzy drinks, all of which Curiosity detested to the point of wanting to puke.

Still, what did she care now?

Her mostly absentee father and status-obsessed mother had no hold over her any more.

She had her figurine. She had her dreams, and dancing, and the growing sense that there was a wondrous adventure to embark upon, just like in her storybooks.

She said no more, and neither did her father until, after a series of traffic light stops, they turned from Regent Street into Piccadilly Circus.

Shoppers thronged the footpaths.

Tourists stood in groups of up to a dozen, taking photos of Eros.

A black taxi and a bus had blocked each other at the junction with Shaftesbury Avenue and, in turn, gridlocked all other traffic.

'Some people might think this a slow way to get to Greenwich,' Daddy said. 'But don't you just love driving through central London in the summer, with the top down and the wind blowing through your hair?'

Curiosity didn't answer. She knew full well that he had only come this way to show off his new sports car. She also reckoned that, by the time they reached London Bridge, his love of driving through central London would be replaced with huffs, snorts, and some ripe curse words.

He glanced across. 'What's that you've got there?'

'It's my ballerina.'

'Doesn't look like much. Where did you get it?'

'I found it at Mummy's dell. It was dirty, so I cleaned it up.'

She felt pride in her deception. She was becoming quite the creator: dream worlds, dancing . . . lies.

The figurine quivered in her hand, as though in approval.

Perhaps she can hear us, Curiosity thought. *Perhaps her*

magical realm is all around, a place that people can't see, but it's there, watching and reading my mind.

Her father glanced across again. 'Well, it looks like a bunch of grubby, old twigs to me. You should throw it away.' He reached out to snatch the figurine from her hands

'Don't touch it.' She clutched the figurine to her chest.

Was there something wrong with his eyes? It wasn't a bunch of twigs. Could he not see how beautiful it was?

He struck out again. 'It's filthy. Throw it away before it makes a mess of my seats.'

'You can't have it.' She hissed.

'Curiosity. Do as you're told.'

'No!'

Daddy snapped his hand back. 'Okay, okay. Suit yourself. It's no big deal. But don't go dropping it in here. I don't want my seats ruined. And who knows what infections there are in that dell? If you catch anything nasty, don't come crying to me.'

The cars in front moved forward. Not by much, though, only a few metres.

Daddy snorted, sighed, grunted then swung the car to the right. He bumped two wheels up onto the kerb, edged around a line of three cars, before he sped along Coventry Street and down into Haymarket, causing shoppers and tourists to hop back onto the pavement as he weaved around the obstructing traffic.

He went along Pall Mall East and onto Trafalgar Square.

It took a while, his bad temper showing in the way he huffed and repeatedly said, 'There should be a ban on weekend drivers,' so many times it sounded like the chorus of a song.

At Duncannon Street the traffic eased, and so did his mood.

'I never liked that dell,' he said out of the blue as they turned onto The Strand. 'It freaks me out. Don't tell your mother, but I tried to go in there once. Years ago. Behind her back. I was putting together a proposal for a possible dig. I've never seen foliage so dense. I would've needed one of those big machetes they have in the jungle movies just to hack my way through.' He laughed. It seemed strained. 'The strange thing was; it seemed to be growing right there in front of my eyes. It's kind of did the same thing again today. It was probably just an optical illusion or the heat messing with my frazzled old brain but, to tell you the truth, the whole place gives me the creeps. Anyway, a well-placed digger would sort it out. People get too caught up with trees and forests but, if you ask me, everything's up for grabs. What use is land if you can't make a bit of cash out of it?'

If it was a genuine question Curiosity had no desire to reply. She hated him for disrespecting nature. It disgusted her. To him everything had a price, but nothing had value. Even at eight she saw this. He was what Faithe Henning called a money grubber. And why he became an archaeologist in the first place bemused her. He never talked about his job; other than how busy he was when it came to picking her up. He never showed any real desire to protect the history he uncovered, just excited, when he would arrive home with some artefact or other that he could sell on.

Apparently, the university allowed him to do this, but she had her doubts.

Her anger rose, but Curiosity sat in silence, caressing her figurine.

They crossed London Bridge, drove through Bermondsey onto Lower Road and stopped at a set of traffic lights, where the car caught the attention of a group of four teenage lads who were sitting, in various degrees of slouch, against a low wall by high-rise housing estate. They looked agitated; all of them wearing thick black tracksuits with hoodies hiding their faces, which Curiosity reckoned to be idiotic on such a sweltering day.

The group rose in unison and strutted over to the kerb. They seemed tense, and skittish, as though they existed in a constant state of edginess. One step away from doing mischief, and another from the watchful eye of CCTV cameras that topped many of the lampposts in both directions as far as the eye could see.

'Sick ride, fam,' the nearest of them said. 'That's one o' them Zagato innit?'

'Yeah, it's dope, bro,' another added, and Curiosity sensed her father's unease.

A moment later, two of the teenagers had gathered by the passenger door. One of them leaned across the bonnet and ran his fingers over the paintwork. He snapped his hand back.

'Piece o' shit car.' He kicked the side wing. Daddy cringed but said nothing. He stared straight ahead.

The other teenagers laughed and Curiosity sniggered.

'You laughin' at me?' the one blowing on his fingers said.

'Yeah, you laughin' at my fam?' another one added, his face creased in a sneer.

Curiosity scowled back, but they ignored her. The rest swaggered closer to the car.

In the driver seat, her father sat with his fingers gripped around the steering-wheel; his hands trembling and his gaze fixed on the traffic lights, as though mentally urging them to change.

Curiosity just stared at the teenagers with distain, for trying to intimidate her, for laughing at her.

Whispers grew in her ears.

An image formed in her mind, of blood gushing from their sliced throats.

She smiled inwardly. Or was it outwardly? She wasn't sure, only that – in the real world – she saw their pupils flare, before they dashed back to the wall, climbed over it and ran off into the housing estate, sending guarded, resentful looks her direction, as though she had given them a terrifying vision of their own death . . . and perhaps she had.

Curiosity felt certain she could do anything, if she only willed it to be.

The lights turned through amber to green, and her father sped off, his sigh audible over the noise of the traffic.

For the next twenty minutes he remained silent.

When they reached the East Gate of the Old Royal Naval College and the University of Greenwich, he exchanged some words with the security guard and drove into the parking area. He pulled into a secluded spot at the end, which was strange choice for her father. He usually liked to park in the open, where his prized possession might be seen and attract the greatest attention.

He must have been rattled by the teenage hoodies.

It pleased her to see him still on edge.

The figurine seemed pleased too. It vibrated, radiating warmth into Curiosity's hands, up her arms, into and through her body.

Daddy got out, dashed around to the passenger side and ran his fingers over the wing.

His mood changed:

'There is no damage. Only the scumbag's footprint. I'll get my valet service to give her the once over. She needs a good clean and polish anyway.' He then leaned in and ruffled Curiosity's hair. She hated that. 'Stay here while I go to my office. When I am done, we can think about dropping you back home.'

'What about the park?'

'What park?'

'Lunch?'

'Oh yes. We were going to have lunch in the park. Do we have to do it today?'

'You promised. It was my birthday yesterday.'

'Oh, that.' He looked put out. 'And I suppose I did promise, didn't I?'

'Yes, you did. And it's eight, if you're trying to remember how old I am.'

'I know,' he said with a tone of confidence.

But Curiosity sensed he was faking it.

'It's just that I'm very busy this weekend,' he said. 'The department is prepping for an important conference. I was going to wait until the next time I pick you up. We can do something really special then.' He smiled, paused then said. 'No. I tell you what, let me get my papers, and we'll get some food from the supermarket. I'm sure I can fit in a quick lunch with my star girl.' He ruffled her hair again. She pulled away. 'I can't stay long though, Spud. Tosca starts at seven thirty and . . .' he checked his watch, '. . . it's five past four now. But, what the hell. Anything for my little birthday princess, eh?'

For a change, he kept to his word and, twenty minutes later, they went through the large, ornate gates of Greenwich Park, each clutching a paper bag filled with: in Curiosity's case a bean salad and a bottle of organic coconut water, her father opting for just a cola.

She placed in the figurine in her pocket.

'Where do you want to sit?' he asked.

Curiosity led him to a grassy hillock, nestled within a crop of trees, dotted with tiny mounds, and where the bushes grew ragged, unlike the rest of the grounds where they were clipped and cultivated.

They sat beneath a blackthorn tree; Curiosity breathing in the scents of the wildflowers; her father texting on his phone as usual.

She recalled another day, when he had been less rushed, had found time to be fatherly.

He had told her about the Roman temple that had once stood nearby:

'This area was a shrine for many centuries,' he had said. 'According to Brythonic folklore, it was a place where the nature spirits were venerated. How cool is that?'

Of course, he went on to state that he wanted to dig up the site, 'if certain authorities stopped being so obstructive.'

But, still, they had shared a moment.

And that moment had been right here, in this spot, among the trees and bushes.

The figurine vibrated in her pocket. It grew warmer. She sensed its approval, whispering in her mind.

It truly was a magical thing.

Ten minutes later, having downed his cola, her father now stood many metres away, talking on his phone and occasionally smiling back at her as she finished the last few mouthfuls of her bean salad.

This was Daddy's definition of having lunch with her.

She lay back and gazed up at the blackthorn tree.

Sunrays danced upon the leaves. A large butterfly landed on one of the branches. It was a Purple Emperor. Cassidy told her how to recognise them. Something leaped between the branches. A small animal, difficult to make out at first but, when it scurried down the trunk, she saw it was a red squirrel. She knew this because Cassidy had told her they had tufted ears and a white underside.

It dropped to the ground and began nibbling at the cobnut it was holding in its paws.

Curiosity craned her head around to get a better view and the squirrel stopped nibbling.

Its fur twitched. Its fluffy tail wiggled. It made a few unco-ordinated darts from left to right, before it skittered off and up an adjacent oak tree. As it climbed higher, it periodically stopped to peer down at her. It looked scared, as if she held its life in her hands.

Maybe she did.

Maybe she had created the squirrel like she had the hedgehog in her bedroom the night before.

Could she really do that? Were her creations and the real world interchangeable?

She smiled at the thought, and recalled earlier in the day when she danced by the dell at the end of the garden. She relived the breeze blowing through her hair, the insects whirling about her head, and how they settled upon her outstretched arms, their touch as soft as silk and the gentle beat of their wings caressing her skin. She remembered the low background hum, interspersed with voices, like a hushed choir, high-pitched, melodic, and oh so enchanting, urging her to go past the old oak tree and walk deeper into the dell.

Something else moved overhead.

Then it dropped down into a shaded spot at the base of the blackthorn tree.

Thinking it to be another squirrel, she said, 'So, there are quite a few of you little guys about here.' She craned her head around. Perhaps she would introduce one into her next dream world.

What she saw was a squirrel, but not as she expected.

Its fur twitched.

Its fluffy tail wiggled.

But there was blood. Lots of blood.

Bubbling from the space where the squirrel's head should be.

THIRTEEN – Concerning a gardener

A short while after Jeremy Portland came for and left with his daughter, Brendan Cassidy finished with the flowerbeds, put the hoe back in the shed, and walked down to the dell.

Curiosity had gone there earlier.

He didn't like that, or anything else about the place. It harboured unhappy memories. And, if truth be told, he didn't know what he might find when he got there.

The trees and bushes, however, rustled as expected. The undergrowth looked dark and dense, but not in any way that might be deemed unusual for a patch so wild with brush and thorns.

Still, a sense of dread niggled.

He turned, left the garden by the side gate, and headed for home. He didn't bother telling Rosina that he was going. She had her friend with her, which meant she had time for little else but lounging around and getting drunk. In his opinion, she was an addict – and, in his time, he had seen more than a few – both to the drink and to the company, beguiled by her friend's strength and influence over her.

To Brendan, the friendship seemed one-sided. *But who was he to interfere in other people's lives?* Rosina Portland's business was her own.

As he walked down Bingham Crescent, his arthritis grated as if there was builder's gravel - not cartilage - behind his kneecaps. This last year or so, he had contemplated packing in gardening altogether. It wasn't as if he needed the money. He was a pensioner now and, unlike others on the housing estate where he lived, he owned his flat outright. To any sensible person, retirement was the logical option. He could take an extended holiday to visit family. He hadn't been home for over twenty years and reckoned he was due a long break, never mind an easier, less painful life. But each time the notion came, he thought of Lily and the self-imposed duty he must perform to honour her memory. Working at her, and now Rosina's home, he kept a little of her with him. It helped him cope with her loss, and deal with the horror of finding her body.

When he reached the corner with Westbourne Grove, his gaze drifted to the burned-out toy shop and the site of so much suffering. He had passed it many times on his way home and, as with each of those, he shrugged, an involuntary shiver rippling down his back as he crossed the street, walked up Colville Gardens, and turned in the direction of his flat in a side street off Portobello Road.

When he got home, he made tea, a tomato sandwich, switched on the television and watched a western where the town sheriff was waiting for his past life to catch up with him.

The distraction didn't work.

The feeling of dread stayed with him. Brendan was scared. He blessed himself.

It was happening again.

His only prayer was that, this time, nobody would die.

FOURTEEN – Concerning the beautiful ballerina

Curiosity woke shivering, her mind trailing remnants of a nightmare where a tiny, spindly creature, with wrinkled, grey skin and pin-like eyes, was decapitating a squirrel with its teeth.

In her half sleep state, it leered at her.

Blood gurgled. The squirrel struggled.

An instant later, she was transported to the dell, where everything stank of rotting vegetation and shadows spread across the tree trunks, cast by the dozens of spindly creatures that were standing on the branches above. They jumped down; falling in a shower of wriggling bodies that, when amassed on the ground, moved towards her.

She willed her eyes to open, but they didn't respond.

She tried again. Her eyes cracked a slit, before they closed again, her dream returning just as heavily as before, with the hideous creatures drawing ever closer.

She tried once more.

This time, she saw daylight. From out of the fug, she made out her wardrobe, her dresser, and the full-length mirror. She was on her own bed. Overhead, on the ceiling, the chandelier twinkled in the sunlight. It shone pretty colours around the room, along with shadows, that seemed friendlier than those from her dream, not so ominous. There was no sound other than her own breathing.

Then, the shadows grew.

They twisted, became silhouettes of the horrid little creatures, and went scurrying down the walls, disappearing into the corner behind the wardrobe. When they appeared again, they clambered over the end of her bed, leaping onto her feet, moving up her legs and onto her chest, still only shadows, but cold, heavy like a wet blanket, weighing her down, squeezing the air from her lungs.

She screamed and bolted upright, her hair clinging to her scalp, her skin damp and clammy. A drip of sweat trickled down her cheek. It felt good, real, something from the normal world.

The bedroom door flew open and Mummy rushed in.

'It's fine. I'm here,' she said and plonked down on the edge of the bed.

But Curiosity took little notice, fearful that this too might be some cruel ruse, that she might still be trapped inside the nightmare. She focused on her wardrobe, and the full-length mirror, both emblazoned by the sunlight surging through the oval window. She noticed her animal welfare posters on the walls, her desk, and her cuddly toy, which her mother now held in her hands.

With each of these landmarks, her fear eased. Warmth returned to her body, bringing with it welcome confirmation that the shadows had indeed gone. Through her renewed clarity, she then remembered screaming at the sight of the headless squirrel and turning to see her father, with his phone still in his hand, charging towards her.

'What's wrong, Spud?' he had shouted. 'What is it?'

'There,' Curiosity said, 'on the ground.'

'I don't see anything.'

'There. A squirrel without a head.'

'What?' His gaze scoured the spot beneath the black-thorn tree.

'It's right there,' she insisted. But it wasn't. The ground was bare, only dirt and a scattering of leaves. 'But it was. I saw it.'

She recalled crying, and Daddy taking her back to his car along with his follow-up phone-call to his girlfriend:

'Lauren – Darling, Curiosity is upset about something. Would it be okay if we cancel Tosca? She might need to stay over tonight. If I bring her home in the state she's in, Rosina will have a right go at me. I'll never hear the last of it.' He paused, listening to Lauren's reply. 'Yes, yes, I know I promised. But she's my daughter. Why are you being like this? She's not attention seeking. She's only a child. No, no, you don't have to leave. I'll bring her back to her mother. I'll be home soon.' He smiled. 'Remember to wear something nice.'

He smacked some kisses and put the phone in his trouser pocket. He then led Curiosity out of park, into the grounds of the Old Royal Naval College, and across to his car.

'Well, you seem much better now,' he said. 'What do you say we get you home to your mother?'

Less than an hour later, he dropped Curiosity back with Mummy and drove away, leaving behind his usual reel of promises of doing something special when he picked her up in two weeks' time.

'Maybe we'll have a celebration. We can push the boat out.

It will be all about you, Spud. Curiosity's belated but extra special birthday party.'

But, from the time her father came running to her aid until he drove away in his car, she gave little credence to anything he said, much less with any conscious thought. Her mind had been elsewhere, caught in the fright of the moment, numbed by it, as though time had stopped.

Now, remembering what he promised, she warranted his words with the usual disregard.

Faithe Henning sometimes called him a 'dumbass'.

With an inward snigger, Curiosity called him that too.

Her mother edged closer on the bed. She smiled, and wiggled the paw of the cuddly kitten, as though levity might dispel the demons, or ingratiate her as being in some way motherly. But, as quickly as it came, that levity disappeared, and she slipped into her standard litany of denunciations:

'Your father is useless,' she said. 'He couldn't even take the time to care for his own daughter. A problem arose and away he went. Poor old Jeremy Portland and his ever so important piece of fluff.'

With practiced efficiency, Curiosity zoned out at this point. Her mother's sympathy was a sham, more about creating a stick to beat her father with than any real concern for her daughter's wellbeing.

There was a knock at the door. It opened and Aurelija stepped inside.

'I'll be going now, Mrs. Portland,' she said. She seemed uneasy, peering around the room as though she expected something to jump out at her.

'Are you finished with your duties?' Mummy asked.

'Yes, I am totally finished.' She glanced at Curiosity, backed out into the corridor, and clutched the crucifix at her neck.

'Then you can go,' Mummy said.

Curiosity reckoned, however, that the Lithuanian woman didn't even hear this.

Before the words had been said, Curiosity heard her rumbling down the stairs and the front door closing with a thud.

As for Mummy, she seemed to have noticed nothing untoward about Aurelija's behaviour and resumed harping on about Jeremy Portland being a useless father, how he had no regard for anyone but himself, and so on and so forth into tiresomeness.

While she ranted, Curiosity reached into her pocket for her figurine. She needed it to take away her thoughts, from the bad dream, from her mother and her endless moaning. It wasn't there and, for first time since waking, she noticed that the whispering voices had stopped.

She panicked, rummaging under her pillow and searching around the bed.

She didn't find it.

She scoured the room, but couldn't see the figurine anywhere.

What if she had dropped it at the park?

What if she had lost it forever? What if the magic had ended?

She made to get up. Her mother stopped her.

'You should rest,' she said. 'Something gave you a bad shock – no thanks to your father.'

'My figurine,' Curiosity said. 'Have you seen it?'

'What figurine?'

'My figurine. Have you taken my ballerina? What have you done with it?'

'I haven't the foggiest idea what you are talking about.'

'I had a figurine. She is my dancing lady. I had her with me when I was with Daddy, but I can't find her now. Oh, please don't be lost,' she said, hoping the magic realm might hear. 'Please don't go. I need you so much.'

'Well, I haven't seen any figurine,' her mother said. 'And who are you talking to?' She was looking towards the door, as if expecting to see someone, perhaps Aurelija, standing there. She then looked back at Curiosity, and frowned, her expression one of curiosity, maybe confusion, as though she was struggling to remember something. 'I didn't even know you had such a thing,' she continued. 'What does it look like?'

Then Curiosity saw it.

The figurine was on the window ledge, blazing bright in the sunshine.

'It doesn't matter,' she said. She rested back onto her pillow. Maybe she had panicked too much and, like this situation, there was also a logical, less frightening explanation for what had happened in the park.

The poor little squirrel might have strayed too close to a lawnmower. Accidents do happen after all. Or it might have been dropped by a hawk and snatched up again when she turned away. It would explain it not being there when she looked back again. And there were hawks in that part of London. She had seen them many times, waiting in Daddy's car, while he conducted *an emergency Saturday tutorial* with one of his female students.

Either way, getting distressed was ridiculous. Death was part of nature. So was blood and dead animals.

Thinking about it, she felt a bit foolish now, for Daddy having to hurry her home, for screaming.

'It's okay, Mummy,' she said, 'I'm fine now.'

'You didn't seem fine when your father dumped you at the front door.'

'Well, I'm fine now. I got frightened, is all. I'm a big girl. I can cope.'

'You all but fainted when you got home. You dashed up these stairs like a lunatic and passed out on the bed. You stayed like it for a good fifteen minutes, until you screamed. It gave me such a fright.'

'Mummy, I'm okay. You don't have to stay. Go back down to Faithe.'

'If your father cared one way or another, he wouldn't have . . .'

'Look, you don't have to stay. Go away.'

Her mother straightened. 'Well, if you are going to be rude, I will join Faithe downstairs. This is the thanks I get for being a compassionate mother. Maybe you need space to think about your manners. It might do you some good to be by yourself.' She left, easing the bedroom door closed as she went.

Mummy didn't do slamming doors. And she didn't do raised voices.

Curiosity was no stranger to being alone. Apart from school and the occasional, mostly unwanted visit from Arabella Heffington Jeffries, she spent most of her time alone. In many respects she had grown to like it that way. She preferred her own company. It was better than being sniped at by Mummy at every turn, and why she collected charm bells. An active mind can ponder a great many things when put to a repetitive task. It has space to wander and invent. She was adept at it, even before she found the figurine, back when daydreams were just illusions, and before she had the power to make them real.

She waited a moment longer, until she heard her mother speak to Faithe downstairs then raced across the room to the oval window. With a gentle grip, she brought the figurine to her chest, returned to her bed and lay down, cradling the figurine in the palms of her hands.

Gazing at the ceiling, she drew in a slow, measured breath, and exhaled in the same deliberate manner. She closed her eyes, took another deep breath, then another, and kept doing so, in slow repetition, until her mind wandered. The whispering voices returned, albeit low-pitched. Through her inner eye she saw the ceiling disappear and become a resplendent blue sky. The shadows from the chandelier turned to clouds. Countless shoots sprouted from the floor, the furniture, her bed, and coiled upwards, reaching for the sun that now blazed in the centre of the ceiling sky. They unfurled, budded, and became wildflowers. They speckled the hills and hollows with vibrant colour, the grass swaying in gentle breeze as though brushed by an invisible hand, liberating sweet fragrances to surge up and fill the air.

The earth shook violently. The floor cracked and fell away. Birch, rowan, and blackthorn burst into being. Thorny briars struck out from the shadows. They set claim to all they touched, weaving their web, encasing this copy of the dell in their tendrils, as though a living entity, and a truly magical thing.

Lost to the reverie, Curiosity immersed herself fully into her creation.

Except, where previously she had only watched, this time she was leaping and dancing, laughing out loud at the audacity of it all, creating life with every step.

One step: buttercups.

Two steps: bluebells, followed by cowslips, foxgloves, snapdragons, and splashes of blue columbine, flowers of all shapes and scents, bursting in her wake and tracing spirals of colour in her slipstream. And, as she created, the figurine vibrated. It felt warm in her hands. It invigorated her flesh and spoke inside her mind.

Come in, it said.

She opened her eyes and discovered that she was standing in a meadow, flowers tickling her heels, grass prickling the soles of her feet, and a soft breeze brushing her face. Behind her, the flower splattered hills rolled back into the distance. Before her, the dell loomed, thick, knotted, but still inviting.

For assurance, she clutched her figurine tighter, but it wasn't there, only her fingers, folding around each other, skin touching skin. The figurine had disappeared.

She opened her hands and, for a few confused seconds, gazed at her palms as though, in doing so, the figurine might reappear there. It didn't and, an instant later, the magnificent vista also vanished.

In the blink of an eye, her bedroom became as it had always been.

She rushed to her bed, threw her pillow and duvet aside, but found nothing. She grabbed the wastepaper basket from beneath her desk, scrabbled around among the scrunched-up balls of paper, but found nothing there either. With frantic swipes of her hands, she went through the drawers of her desk, scouring through pencils, pens, erasers, and other desk-stuff. She ran to her dresser and cast her clothes to the floor. She threw open her wardrobe, got down on her hands and knees to search behind the upright mirror, but the figurine was nowhere to be seen.

Her heart sank. She returned to her bed, buried her head in her hands, and cried.

Her ballerina was gone.

The magic was gone.

Something sparkled on the window-ledge.

She wiped the tears from her face and looked up to see her figurine blazing bright in the sunlight. But not posed like a ballet dancer. She was standing upright. The fronds of her tattered green dress hanging downwards, ruffled as though made from real cloth. Her arms, where they had previously been raised above her head, were now folded at her chest, her copper hair flowing down the length of one bare arm, the wings on her back fluttering.

The tiny figure was looking straight at her.

Her eyes were wide open, and blinking, but Curiosity felt no fear, just amazement and happiness that her fairy ballerina had returned, had come alive to her.

Part of the magic. Part of the wonder.

'Oh, you are so beautiful,' Curiosity said.

In response, the little fairy glowed, and Curiosity chuckled.

She held out her palm. The creature looked down, as if gauging how to step onto it, but didn't. Instead, it – *she* – gazed at Curiosity, her features creased, as though assessing the larger, human creature standing before her.

'You are my beautiful ballerina,' Curiosity said. 'My fairy-lady. And I love you with all my heart.'

With that, the fairy-lady rose up and went flitting around the room. She darted from corner to corner, randomly coming to rest upon a piece of furniture, before she whisked away again, sometimes spiralling upwards like a spinning top, sometimes twirling downwards, skipping across the carpet like a pebble across a pond. Awestruck, Curiosity watched as the tiny creature tumbled, looped, and danced upon the air. She was mesmerised by the acrobatics and enchanted by the trails of sparkling dust that streaked in her wake. She laughed. She clapped. She hoped the show would never end and, for many minutes it didn't until, after a few last circuits of the room, the fairy-lady just stopped. She fluttered down to hover centimetres from Curiosity's nose. She wore a quizzical look on her little face, as though searching for something in Curiosity's expression. Perhaps for kindliness, or maybe for the love that she had professed only moments earlier.

The fairy-lady smiled and Curiosity's heart quivered.

It trembled again when the creature hovered by her ear.

The whispering, that up to now had sounded more subdued than usual, got louder. The room filled with insect-like buzzing, quite loud and unpleasant to hear. Within it were the hissing voices she had become familiar with. Curiosity, however, disregarded the unpleasantness, for she was taken.

She knew she would endure anything to be with her fairy-lady.

That she would follow her anywhere.

As if knowing this, the fairy-lady zipped across to the door. She circled the knob, which turned unaided and, when the door opened, she floated out into the corridor. With one tiny hand, she beckoned Curiosity to follow her, and she did, out to and along the first-floor landing.

The fairy-lady guided her, past her mother's bedroom and two guest bedrooms, to the recessed staircase at the farthest end of the corridor. There were no windows here. The stairwell was dimly lit, chillier than the rest of the house, and yucky, grey cobwebs matted the banister rail leading up seven treads to a door, which in turn led to an attic room, where Curiosity had never been and never had cause to want to. She might be adventurous but was still wary of dark places. Well, until now.

The fairy-lady hovered mid-air. She was pointing up the stairs to the door.

'Do you want me to go to the attic?' Curiosity asked.

She was certain she had heard a hissing voice say, *'Surprise.'*

The fairy-lady flew up the stairs. Midway, she turned, her glow illuminating the recess, and gestured for Curiosity to follow.

Taken as she was, Curiosity went with her. She climbed the stairs. When she reached the last step, the fairy-lady circled the knob and the door opened.

The room looked much gloomier than even the stairwell.

It smelled stale, like clothes left too long between washes.

Above her head, rafters sloped down from a thick cross beam, inclining back into the shadows at the far end of the room. There was dust, lots of dust. It covered the floor and drifted on the air. It created a curtain in the doorway, through which she could make out cardboard boxes, about five in all, maybe more to the rear, she wasn't sure because, although some sunlight managed penetrate the room's single skylight window, it was feeble, muted by dust and the grimy cobwebs that fogged and dirtied the glass.

As her eyes adjusted, she made out some furniture: four kitchen chairs, placed two on top of two, a threadbare sofa, a tall dresser, a wooden clothes rack, a mannequin wearing an old coat and a floppy hat, and a wooden trunk, sitting a few metres inside the door.

The fairy-lady hovered over the wooden trunk.

She was glowing brighter than before and, again, Curiosity thought she heard the word *surprise* being whispered in her ear.

As she stepped inside, she remembered Mummy had forbidden her from coming to the attic. She said it was a grubby place, that she didn't want her trailing dirt down and over her expensive carpets. But, as with all adventurous children who are prohibited from doing something or other, Curiosity cared little for what her mother did or didn't allow. The wooden trunk intrigued her. The wood looked shabby and pitted. It had an iron clasp keeping the lid shut. It reminded her of a treasure chest in a pirate movie.

Mostly, however, it was just there, all but urging her to look inside.

So, she did.

She flipped the clasp and pushed the lid upwards. The hinges creaked. A waft of dust and musty air rose up and she pinched her nose.

The fairy-lady flitted away to the other end of the room, still in view, but hovering back among the shadows, arms folded, like a tiny teacher waiting for her pupil to solve a puzzle.

In the trunk, Curiosity found a bundle of patterned, brightly coloured cloth. Three kaftan dresses, which she supposed might have belonged to the woman Mummy sometimes talked about and called her 'Aunt Lily'.

She folded them neatly and set them aside.

Two books lay beneath them. The first one was titled: *The Magic in the Groves.* On the cover was an elaborate painting of trees and bushes. It looked similar to the dell, and the pages inside were laid out much like her other storybooks, with colourful illustrations of fairy folk, goblins, imps, and pixies, with short stories to complement each.

She liked this book.

It was much like her others.

The second book had no images at all on its olive-green cover, just the title: *Ways of Seeing – a Treatise on Crossing to the Otherworld.* Its pages held no illustrations either, only long paragraphs of text that looked wordy and boring.

Near the back, a page had been torn out and only a ragged remnant of paper remained, but Curiosity didn't waste time to speculate on what the page might contain. Her curiosity was pricked by the A4 sized sketchpad set edgewise at the back of the trunk.

She put the books aside.

She lifted out the sketchpad and flipped open the cover.

A coloured pencil drawing commanded the first page, depicting a naked, pale – almost opaque grey – skinned girl sitting among flowers. She looked as thin as a rake, had flowers in her hair, and four, multicoloured dragonfly wings flared from her back. She wore an impertinent expression, as if challenging the artist to capture her image, and she reminded Curiosity of her fairy-lady, albeit less refined.

The page was bordered with sketched coils of bright, green ivy and, at the top, the words *tylwyth teg* and *aes sidhe* had been written in black pencil, with the word *faerie* written below.

Curiosity speculated that this was the correct way to spell *fairy*, and vowed to do so from now on.

As she continued through the rest of the sketchpad, on each page there were drawings: some depicted flying insects similar to daddy-longlegs, like the ones she saw when she had been dancing down by the dell, only with humanlike faces and bodies. There were creatures that looked like emaciated squirrels or hedgehogs, and others that had impish features, with tiny pin-like eyes and pointed ears and noses. Some wore foxgloves for hats. Others had grass growing from their backs and acorns for skulls. The daddy-longlegs types were sketched in flight and, those without wings, were depicted frolicking though wildflower meadows, or congregating along the branches of trees.

It struck Curiosity how beautiful they all were, weird to be sure, but so attractive.

Some of the pages she flicked through had more writing on them: *cyhyraeth, an cat sídhe, gwyllion*, and *pwca*. She assumed, like the first page, these must be the names of the bizarre creatures, written in a language that wasn't English and she didn't at all understand.

There were also long paragraphs she didn't bother to read.

Inside the back cover, a page – which she assumed to be the one from the green book – was paper-clipped to the cardboard, along with an old, orange-tinged photograph.

She pulled them off.

The page fell free and dropped into the trunk. She left it there. Her attention captured by photograph.

It showed a child, a girl.

She was dancing at the end of the garden by the dell. Behind the girl, faint lights glowed in the bushes. The closest ones looked like eyes and faces.

Curiosity reckoned the girl to be somewhere around her own age. She had red hair, wore a white ballet tutu with fairy wings, and was holding her arms arced above her head, like the ballerina figurine.

The girl looked a little like her, and also a lot like Mummy.

Curiosity felt angry. The figurine, the faerie-lady, dancing, the dell, these were *her* things. They were *her* fantasy. They were *her* magic.

Was Mummy going to spoil this for her too?

The faerie-lady burst from the shadows.

She screeched and, startled, Curiosity dropped the sketch-pad and photo into the trunk.

She took a step back.

The faerie-lady came across, smiled, hovered above the open lid and, with her tiny index finger, pointed down to a bundle of nylon tulle that was lying at the bottom of the trunk.

Curiosity stepped up. She bent down and picked up the bundle.

The faerie-lady screeched again. But it sounded softer this time, like delight or excitement, and she darted off, flitting from rafter to rafter, sending plumes of dust spinning on the air behind her.

Curiosity's anger at her mother disappeared, replaced by curiosity.

She was holding a tutu. The tulle was torn in places, the white cloth had yellowed with age but, in the main, the garment appeared intact. When she shook it out, a pair of gossamer fairy wings fell to the floor, shaped out of wire, and covered with the same nylon tulle as the dress.

It was the ballet costume her mother was wearing in the photo.

Now it was hers.

The faerie-lady stopped mid-flight.

She fluttered back to hover at Curiosity's ear.

Again, she heard the word, *surprise*, whispered in a familiar hissing tone that she ignored for its unpleasantness, but took to be a prompt to put on the tutu and wings.

The dress fitted well, as if it had been tailored for her.

The wings fitted likewise. And she spun around as though admiring her reflection in an imaginary mirror, brushing out the wrinkles with the palm of her hand, ruffling out the skirt, and feeling the fabric against her skin as if it was meant to be there.

Was this what normal girls do?

The type of normal girl Mummy would approve of?

Perhaps, but she didn't care. She only wanted to spin and never stop dancing.

The door slammed shut. The room dimmed.

Through the skylight, a lightning flash lit up the attic and, a second later, the accompanying thunderclap shook the walls, as a downpour crashed against the roof.

With the next lightning flash, Curiosity screamed.

Beneath the clatter of the rain, however, nobody heard, except for herself, the faerie-lady hovering at her shoulder, and the woman, standing at the back of the attic, the roof timbers visible through the vaporous constitution of her body.

FIFTEEN – Concerning the careful wish

Having left Curiosity in her room, Rosina went out to join Faithe on the patio. The child was wilful. The child was obstinate. She was just like her father, and he was – well, Rosina had many, variegated words to describe her ex-husband. She also had a few for his frequent and ever youthful girlfriends.

Faithe, on the other hand – who, while Rosina was upstairs, had stayed on her lounger sleeping off the effects of her Kahlúa eclipsed coffee – exhibited even less grace when speaking of Jeremy Portland and his dalliances. All of which, someone as prudish as Rosina could never consider saying yet enjoyed for their total vulgarity.

She admired this trait in her American friend. She envied her whole-scale indifference and how she disregarded the subtleties of taste or breeding. The very same American who could, quite easily buy, sell, and hawk every one of the feigned highbrows of the Westbourne Grove Ladies Forum, a hundred, maybe a thousand times over.

Faithe Henning (maiden name: Sibourne) came from and possessed big money. *Black card* or *old money* they called it in her neck of the woods. She also held a lineage traceable by centuries back to the first Sibournes to colonise North

America, a rare heritage nearly as old as The Mayflower, with Faithe the only lasting descendent.

When it came to her fractious marriage to Dayton Henning, she simply stated that plain old commerce had dictated the match.

'An exercise in good business,' she said, 'especially for a woman with no living family to fall back on.'

What Rosina didn't like, however, was how Faithe put her in her place. How she made her feel small and petty. As though, with the completion of her house, she had all but given up on any ambitions for her own life, and had forced her aspirations onto her daughter. In many ways, Rosina had to agree, even if such admission made her feel even smaller, and pettier. But Faithe's constant fault-finding angered her, a left-over trait from a childhood urgency to achieve so much.

Faithe was overcritical. She was opinionated and pushy. Sometimes, it seemed like she didn't care at all, and only turned up at Rosina's to drink her booze, to put her down, and then fall asleep as though her feelings meant nothing. At this very moment, looking at Faithe and listening to her snore, Rosina felt angry with her friend. She felt angry with Curiosity. She felt angry with Jeremy, and the clouds gathering overhead that threatened to ruin her sunny day.

Most of all, she felt angry with the many inadequate turns her life had taken.

Rosina hadn't always been just Curiosity's mother, or indeed anybody's wife.

Back in her childhood – a time she now struggled to remember – she had been Rosina Warren, a child with a mission – no, she was a child with a vision, to achieve something, to be someone.

Determined not to end up like her mother, whose death by gin was the reason she came to live with her great aunt in the first place, she quickly formed the opinion that an old cuckoo such as Aunt Lily might be an equally bad role model. Made even more evident by how she didn't embrace the hippy lifestyle until she was thirty-five, throwing away, into the bargain, a successful career as a dancer.

And it was that life, the one before the tie-dyed t-shirts and kaftans that Rosina found so alluring. In particular the glitz and celebrity, the West End theatre contacts, the mingling with the stars, gentry, and royalty. If only she had refused that invite to the 1968 Isle of Wight Festival, maybe things might have been different for a budding social climber like Rosina Warren.

Because she was a driven child. Some might say obsessive.

And standing here on the patio, looking down what had once been Aunt Lily's garden, she recalled a summer afternoon. She was seven. Aunt Lily was out in the shed with the gardener Cassidy. She went there often, and tended to stay a long time.

Rosina was sitting on the lawn, flicking through a magazine that she found in a box under Aunt Lily's bed. There were many magazines in the box. And they had the same title: *Ballet Preview*, all dating no later than the *Midsummer Issue 1968*.

On the cover of this particular issue, an elegant lady stood poised on the tips of her toes, while two other ladies danced across a curtained stage behind her. They wore frilly white bodices and tutus. They looked graceful, angelic, and everything she wanted to be.

From that moment, Rosina was smitten. Ballet became her single-most obsession.

She at once badgered Aunt Lily to register her at the Sophia Aleyev School of Ballet.

She spent every minute available in practice; both at home and at the Sunday evening lessons. Miss Aleyev, as Sophia insisted 'her girls' called her, was methodical. She was strict. She encouraged her students to dance by candlelight, stating that the soft glow added ambience and aided in the development of style. Aunt Lily even paid the exorbitant fees, her only reservation being the elitist tendencies of Sophia Aleyev herself. Objections supported by her revelation that, during her time with The Royal Ballet, they had once danced together.

'Sophia has a stick up her arse,' she said, and did so often.

The memory made Rosina smile.

She remembered training hard.

With diligence, she attended every single lesson at the ballet studio situated above the toy shop on the corner of Bingham Crescent and Westbourne Grove. She studied the steps. She worked on her poses, twice as hard as any other of the budding ballerinas, and to the point of aching muscles and bleeding toenails. The tragic truth was, however, although Rosina had passion enough to light-up the night sky, she had no natural talent.

The spark one might say.

Clarissa Heffington (snootier twin-sister to snooty Ophelia Heffington) had natural talent.

Both Clarissa and Ophelia Heffington had the spark.

Each of the other four girls in the class: Evelyn Willoughby, Sarah Penthorpe, Hillary Downshire, and Millie Beecher were better than Rosina, although not one of them put in a fraction of the work she did.

And still, as the weeks passed, she practiced every day in her room and in the garden.

She read books.

She watched videos to study the greats, and even convinced Aunt Lily to fit a barre along the wall of her bedroom. She persisted, but her awkward feet – *Warren clumpy clodhoppers*, Aunt Lily called them – and a lack of basic prowess, kept letting her down.

Most nights she cried herself to sleep for failing a demi-plié, or because the other girls had sniggered behind her back. Most times they sniggered to her face. They called her *gingernut*, and *clown feet* because of her wider than normal toes.

Ophelia called her *Little Miss Bumble*, because sometimes she would stumble during a difficult pose, usually when Clarissa pushed her. And Rosina would thump to the floor, hurt her knee, or go home with a bruised hip, or both. Mostly though, she would feel humiliated in front of the other girls, and Miss Aleyev, who would glare at her with disapproval.

Clarissa was the meanest of the twins.

Even all these years later, Rosina remembered when Clarissa pushed her into one of the candle-stands that were placed down the centre of the room. Her hair caught fire. And, while Rosina screamed and tried to pat out the flames,

Clarissa just watched and giggled. The other girls just watched too, although in silence. They looked vexed. Even Ophelia.

Luckily, Miss Aleyev doused Rosina's head with a fire blanket, leaving her physically unscathed but more mentally crushed than ever. She told both Miss Aleyev and Aunt Lily that it was her own fault; that she had lost her footing and had veered too close to the candle-stand, a false admission that added to her growing list of embarrassments.

Clarissa laughed a lot that day, and Rosina hated her.

She never told Aunt Lily about the bullying. She was scared she would take her out of the class. With each put-down, her anger and determination grew stronger. She studied more. She worked all the harder. Sadly though, even with her persistence Rosina would never be good enough.

Why?

Because she just couldn't dance.

And, when she was told this – by Sophia Aleyev no less – the news left a devastated little girl in its wake. Her goal was crushed, not wholly by her lack of ability, but by the sniggering girls at the Sophia Aleyev School of Ballet. A humiliation Rosina felt unbearable to the point she hated them and wished them all gone.

That hatred rose up again, now, as sure as if the years had rolled away but, as always, she pushed it down. Memories were dangerous. They should be suppressed, locked away, and never countenanced.

With regard to Faithe Henning, however, of course Rosina could never wish her best and only friend gone. No matter how displeased she felt with her. She was having a bad day. It happened a lot since she had stopped the medication.

Her anger, on the other hand, seemed to be getting worse. No one would ever see it, though. Propriety dictated such. Something both Curiosity and Faithe failed to grasp.

She went to the kitchen, uncorked a bottle, poured some wine, and took a swig that emptied half the glass. She topped it up, left the bottle on the counter, and went back out to the patio.

Drinking had become a bit of a habit since Jeremy walked out.

Wine was a crutch, but a moderately acceptable one, especially for a societal mother.

Or so she told herself.

Irony was indeed the saddest truth.

Overhead the sky darkened. She felt the spits of rain on her skin and roused Faithe to go inside. Faithe seemed not at all pleased at being wakened. She groaned and, on the way into the kitchen, dragged behind like a child at bedtime.

They had only reached the patio doors when lightning struck. A second later, the accompanying thunderclap shook the walls and a downpour crashed against the roof.

When the next lightning flash came, they were both inside, with the door slid shut.

The next thunderclap made her jump, and she thought of Curiosity upstairs and whether, like her, the thunder had frightened her.

Nature was terrifying.

By its own will, it came crashing in at any time, changing the look and feel of a day. It altered moods. Like Curiosity had changed. These last few days, her mood had become gloomier and more standoffish. Not as sudden as the downpour raging in the garden, yet there, niggling like Faithe's criticisms, prickling Rosina's anger, drawing her thoughts and attention to the dell at the bottom of the garden.

Watching the rain pummel the trees, she recalled her own strangeness as a child, and her rage at failing to be a great ballerina. Feelings that might have stayed hidden but for the deluge churning up a memory of another stormy evening, when she stood beside her enchanted pool, her clothes and body drenched, shivering, terrified, but mostly angered. Seething hatred that she put behind her, buried beneath years of therapy, prescriptions, and drink . . . or so she thought.

SIXTEEN – Concerning the orphan's curse

Swirls of steam billowed up to form a thick cloud, hugging the ceiling and speckling the white tiles of the shower cubicle with drops of moisture. Hot water cascaded down her body bringing the fresh touch of cleanliness. A purging of sorts, to rid her flesh of the malignance she sensed back at Rosina Portland's house. Aurelija scrubbed her skin with soap and lather. The bubbles felt good, soft, and gentle. She touched the crucifix at her neck and mumbled a thank you to the Virgin Mary for having protected her this day, and for giving her the strength to see wickedness when it manifested.

The Republic of Lithuania was a modern country, a progressive country, and still – in the rural region of her family home – superstitions around *laumės* held fast. They were the woodland fae, the guardian spirits of orphans. Orphans like Curiosity Portland, where emotional abandonment had left her all but parentless. And *laumės* caused hail, storms, and rain by singing, curses, or by dancing. They had compassion but also a malicious streak, especially to those who live their days in envy of others. And, when crossed, their revenge was as savage as the full power of nature that spawned them.

Laumės were better left alone.

Beings to be placated and, better still, avoided if at all possible.

She turned off the faucet, reached through the shower curtain for her bathrobe, put it on, and stepped out onto the bathmat, taking care not to slip on the shiny tiled floor. She dried her body with a towel, working from head to toe as best she might in the tiny, boxlike room, wrapped it around her torso and then folded another around her hair, before sitting down on the toilet seat.

She blessed herself, kissed her crucifix, and thanked the Virgin again.

She crossed and uncrossed her fingers to mimic the divine knot that warded off evil spirits. This she did three times, as in the Holy Trinity – the three hypostases of God – and to encourage the Holy Spirit to protect her soul.

Leaving the shower room, she picked up her phone from the table by the front door of the living-cum-kitchen-cum-bedroom that constituted ninety percent of her and her partner's studio flat. She glanced across to Matis sitting on the sofa-bed. He was watching football on the television and appeared content and, at the same time, agitated, his expressions alternating between frustration and elation as his gaze flitted to every corner of the screen. She then peered up to the painting on the wall of the Christ Jesus comforting a crying child, and she felt the succour of it.

She phoned Rosina Portland.

'I can't come to clean anymore,' Aurelija said when the woman answered.

'What do you mean you can't come to clean anymore?'

'I'm finished, Mrs Portland. I want to find a job somewhere else.'

'But you mustn't leave. I need you to do the ironing and keep the house tidy.'

'I can't come back.'

'And why is that?' The woman sounded angry and put out.

'I just can't.'

'Well, that's just great,' Rosina said. 'What do you expect me to do?'

'I don't know. Matis, my boyfriend, he will call to your house to collect my last wages.'

Rosina Portland didn't reply. The phone went dead and a weight lifted from Aurelija's heart.

'Kas paskambino?' *'Who called?'* Matis asked glancing away from the television for a split second.

'Tai nesvarbu.' *'It's not important.'*

And it wasn't – now.

She had left.

Money would be tight. She would need another job and sooner rather than later, but the fear she'd felt when she saw Rosina's daughter poking around at the end of the garden was gone. Well, maybe not gone. But set aside, shoved to the back of her mind like all the scary stories that the nuns had told the orphans at *Gailestingumo Seserys,* by way of a warning and to ensure they always kept to their nightly prayers.

SEVENTEEN – Concerning the spirit who desires

It was a different Curiosity Portland who had entered the attic room to the one who left. When she finished screaming, she was more acceptant of the scary events happening to her, every bit as much as she had accepted those that were magical.

In the most, she remembered little apart from being plunged into darkness, the thunder, the lightning, and the whispered voice of her faerie-lady hissing in anger, before the tiny creature disappeared altogether.

There was a vague comprehension of something hazy yet human-like gliding towards the door, but no awareness of it opening, or her walking back to her room and getting into bed.

What became real to her, though, was the dream she had many hours later.

She was back in Greenwich Park, lying on the mound. A squirrel was looking down from a branch overhead. On second glance, she saw it was the same spindly, grey creature from her earlier nightmare. It was grinning. Its jagged teeth dripped with blood. This time, however, the creature didn't frighten her and when she woke, she looked around the bedroom for her faerie-lady.

Whether lifeless figurine or an actual flying creature, it – *she* – brought her comfort.

She was the only thing Curiosity cared for.

A green glow was pulsing outside the oval window.

She got out of bed and went to investigate, noticing that she still had on the ballet costume that she found in the trunk in the attic. In the garden, dozens of tiny, green lights sparkled, as though emerald fireflies had gathered to swarm upon the air. Where there had been lawn, a meadow of long grass and wildflowers now flanked a pathway of lucent stepping stones that ran all the way from the patio, down to the dell at the end of the garden. In the centre of the dell, the oak tree stood tall and wide, its massive limbs outstretched. And, on the other side of the window, her faerie-lady hovered. She was gesturing for Curiosity to come to her. A beautiful, shining entity, bobbing and beckoning, blinking and smiling, filling Curiosity's thoughts with enchantments she found too bewitching to resist. She heard the whispers. They were, as always, unpleasant but intoxicating. They sounded harsh and guttural, yet melodic, a song of sorts, punctuated with the word *'surprise'*, that repeated in her mind and heart, both of which she felt recourse to give over completely.

She dashed out of her bedroom to the top of the stairs.

'I'm coming,' she shouted, a little too loudly.

Her mother – who left her bedroom door open at night – groaned then shuffled in her bed. It was followed by a long, throaty gurgle that sounded like Faithe Henning. On the occasions when she and Mummy were too boozed up to call a taxi, Faithe often slept in one of the guest bedrooms.

Keen to avoid another lecture, Curiosity slowed her pace.

She waited until she heard the two women settle, noting how Faithe's throaty gurgle hadn't come from a guest bedroom as she had first thought, but from the floor of Mummy's room. They must have really put it away this time. She brushed it off. They would probably be back at it again first thing in the morning, when they both woke with a hangover and Mummy needed something strong to deal with her tetchy, snippy mood.

Curiosity continued down the stairs, making sure to take controlled, quiet steps.

When she reached the circulation space, the green light had effused the whole kitchen. It glinted off the shiny chrome fittings, and danced bright streaks across the polished granite counter, glittering like the dying sparkles of a bonfire-night firework. Outside, along the full four metres of the patio doors, numerous twinkling creatures had gathered, like festive lights strung across the glass. The hissing whispers, that Curiosity carried with her most times these days, grew in intensity, and among the little creatures, her faerie-lady hovered in centre place, as though waiting to greet her.

Curiosity felt unafraid.

She had become unafraid of most things since her visit to the toy shop.

She went to the patio doors and pressed a button on the wall. The motor whirred and two large, central sections of glass door slid apart. Air rushed in, filling Curiosity's nostrils with the sweet scents of lavender, meadowsweet, and other flowers she couldn't identify but breathed in for all their delight.

The creatures swarmed into the kitchen.

Like water pouring through a breach in a dam, they surged past the faerie-lady, who remained hovering outside, flowed over the counter and cupboards, and went whooshing around the downstairs areas of the house in waves of sparkling, green light.

Curiosity smiled at the thought of Mummy's house being invaded by such wondrous things. She watched them roll and flow. She saw them rise up and fill the room, as though investigating every nook and corner. Some landed on the furniture and poked at the wood. Some plucked the fabric on the sofa. Others jumped in, out, and over Mummy's precious ornaments: her expensive Murano glass vase, the maple-wood fruit bowl on the coffee table, and the crystal goblets that stood on a designer console table which cost more than Curiosity's annual prep-school fees, or so Mummy kept telling her.

Three of the little creatures were pulling on the handle of a kitchen cupboard. The door opened a crack and they fluttered inside. There was a thump, and the door flew ajar to a flowing cascade of granola and oat flakes that spilled out and showered down over the floor. Behind her by the patio doors, another creature was pressing the button on the wall making the doors slide open and closed again. It did this repeatedly, smiling as though something it had never encountered before.

There was a crash in the circulation space.

One of Mummy's goblets was on the floor, in pieces, with a group of creatures flitting around the scattered wreckage, darting up from and down to the crystal shards, before they fluttered away to circle the Murano vase which Curiosity reckoned, without much effort, might end up meeting the same fate.

And she wasn't at all worried that her mother's precious furnishings were being broken.

She couldn't care less if the whole house was destroyed.

She hated it here.

The creatures were amazing and, when one of them flew close, she held out her upward palm, in the hope that it might land there.

It did.

It looked like a creature depicted in the sketchpad. One of the same daddy-longlegs creatures she had danced with in the moments before Daddy arrived to take her to Greenwich and the park. It was human-like, five centimetres tall, with stick-like limbs and a thin, translucent body. The wings on its back fluttered. Its needle-like fingers stroked the air like a swimmer maintaining buoyancy in a pool. It smiled, a gentle crease that enlivened its oval-shaped face, and its nostrils – no more than slits – opened and closed in tempo with its breaths, its green inner light throbbing with the rise and fall of its chest.

Curiosity smiled.

The creature pulsed faster. As did all the others, still flitting around the circulation space and kitchen, or massing like a colony of bees on the countertop, cupboards, and furniture. They glowed brighter. So bright, Curiosity had to shield her eyes. She giggled. The intensity didn't bother her.

What could, in the face of something so magnificent?

The faerie-lady drifted from the patio into the kitchen. The creature on Curiosity's hand took flight and joined the others. Still pulsating, they moved apart, as though two giant, invisible hands had struck out to separate them. The faerie-lady flew slowly through the middle, like a queen in a street-lined procession. She stopped halfway, gestured for Curiosity to come with her, then turned and flew back out to the patio.

Curiosity followed, amazed to see the garden transformed from plain lawn to a colourful blaze of wildflowers. She chuckled, skipping from one luminescent stepping stone to another, each one brightening when her foot landed. She laughed aloud. A trickle of spit dribbled down her chin, and she wiped it away with the back of her hand, laughing louder at her goofiness, and not at all worried that her mother might hear her, waken, and scold her for being out of bed.

As she skipped, she threw her arms out wide. She spun circles, kicked her feet into the air, and danced.

From above in the sky, specks of glitter rained down like a waterless shower and reminded her of her favourite painting, Vincent Van Gogh's *Starry Night*. As the specks settled, they dusted her arms, her face, hair, tutu and fairy wings with a fine glistening powder that made her skin glow, illuminating her body like the flying creatures.

Floating a few metres ahead, the faerie-lady urged her onwards, down the garden, towards the dell and the oak tree at its centre. The great tree also glistened. A golden door had opened up in its trunk and lay ajar, with a bright white light shining from a place farther within. As she drew closer, the hissing voices grew louder. At the same time, the shining creatures congregated in two hovering lines to either side of the luminous path. Their glow had dulled. Their hue alternating between vibrant green and the dull grey colour of dirty pond water, the latter becoming more prominent as the hissing intensified. They seemed excited, buzzing and burbling like bees frenzied by an intruder to their hive, all except the faerie-lady, who hovered in the middle and, as still as moonbeam, with only her tiny hand moving, ushered Curiosity forward.

In reality, Curiosity paid little heed to the creatures' fluctuating appearance, because her thoughts were lost to the wonder of the scene and the speculation of what might lie beyond the golden door.

She danced a few more steps and stopped a metre or two short of where the lawn gave over to the dell. On the other side of the opening, a hedge lined pathway led to a circular pond, its low stone walls festooned with all manner of colourful flowers and plants. It shimmered as if burning with cold white flames and, at its centre, a marble fountain topped with a statue of a *faerie* – not unlike the figurine – trickled water from an urn. The sound played music to her ears. It was a bewitching tone. She wanted to hear more, to be closer, to go through the door and experience the many wonders within.

Come in, the voices said. *Come in.*

Curiosity heard the words as sure as if they'd been spoken aloud. They came from the dozens of imp-like creatures who had appeared from nowhere, and were dancing naked and in time with the melody of the trickling water. These creatures, with sniped noses, pointed ears, and purple foxgloves adorning their heads, cavorted in and through the chiselled hedgerows. They spun in circles amid rings of red and white toadstools. Some swayed, their little nude bodies glowing bright and white, while others jumped and tumbled over the stone walls of the fountain.

Outside in the garden, the ranks of daddy-longlegs-like creatures had collapsed and now swirled around the opening like leaves caught in a whirlwind. The faerie-lady beckoned. With a delightful melody she urged Curiosity to follow her.

Come in, she sang. *Come in.*

Curiosity resumed dancing. She skipped closer to the door. Steps not taken through any conscious decision, but by way of joyful feelings seeded in her thoughts.

A sudden chill stopped her mid-stride

A woman appeared and blocked her way.

Curiosity stumbled backwards. She tripped and fell, the woman shimmering, heavier than mist but cloudy, the trees of the dell visible through the half solid composition of her body. She wore a sodden kaftan dress, reaching to the ground. Her skin was pallid and puckered. Her black eyes all but hidden beneath strands of dank hair and pondweed clinging to her face. She stared, straight at Curiosity, with one hand held high in a visible instruction to go no farther. And her lips were pursed, as if uttering in a sustained but silent, 'No!'

When Curiosity realised what she was looking at, her body numbed, and her heart thumped so strongly it rolled like a stone into her gut. She needed to pee. She almost did, but pushed back the urge, fearing she might not withstand if something else happened to shock her.

The flying creatures changed.

In a matter of seconds, they lost their sparkle, fully transforming from glowing green to the opaque grey they had only hinted at before. Overhead, the glistening shower also lost its sparkle. It was now rain, a torrent, and Curiosity felt the abrupt coldness of being soaked to the skin.

The creatures swooped and set upon the ghostly woman.

Then others appeared, larger than the flying creatures, with gangly bodies, ovoid heads, pointed ears, and slit-like eyes. They rose up en-masse from the undergrowth and clambered across the branches of the oak tree, now devoid of its golden door. The bright and airy scene of only moments before had gone, smothered beneath coils of thorns, branches, and bracken that curled outward from the dell and across the lawn. The creatures advanced; an army of scuttling things. They scrambled up from every nook and hollow. They burst from the sodden earth and, as a single enraged mob, fell upon the apparition, spitting and hissing with a loudness that made Curiosity clamp her hands over her ears. They hacked at the woman's ghostly body. They sliced with their clawed fingers, stripping away parts of her ethereal arms, chest, and face, purls of which spun upon the air before floating down to dissolve like fog into the earth. And, throughout the onslaught, the apparition stayed her ground, her agony evident by the way she roiled and the voiceless scream that stayed steady upon her lips.

Curiosity wanted to run, to escape back to the house, to her bedroom where she could bury her head under the duvet and pretend this was all a bad dream. She wanted her faerie-lady. She needed her to make the ugly creatures go away and the ghostly woman to disappear.

Then she saw her, hovering above the melee.

She was naked and had lost her glow, her skin now grey, leathery, and opaque as if pulled taut over her bones. Her multicoloured wings had blackened. Her once graceful face contorting, stretching, became ovoid, ears elongating, as her pretty nose retracted beneath her now slit-like eyes and became two clefts in the centre of her face. With jagged teeth, she snarled. Her once enchanting voice mutated to a dirge so loud and unpleasant it hurt, even through the hands Curiosity held clasped to her ears.

The creature hissed. And Curiosity's heart sunk to see her once beautiful faerie-lady deformed into such a thing. It looked hideous, angry, and joined the others in their attack, encouraging them with violent gestures to set upon the apparition below.

A battle as strange as if it came from the pages of a storybook.

Was it real? Was it happening? How could it be?

Those were just stories. Yet, here she was witnessing the battle nonetheless. A disturbing thought for sure, and troubling enough that, for a few seconds, she pushed away her fear. Her initial shock waned, and she jumped to her feet, dashing up the garden towards the house. She expected that she might get only halfway before the mob of creatures came after her, envisaging slews of the tiny creatures scuttling up behind and around her. In her dread, she imagined them clambering over her shoulders, smothering her face, and their fingers clawing at her flesh.

The creatures, however, didn't come and, when Curiosity reached the patio, she stopped before entering the house. She turned, quickly, unsure if they might be playing a trick on her, or that she might look down and see them congregated across the lawn, waiting to pounce and drag her down to somewhere underground that she dared not think about.

The garden was empty.

Apart from the downpour, nothing moved. The only noise was the sound of raindrops pattering against the flag-stones. Where the battle had raged there was stillness. The apparition was gone. The ugly creatures were nowhere to be seen. She moved into the kitchen. The cupboard door was closed, the floor tidy of strewn cereal and, in the circulation space, Mummy's goblet was back in its place on the console table, unbroken, with no shards of crystal scattered over the floor. Curiosity gazed down to see if she was still wearing the tutu and fairy wings. She wondered if they too were no more than another vivid dream.

Upon seeing that she still had on the costume, she then speculated that there might be a more realistic and troubling answer to all she had seen and heard of late. A fear founded in the notion that her beloved faerie-lady, the wildflower meadows, the ghostly woman, the ugly creatures maybe even the sodden black tomcat peering out from beneath one of Mummy's loungers – might be part of some frightening illusion created only by her thoughts.

Even at only eight years old Curiosity knew enough about insanity to think it might afflict her. Even as a mere child she could sense, given all the crazy things she had seen and dreamt these last few days, that she – as her mother had in her childhood – might be going mad.

EIGHTEEN – Concerning Lauren's ruse

When they arrived home to Jeremy's Holland Park Avenue apartment, Lauren went straight to the bedroom. She hadn't taken a jacket to the opera. Her clothes were wet. Her hair ruined.

Jeremy followed.

'Did you enjoy that?' he asked. 'Did it make you feel romantic?'

She edged backwards. He went with her, his arms enfolding around her waist. She pushed him off, walked across to the other side of the bed, said, 'Not now,' and then, to punctuate her rebuff, turned away.

'Why not?' he complained.

'I'm not in the mood.'

'Not in the mood? You must be.'

'I'm not.'

He threw his hands in the air. 'Jesus. What is it with you? We've been to the opera. It's sensual. It's supposed to make you feel romantic.'

'I'm soaked,' she said. 'Way too tired, and I've got a headache.'

'Jesus. You've got a headache. If it wasn't such a cliché it might be funny. If you even know what *cliché* means?'

Lauren didn't reply.

'Okay then, suit yourself. I'm getting a drink.' He stomped into the living-room, lifted a bottle and a glass from the drink's cabinet, poured himself a large brandy, and flopped down onto the couch.

He was mumbling to himself.

She smiled.

Lauren Alcock cared little what Jeremy thought, desired, or mumbled about. His usefulness claimed no more importance in her life than a means to advancement: a meal ticket, a way to secure better grades, gained by employing her other, less mentally taxing skills. That is, of course, if she counted being with Jeremy Portland less mentally taxing than pursuing her studies.

Most thought she was stupid, that she lacked academic aptitude, but it was what she wanted them to think. She saw herself as the ultimate independent woman, using whatever and whoever might help her climb to success without the exhausting effort. The whole thing was a con, the *dumb bimbo* ruse. Even Jeremy's kid was convinced.

Why study when men were so easily manipulated?

And it worked particularly well on older men. Men like Jeremy Portland. Her lecturer for Archaeological Theory and co-ordinator for her whole course. He thought he was so smart but, with his well-known skeeviness, he was an easy mark: a flash of a smile here, a brushed hand there and, once duped, the occasional denial was a major part of the play.

To this end, Lauren walked into the en-suite bathroom. She left the door ajar so Jeremy could see her from the living-room. Temptation was the most important piece on the board. It kept them eager. In the game, so to speak. And, when they were both, a girl could ask for whatever she desired, as long as she showed a little interest now and again to sweeten the deal.

Standing in front of the mirror, she dried her hair with a towel, lifting and letting it fall with the greatest performance, but Jeremy didn't stir. He just sat there, staring into his glass with an angry but indifferent expression on his face.

Lauren couldn't have that. It wasn't part of her scheme. She moved – or rather, swished – back into the bedroom, positioning herself close to the door with her back to Jeremy, where she could fully exploit his eyeline from the couch. Turning to see if he was watching, she noticed a doll-like object lying on the floor by the bedside cupboard. It was weaved from twigs, shaped like an angel or a fairy. She assumed it belonged to Jeremy's daughter. The snooty little brat was always leaving her stuff behind when she stayed over. And she stayed over one Saturday in every month, which was far too often. The daughter didn't factor in Lauren's plans. She was a link to his old life, something she must detach, so he could focus on her, and her grades. It was why she had zeroed in on him at the start of her second semester, and why she was now performing her best routine.

He wasn't bad looking either, for an older guy, owned this fancy loft flat, had a fair bit of money into the bargain, and shared her liking for ancient things that could be sold for cash. It was why she decided to study archaeology in the first place. A chance discovery of an old family heirloom had made her a tidy penny, and she saw in Jeremy Portland as someone who would equally sell his own mother if he thought there was money in it.

He was a worthwhile use of Lauren's time. A good investment.

If he played his cards right, he could even become a longer-term venture. Of course, she knew she had the skills to deal with a needy daughter and, when working her wiles to full effect, distancing Jeremy from his old family had proved a piece of cake. She just needed to make sure of it. So, he wouldn't want to return.

Something his ex-wife made all the easier with her never-ending nagging.

She kicked the twig doll under the bed, uttered an obvious and attention seeking cough but Jeremy didn't respond. He didn't even look her way. Apart from slurping his brandy, he didn't make a sound, or say one word.

He could be a real prick sometimes.

There was, however, another sound. It came from the other side of the bed. A harsh, unpleasant buzzing noise, as though insects were swarming beneath the mattress. A shadow moved across the wall. It was followed by another, and then some more. A row of tiny stickmen creeping over the exposed brickwork before disappearing beneath the bed.

Lauren kneeled, lifted the edge of the duvet and, at first, she saw nothing of any consequence: her pink slippers, a sock, a condom wrapper, and some dust bunnies that Jeremy's cleaner had missed while vacuuming. Then something moved. Perhaps a few things. They skittered across the hardwood floor and disappeared behind a bed-leg.

Her first suspicion was that they were mice, which might

frighten other, more excitable people, but they didn't daunt a stiff willed character such as Lauren Alcock. She saw only the competition. They were invaders. They were vermin. They needed to be eradicated, and in the most vicious way possible; traps, poison, being thumped with a heavy boot, anything that made her feel superior because she had beaten these tiny animals a fraction of her size.

She moved farther underneath, disgusted by the dust that was clinging to her clothes and making a mental note to tell Jeremy that his cleaner had to go. It was then she discovered that her mouse suspicion was very wrong. In an instant, dozens of tiny, skeletal creatures charged at her. They came as a single mass. They looked like the little monkeys she had seen at London Zoo, only smaller, with their teeth stripped and claws bared.

She screamed.

Jeremy dashed into the bedroom.

When he got there, she was cowering by the bed.

She didn't look up. She didn't say a word. Just stared in disbelief at the slashes on her blouse, and body, and the rills of blood pouring down her arms and chest.

NINETEEN – Concerning Brendan's beloved Lily

Brendan Cassidy didn't consider himself the type of man to go running around scaremongering people. And his dreams about Lily Warren were usually pleasant: scattershot images of being younger, of holding her close, giggles, kisses, and making love atop the potting table in the garden shed, while little Rosina played, danced, or read magazines on the lawn outside. No matter how many folktales or superstitions he bought into, he didn't believe that the ghosts of the dead came to visit grizzly old men in the middle of the night. Yes, sure, they existed, but for others, people in grief, who needed the comfort of knowing their loved ones hadn't truly left them. And still, if asked in confession, he would swear to the lord above that, sometime after midnight, Lily was standing by his bed. She appeared as he had found her on the night she died. Wan skinned. Her hair and clothes dripping with pondweed and water. She was staring straight at him, and fear gripped him as sure as if she had reached into his flesh and clasped her cold hand around his gut.

Then she vanished.

Somehow, he slept all the way until dawn and woke, not so much troubled at how the mind can accept just about anything – even the prospect of the dead returning to the living – but how easily he had embraced her presence, bringing her down with him into his dreams where she slid into the bed alongside him and her cold but gentle touch crested away the years. Then she shouted. A muted order heard only in his thoughts. Angry and urgent words, coming to him as impulses, to rise, to go to Rosina Portland and warn her.

He got up and made tea. At least it was Sunday. The Lord's Day. He searched for his beads at the back of the sideboard drawer and, with trembling fingers, said a rosary, followed by two more.

It had been a while since he had asked for intercession.

After a few hours of staring out of the window, watching the morning sun creep to prominence in the sky, he went back to bed and tried to sleep, but the image of Lily's emaciated face refused to leave.

Since yesterday, the whole business of Curiosity going into the dell had unnerved him.

More so than before, all those years ago when Lily thought malign creatures had targeted Rosina and she took her own life. Or so the coroner said. And then there was that fecking black and white cat that was always lurking around. It was like a story from one of his mother's folktales which, if Lily's ghost appearing to him was to be believed, might very well prove to be more than just yarns.

His mother – God rest her soul – said they were cautions. Warnings. But, if the truth be told, he never really believed her, even when Lily had been so certain. Now, he wasn't sure. Through some coincidence, just like Rosina years before, Curiosity had drawn the attention of powers that were persistent and, once aroused, couldn't be deterred.

Brendan's mother spoke of how they possessed a sense of humour, a wicked streak seeking to toy with those too fond of adventure. How they placed temptations and deceptions to trap those with too much inquisitiveness in their hearts.

Inquisitive children like Rosina, when she was a girl, and now her daughter.

Half an hour later, he was at Rosina's door.

When she opened it, she said, 'Cassidy. What are you doing here? It's not your day. I told you to leave the lawn until next week.'

Rosina's friend, Faithe Henning, was inside, sitting at the kitchen counter reading a magazine. She looked sleepy; her hair tossed as though fresh out of bed. She glanced his way, but there was no emotion in her expression, only indifference. As for Rosina, she was dressed as immaculately as usual, nice blouse, smart skirt, even makeup, but her bloodshot eyes, the shake in her hands, and the stink of stale alcohol on her breath cast a grubby pall upon her efforts.

'I'm not here to cut the lawn,' he said.

'Then why are you here? It's early. I have breakfast to prepare.'

He paused and drew a breath. 'Well, I don't want to make a big deal out of things. And you know me. I'm not one for getting worked up or alarming people. But I've got something to tell you. Something you might think sounds strange.'

'Like what? If it's about the garden, or an increase in pay, we can talk about it next Saturday.'

'It's not about pay, or the garden.'

'Well, what then?'

'It's about you, and Curiosity. She's in danger.'

'What are you talking about? Don't be silly. How could she be in danger?'

'Just believe me.'

'Believe what?'

'It happened before.'

'What happened before?'

'They happened before. You must have forgotten.'

'They? Who happened before? What the hell are you talking about? Are you drunk? I know I'm partial to the odd morning glass but . . .'

'I don't drink. Just tea. And all I'll say is that it's happening again.'

'What's happening again?'

'Curiosity is in danger. You're both in danger. Lily came to me. To warn you.'

'Lily? My great aunt Lily? My *dead* great aunt Lily came to you and now you are here to warn me about . . . well, what exactly?' She laughed. It seemed forced, as if his words had touched a nerve.

'I don't know.'

Rosina scoffed. 'Jesus, first Aurelija calls to say she's resigning, and now you come around here blabbering nonsense about seeing my great aunt Lily.'

'Aurelija has left?'

'She handed in her notice. She won't be back. And good riddance, I say. She was always too damned full of herself for my liking.'

Cassidy mused on this.

Had Aurelija sensed the same as him? Or seen Aunt Lily?

Either way, she was better off out of it.

'Aurelija was a good worker,' he said. 'And she was right to leave. And so should you. Take your daughter and get as far away from here as you can.'

'Good lord, man. I know you have a soft spot for Curiosity, but this is ridiculous.'

'It's not ridiculous. You should take heed.'

She pushed the door to close it.

He blocked it with his boot. 'Believe me. You're not safe. Curiosity isn't safe.'

Rosina looked angry now. 'Go home, Cassidy. Sleep off whatever crazy Irish jungle juice you've been drinking.' She peered down at his foot.

He drew it back and the door closed with a slam. But, by her reaction, he sensed she was fighting something, perhaps a memory, of Lily, of the fire, of the entities that had led her so astray. He went out to the street and looked up at the peaked roof over the doorway and then to the windows. Nothing stirred. Everything appeared normal. He wasn't even sure what he was looking for. Then, for the first time since Lily's death, he went to chapel.

It felt strange to walk through the vaulted doorway, awkward, coupled with a sense of not belonging.

The priest said Mass.

Brendan sat in silence.

The congregation recited Psalm 94:19:

When anxiety was great within me, your consolation brought joy to my soul.

The priest went on to talk about how, when a person fears

the future or worries about events outside of their control, they must give that anxiety over to a higher power, but Brendan heard only parts of this, his thoughts were elsewhere and, when Mass finished and the rest of the congregation left to continue with their day, he lit a candle for strength, another in memory of Lily Warren, and one each for Rosina Portland and her daughter Curiosity.

What more could he do? He had tried his best.

He gave over to a higher power.

He knelt and said a prayer, followed by many – because, where he came from, when evil drew near and hope was lost, prayers were all a person had to cling to.

'That was weird,' Rosina said.

'What was weird, Sugarplum?' Faithe asked, sipping a cup of coffee and leafing through a glamour magazine. She stopped at a page titled: *The Independent Mother.*

'That really is a good article,' Rosina said. 'Shows how a woman can be both a mother but not lose herself in the process. Very captivating.'

'I know that,' Faithe said. 'It's why I gave you the magazine in the first place.' She closed the cover and looked at Rosina. 'Anyway. What's so weird?'

'Oh, it's just Cassidy. First, my housemaid quits without notice. Then my gardener turns up at the door spouting nonsense. I always thought he was a bit unusual. But, then again, isn't every old man? It's as if, when they reach a certain age, they all develop strange habits.'

'I wouldn't know. I don't do old men.' Faithe laughed.

'No. You wouldn't. But he just told me the craziest thing. That Curiosity was in danger.'

'Danger?'

'Yes. Danger. He said I must get her out of the house.'

'I wouldn't worry. It's probably something to do with the garden. Or that dell. He is the gardener after all. Maybe he's just worried she'd get caught up in the thorns. She did go quite far in yesterday.'

'Maybe. But he seemed distressed. I've never seen him like that. I think I liked him better when he didn't say much.'

'Well, as you say. Old men have strange habits.'

'I suppose.' Rosina shrugged. 'Do you want breakfast?'

'I have breakfast.'

'I mean solid breakfast.'

'No. I'm fine as is. I need to leave room for the booze.' Faithe laughed again, opened the magazine, returned to page with the article and mumbled as she read.

Rosina fixed herself a bowl of granola and sat at the counter. She mulled over Cassidy's warning and then discounted it. But his words niggled. Memories were returning, churning up unhappy feelings, and anger, where a part of her fought to keep them hidden, and another wanted them to be revealed.

TWENTY – Concerning the changing girl

For the whole of Sunday afternoon, after Faithe Henning had left for home and Mummy sat reading, Curiosity waited by the dell, in vain, for her faerie-lady to reappear. She needed to see her again. She needed to know the magic was real, not least to prove that she wasn't going mad. Of course, anyone with a sensible head might assume the frightening battle she had witnessed would prompt her to throw off such fascination. But Curiosity's obsessions never did match up to logical thinking and, although she lacked the courage to fully enter the undergrowth, she saw no danger in venturing close to the oak tree. It conjured up sweet memories of the rain of sparkles and the beautiful glowing creatures that had swarmed around her.

In the evening, before sleep, she danced around her bedroom, hoping this too might encourage the faerie-lady to come to her. She did so, dressed in the ballet tutu and wings, but only in her bedroom, secretly, in case Mummy found out that she had been poking around in the attic.

Again, nothing wonderful happened.

The faerie-lady didn't come, and Curiosity feared that the magic was gone.

On Monday, she didn't go out to the garden at all. She

stayed until evening in her room, still in her pyjamas, reading her storybooks, counting her charm bells, and feeling despondent for her loss. At some point, she fell asleep and woke feeling groggy, her thoughts trailing the embers of a dream where the faerie-lady danced on the edge of her pillow. In her semi-awake state, Curiosity felt the delight of it. She felt empowered and fired up with the determination to make everything right again.

She got up, and was about to change into black shorts and one of her charity-shop t-shirts when she stopped. It was the t-shirt her mother hated most. It was washed-out and had the words 'Party On' printed in bold letters on the front. Usually, she would take great pleasure in arriving downstairs wearing this. The look of disgust on Mummy's face was always priceless. But, if she was to entice the faerie-lady to come out from the undergrowth, she needed something brighter and much more colourful.

She went to the dresser, opened the bottom drawer, and rummaged through some older clothes that were now too small to wear. She removed a plastic package. It was the first she found and one of many. She ripped open the wrapping and shook out one of the floral dresses that Mummy had bought for her. When she put it on, she looked at herself in the mirror. The dress looked good. She liked it. More so than her shorts and t-shirts. She straightened the hems, fixed the collar flat, and went down to the kitchen. She didn't bother with shoes.

The look of astonishment on Mummy's face was just as priceless as when she wore the shabby t-shirts. But Curiosity didn't say a word. She walked straight past her mother, who was sitting at the counter drinking wine, ran out to the patio and down the garden. Once there, she danced, skipping all the way to the edge of the dell, in the hope that the colours and flowery pattern of her dress might please the faerie-lady enough that she would come out to greet her.

She had danced for only a moment when Mummy shouted, 'Come in from there. You must be starving. You haven't eaten a thing all day.' She was standing on the patio with her arms folded, and Curiosity felt certain she only called her back to ruin her fun.

When she reached the kitchen, her mother followed her inside. She was smiling.

'That dress looks nice,' she said. 'It suits you. It makes you look like a normal girl.'

But Curiosity ignored her. She took a bean burrito from the freezer, peeled off the wrapping, popped it into the microwave, and turned the dial to one minute.

The doorbell rang. Mummy went to answer.

The woman at the door said she was a police appointed psychological investigator. She had a midlands accent, introduced herself as Acacia Okeke, looked about forty years old, wore a plain, cream dress, and had a nice smile and a kind face. When Mummy had finished checking her credentials, she ushered the investigator inside, directing her to sit on one of the circulation space sofas. Mummy sat on the sofa opposite, instructing Curiosity to put down the burrito she was eating and to come and join her.

She did so by patting the cushion, as though they often sat together:

'We must deal with these people as a family,' she whispered, 'even if there are only two of us.'

Curiosity sat. She wiped the dirt off her bare feet, which Mummy didn't look at all pleased about, but said nothing. Curiosity then wrapped her arms around her legs, hugged her knees to her chin, and waited, hoping that the woman – even though she seemed nice – wouldn't ask any awkward questions, or, better still, that her faerie-lady might suddenly appear and magic her away from this uncomfortable situation.

'I've already spoken to the police about Jeremy,' Mummy said to the woman. 'Two officers came by yesterday. They asked a lot of questions. They were very thorough. And personal.'

'I know,' Acacia Okeke said tapping a small, soft-covered briefcase on her lap. 'I have copies of their notes. And I apologise for the inconvenience. But my job is to approach the attack on Jeremy Portland's girlfriend – if that's what it was – from a psychological point of view. In the hope it helps to establish intent. If there was intent, or even a crime for that matter.'

Mummy didn't say anything to that.

'Jeremy is your ex-husband, yes?'

'Yes.'

'But he doesn't live with you anymore?'

'No, he has his own apartment. But I'm sure you know that already.'

'And would you say that he angers easily?'

Mummy scoffed: 'Good Lord, no.'

'How are you so certain?'

'Because *Jeremy* has the emotional range of a housefly. He would have to feel something to get angry.'

'So, he has never physically harmed either yourself or your daughter?'

'No. He isn't like that.'

'I see. That's what I thought. You did, however, mention to the interviewing officer that there might have been an incident at Greenwich Park involving Curiosity here.' She smiled, and Curiosity smiled back. 'Do you think he might've prearranged something to frighten and control her? Or has he ever done anything like that before?'

'What? That thing with the dead squirrel? No not at all. My daughter is always making things up.'

Curiosity didn't respond to that. She didn't care what her mother thought of her.

'And, anyway,' Mummy continued, 'to do something like that would require Jeremy thinking about his family. He thinks only of himself.'

'I see,' Acacia said again, 'I'm sorry to ask, but we have to be sure. The incident at his flat was on the same day, and it has been difficult to get any cogent information from his girlfriend, Lauren Alcock.'

'Lauren Alcock? How very colloquial . . . and fitting,' Mummy said. 'I didn't know her name. Then again, I never do with any of them.'

'He is flirtatious?'

Mummy sniggered. 'That would be the understatement of the year.'

'Ah. In that case, do you think Jeremy's amorous behaviour,

for want of better words, could cause him to be violent? Are there issues with old girlfriends? Yourself? Perhaps a jealous husband? Situations that could make him fly off the handle.'

Mummy sniggered again. 'That would be a stretch. For Jeremy to get violent, he would have to possess emotions, maybe even a heart. As I said before, emotions aren't his thing. He's as cold as a snake, and just as unapproachable.'

'Yes, that's the impression I got when I interviewed him. He's a very distant man, and certainly doesn't like, and I quote: *some snotty-nosed shrink poking around and asking stupid questions.*'

'Is the young lady okay?'

'Miss Alcock had quite a shock. But the doctors say her injuries aren't serious. Some of the cuts go quite deep, but they will heal soon. It's just difficult to believe that some-one – with no previous history of self-harming – could hurt themselves so badly.'

'You think that is what she did? Cut herself?'

'We don't know, yet. She stopped answering questions pretty much after telling us that she was in the bedroom getting ready for bed. She seemed very troubled. And ter-rified. That's why I have to ascertain if there were control issues. Whether Jeremy might use violence as a means of subjugation.'

'I doubt it. Violence would be far too brash for Jeremy. Apart from money, he is only interested in one thing, and that's younger women, which he achieves by laying on the charm. He really is quite the charmer. If he was still living with us, I'm certain he would have tried it on with my housemaid by now. You never know, she might have even let him. People are always letting me down.' Acacia Okeke didn't respond to that and Curiosity noticed how her mother looked disappointed at her lack of reaction. 'Look, as you have seen for yourself, Jeremy is a cold fish, and annoyingly academic. He never embarks upon anything without a qualified reason *why*; and then only if it serves the narcissistic wellbeing of Jeremy Portland. Money is his usual impetus, along with anything in a skirt. But, has he ever been violent with me? No, he hasn't. Charm is his weapon of choice.'

'And what about you, Curiosity,' Acacia asked. 'Has your father ever been angry with you, or perhaps told you off a little too loudly?'

Curiosity sat up straighter: 'No.'

'Are you sure? Maybe on the days he picks you up? Has he ever come too close to you, touched you, or yelled when you've done something he thought was wrong?'

'No.'

'You're sure?'

'No. He has never shouted at me. At least not like you say. He hasn't yelled.'

'So, he has shouted at you?'

Curiosity didn't reply.

'Please, you can tell me. I'm not the real police. I just kind of help out.' She smiled. 'Anything you say will stay between us. I promise.'

Curiosity waited a few seconds before answering, aware that by doing so she was goading the tenseness. 'Only once,' she said, 'on Saturday, on the way to the park. When I wouldn't give him my figurine.'

Mummy perked up at that, looked angry, then confused, but said nothing.

'And did your daddy do anything else?' Acacia asked. 'Did he raise his hand or threaten to hit you?'

'No.'

'Are you certain?'

'Yes.'

'If he did, you can tell me. It won't go any further. I promise. Cross my heart.'

'No!' she snapped. 'And stop asking. He didn't hit me. Daddy would never hit me. He doesn't even hug me. Because he doesn't love me.' Tears welled on her eyelids. She pointed at Mummy. 'And neither does she.'

TWENTY-ONE – Concerning the guilty memory

In the space of a few seconds, Curiosity had jumped over the back of the sofa, dashed through the kitchen, and was half-way down the garden. Watching her daughter run off like that, Rosina felt more than just anger at her unmannerly exit. There was wariness, with an undercurrent of fear, brought on by the mention of a figurine, and a guilty memory that was fighting to get through.

'She seems very independent,' Acacia said, interrupting the thought. 'Does she often react this way? She seemed very distressed. Then again, I suppose the marriage break-up has been tough on her. It always hits the children hardest.'

Rosina answered with a simple, 'I hear they say as much. But young ladies need to get used to let downs. It's the way of the world, and Curiosity will face many in her lifetime.'

'And does your ex-husband agree with this viewpoint?'

'Jeremy? Not at all, he would smother her in chocolate if it there was something in it for him. Sadly, though, there isn't. He hardly bothers to pick her up when he is supposed to. She is of no value to him.'

'Still, it must be tough for her?'

'Well, it will do her good to see both him and the world

for what they are.' She stood. 'So, do you have any other questions? I'm very busy.'

'No, that's it.' Acacia said and got up. 'But, please feel free to call me if you think of anything else.' She reached a business card from her briefcase and set it on the coffee table. 'Or you can contact the station directly, if you prefer. Either will do. They patch any important calls straight through to me.'

'There really is nothing more to add. I know nothing of what Jeremy does.'

Acacia smiled and nodded.

Rosina stood, ushered the investigator to the front door, and let her out.

Once outside, Acacia turned, still smiling. 'You have nice gardens. They're very pretty.'

'Yes. Cassidy is very good. If not prone to talking lunacy on occasion.'

'Cassidy?'

'He's my gardener.'

The investigator perked up. 'And do you have an address for Mr. Cassidy? I would like to speak with him too.' She reached into her briefcase and took out a pen and notepad.

'No. I don't get too familiar. But I think he lives in a side-street off the Portobello Road.'

Acacia placed the pen and pad back inside the briefcase and zipped it closed. 'Does he have a first name?'

'Brendan, I think. Look, I am very busy.'

'I'm sorry. Absolutely. I will leave you alone now.' She walked down the drive. 'Please say goodbye to Curiosity for me?' she shouted back as she went through the front gate.

Rosina didn't reply.

When Acacia reached the street, Rosina watched her side-step the black and white cat that was sitting just outside the gate. It was the same one that had crept up on her a few days before.

The cat didn't budge.

It sat staring at Rosina, and mewled, before it followed the woman down Bingham Crescent.

Rosina closed the front door with haste, walked through the kitchen to the patio, and looked for Curiosity down the garden.

She was standing amid the bushes of the dell, dwarfed by the oak tree and indistinguishable from the trunk but for the faint trace of amber twilight illuminating her silhouette. The scene brought forth a memory, once buried in Rosina's psyche by way of drugs and dependency, and now loosened by Curiosity's mention of a figurine.

She recalled a night when she too had rushed in anger to the dell.

It was nine years earlier. Faithe had advised her to organise a party to celebrate the completion of her triumph home.

'To impress friends,' she said. 'And silence foes.'

In particular the supercilious Ophelia Heffington Jeffries who, up to then, had mocked that 'the rubble of bricks' was beyond repair.

The party had been going well too. The numerous exclamations of 'wow' and 'wonderful' had Rosina beaming with delight. She was in 'hog's heaven', as Faithe said. That was until Jeremy ruined everything by exhorting a university associate to back an excavation at the pool in the dell.

'It might be Neolithic,' he said to a man with a grey beard

who Rosina recognised as Jeremy's closest colleague. 'Which means there could be finds. Or it could be Bronze Age, maybe Iron Age.' His speech was rapid, the words tumbling out in that excited way they did when he thought there was covert money to be made.

The man nodded, nuzzling his beard. 'There's certainly evidence of a number of settlements around West London and the Thames Valley area in those time periods. The region appears to have been habituated long back into antiquity. In the nineties, we conducted a dig not far from Staines and unearthed an Iron Age roundhouse. We also discovered a votive pool nearby, where we brought up a bronze axe, the remains of two sword pommels, and a gold torc, amongst other treasures. They are part of the British Museum collection now. It's certainly worth an investigation. You should write a proposal. Submit and see what happens. It never hurts to ask.'

Jeremy's eyes glistened.

Rosina overheard and saw red.

'You can't,' she yelled. 'You absolutely can't. I won't let you.'

'Oh, don't be so melodramatic,' Jeremy replied. 'We're only talking. Nothing has been set in stone. You're getting overstressed again. Maybe you should take some of your tablets and have a lie down.' He grinned.

The rest of the guests just stood and watched.

Even Faithe smiled as she filled her glass with wine.

Rosina remembered hoisting the hems of her evening-gown and dashing down the garden. She recalled her anger and wanting to hurt him. Jeremy was always humiliating her. Everyone knew about the other women. It was evident in their sideways glances and the way they asked, 'and how are things?' their pitying expressions betraying their true regard for her.

In her mind's eye, she relived running unfazed by the October chill to the edge of the dell. Not so much as a memory but as an emotion, of being attracted to the trees and wanting to hide deep within them. Back at the house, the party she had organised in her own honour was continuing without her. No doubt, with the ever-charming Jeremy as the master of ceremonies and all the more entertaining for her absence.

A man stepped out from the bushes and startled her.

He was standing in shadow, his body half concealed by the trunk of the oak tree, his white bowtie in contrast to his dusky skin, black tuxedo and shirt.

'Are you feeling all right?' he asked. His voice sounded coarse and guttural, but not unpleasant. He walked out into the moonlight and peered up at the house. 'You shouldn't waste your valuable time and energy on those people. They are probably just jealous of what you have achieved. It's often said that children can be cruel. But I think that spitefulness is a trait more aligned with the undeveloped adult. And by *undeveloped adult* I mean most of the human populace over the age of twenty, who lack the imagination to create something as wonderful as your house.' He laughed, with gusto, and a flash of sharp uneven teeth that revealed the roundness of his face. A handsome man, even though, if asked to describe him in detail, Rosina felt certain she couldn't. Except for his eyes. They were almond shaped and yellow. His pupils were large, like deep pits, and welcoming.

The man had held out his hand:

'Forgive me. My name is Robin,' he said, 'Robin Good-fellow.'

In response, Rosina offered her own hand, which he shook with vigour before she pulled it back and uttered a curt, 'Hello.'

'Your house is a triumph.'

'Thank you. You are very kind.' She looked him up and down. 'I don't think we know one and other. I invited so many people to my little gathering, but I don't think we've met.'

'We have met, but it was a quite a while ago. You could say that I am here on behalf of these trees and bushes here.'

'Oh, I see.' Her anger grew again. 'That would figure. You're another of Jeremy's colleagues, making an assessment for an archaeological dig. Well, you can forget that right now. The dell stays as it is. No one will be excavating anything.' She turned to walk away.

The man grabbed her arm. 'Please don't go. I'm not here to assess anything. Except for yourself that is. In fact, I think the dell is a marvel. And I'm the last person who would want to see anything happen to this magnificent copse of trees. Call me a traditionalist, if you like. I'm all for preserving nature, what little of it there is left.' He smiled. 'Look, perhaps we've gotten off on the wrong foot here. And you look cold.' He removed his jacket and wrapped it, along with his arm, around Rosina's shoulders. 'You see, I only want you to become everything you were destined to become.'

His words were soothing and seductive. The warm touch of his hand sent tingles down her spine and, when he pulled her closer, she felt carefree, somewhat sinful for letting him do so.

'Sometimes, ladies like you get a raw deal,' he continued. 'But I am here to turn your dreams into reality. Don't fret over those who would bring you down. My gift is something magical, and just as nature intended.'

At this point, the memory became a patchy jumble of images and emotions.

She recalled talking for hours, or maybe only minutes. She remembered feeling reassured and desired, to the point of re-experiencing those very same sensations to their full intensity now, almost nine years later. The emotions became more distinct. Through the lens of recollection, she could feel the stranger's arms around her waist, as if her present reality was gone and only the dreamlike memory remained. Because, whether this was remembrance or reverie, she needed to re-live her time with this stranger; a long-gone happy event punctuated by an insect-like thrum that had risen up around them and replayed again now, like a favourite but forgotten tune. Her awareness of the world disappeared. All sense of time vanished. In an instant, she felt as light as a feather and too heavy for the ground to support her. She wanted to sink. She wanted to stay just here, in this recalled moment where, as with then, she saw herself gazing into his yellow eyes, sucking-in the earthy stench of his breath, taking all the transgressions he offered: the thrill of spontaneity, the freedom of unreservedness, and the desire to live a different life, if only for a moment.

The memory dissipated, and Rosina reached out to steady herself against the patio doors.

She felt lightheaded, weary.

As her thoughts cleared, however, the guilt rose. A confession of sorts. Remorse for breaking her vows. For eight years and nine months, she had kept this guilt suppressed, hidden in the rearmost chambers of her mind behind her haughtiness and self-reproach but, as with all shameful secrets, it was always there, creeping slowly into the light.

TWENTY-TWO – Concerning the dance and the disorder of nature

Curiosity had gone only a couple of metres into the dell, before she stopped running. She'd never been farther than this. The prospect vexed her. But, if the faerie-lady wouldn't come to her, she must seek her out. She craved to see what lay beyond the oak tree, now devoid of its golden door and looming tall and broad before her.

She pressed on.

Barefoot and protected only by the thin fabric of her cotton dress, she ignored the wounds afflicted by the thorns to her arms and legs. She moved past the tree into the undergrowth, her skin streaked with the cuts meted out by briars that seemed, by a will of their own, to lash out at her legs, body, and face. She ignored the pain. Perhaps her ordeal was a test, a means to gauge her commitment to leaving her unhappy life with her squabbling parents and discovering the newer, magical world ahead.

Her excitement grew. She anticipated that, by delving deeper, she must come upon the pond where the creatures had danced. She longed to go to the magnificent white stone fountain. She wanted to spin and frolic to the tune of the water that trickled from the statue at its centre.

As she pushed deeper into the dell, however, she found only more bushes, thicker branches, and bigger thorns. She turned to look behind. Under the fading sunlight, briars grew and coiled around the trees. They weaved around and through each other, creating a barrier of tendrils that obscured the path she had taken. The lawn outside was out of view, lost to the foliage. Even the sky above was hidden by a thick canopy of branches and leaves that grew as though time had speeded up and a whole season of growth had passed in mere seconds.

For the first time since entering the dell, she felt the pain of her injuries. Deep gashes that dripped blood down her legs and arms. The ground was littered with barbs that pricked the soles of her feet. The cuts on her face stung as sharply as a dozen paper cuts. She felt scared, trapped by the twisting fronds, intimidated by the thorns, and terrified by the shadows. With all her heart and hope, she wished that her faerie-lady might come to her, that her magic would turn the fronds to feathers, the thorns to threads, and the shadows into sparkling light.

She longed to be freed and to see her again.

With a whimper she said, 'Please come. Please don't be gone.'

As the sunlight dimmed and the briars wormed their way ever closer, the faerie-lady didn't come. The thorns coiled around her ankles. They gripped her limbs and stabbed her skin. As they tightened, Curiosity shrieked in pain, and she wept. She felt alone in here.

She felt alone just about everywhere.

Sometimes, even when counting her charm bells. Now,

even the thought of that gratifying pastime held no comfort, because, over the past few days, her insular universe had changed, perhaps for good or perhaps for ill but – with certainty – forever. She had run to the dell in an attempt to embrace something magical, to find a place to belong but now, trapped, with barbs biting into her flesh, she feared the magic had gone.

This proved to be the loneliest feeling of all.

And yet, there were voices here, faint, and whispered.

They spoke over and through each other. Unintelligible for their gibberish, but there, coming from somewhere within the undergrowth, confusing her thoughts and heightening her fear. Trapped as she was, she panicked. She struggled against her bonds, flexing her shoulders and waist in an attempt to wriggle free, but the tendrils gripped tighter, coiled around her throat and chest, squeezing the breath from her lungs. The world dimmed. Her head went light. Her legs gave way and she slumped, causing the barbs to pierce deeper and with greater agony. Her mind blanked but, as her sight and senses left her, up ahead, she glimpsed something twinkling through the encroaching darkness: a faint glow, moving towards her, fringed with an aura of pulsing, green light.

For a second, her mind cleared, causing her pain to stab with greater ferocity. But Curiosity endured and watched as the light bobbed from bush to bush, tree to tree and, with each contact, faces appeared. They had sniped noses and pointed ears. They emerged from the bark as though initially part of the trunks and branches, then stretched outwards, became fully formed creatures, dropping like melting candle-wax onto the dead leaves at the roots of the trees, before scurrying away into the bushes.

Although she couldn't see them, she sensed their eyes examining her.

It felt like insects crawling over her skin.

The thorny briars also responded to the touch of the light. They relaxed their grip, snaked back into the shadows, and she winced when the barbs withdrew from her flesh, but also felt the comfort of having them gone. The pulsing light darted closer. Curiosity stepped backwards. It hovered before her face and, within the swirling hues of green, a figure formed, with a tiny body, limbs, a head, a face, and fluttering dragonfly wings on its back.

Curiosity's heart leapt. She chuckled.

Her faerie-lady had returned.

The whispered voices grew louder and more distinct. The dell became alive with them, speaking the words:

Come in. Come in.

When fully formed, the faerie-lady flitted from side to side. She spun on the air and did so many times, before flying up to hover overhead. At the same time, the trees of the dell creaked and groaned. They folded to either side, as though blown by a windless storm, and revealed the same hedge-lined pathway that had appeared two nights earlier. The whole vista capped by a blue and cloudless sky.

The faerie-lady smiled.

She turned and floated along the path towards the white light at its end, gesturing for Curiosity to follow, which she did, with eagerness. She dashed along behind the faerie-lady all the way to the circular pond, amazed by how its stone walls shimmered as though on fire but felt no heat from the flames. Surrounding the pond and set into a lawn of cropped grass, a circle of varicoloured flagstones gleamed as if lit from beneath, and the walls were festooned with so many different plants and flowers she gave up identifying them all. Cassidy might know but she could never tell him about this place.

Rising up from the centre of the pond, a plinth of white marble stood, topped with a statue so lifelike it might be mistaken for a once living faerie – or fairy – or fae, whatever the right word might be – as though it had been turned to stone while carrying an urn across the water. She rushed to it, reached up to the urn, and thrust her hand into the trickling water. It lapped over her skin and soothed the sting of her cuts and scrapes, its gentle babble combining with the whispering voices, creating a sound so melodic it calmed her, bringing an overwhelming desire to stay.

The water turned colder and she removed her hand. Her cuts were still there but had ceased smarting. With the pain gone, she looked around, eager to miss nothing, to see and experience everything. While she took it all in, the faerie-lady hovered a few centimetres above her shoulder. And other creatures – dozens of them – that had since come out from the undergrowth, now peered from within the pristine hedges with tiny, inquisitive expressions. Some were thin. Others were pudgy, with roundish faces. Some had pointed noses and ears. Some wore upturned foxgloves or acorns on their heads. They all had almond shaped eyes and, apart from their headwear, were totally naked.

Overhead, a horde of the glowing creatures she had seen before swarmed.

They swooped and flew around the clearing, where red toadstools with white spots sprouted in their wake. They brushed the petals of the flowers. Clouds of sweet-scented pollen puffed upwards and spiralled on the air before falling down upon other, different flowers that did likewise. Within moments, the whole area around the pond shimmered with clouds of colour as bright as the white stone, and scented with fragrances so intoxicating that Curiosity felt dizzy.

She threw her arms into the air.

She skipped and reeled from one clump of flowers to another, caressing them with her fingertips and keeping time with the babble of the trickling water. She danced steps that were previously unknown to her. She lowered into a demi-plié and spun a pirouette, as naturally as if she had studied them for years, or maybe just knew how to do so. A trait as inborn as her chestnut-coloured hair, or her freckles, or her Warren clodhopper feet that now tingled with the want to chassé, jeté, and many other steps she knew how to perform without thinking. Curiosity's whole body tingled. The same energy she had felt when creating her dream worlds, natural, unbridled, and emanating from deep inside. Frolicking along the flagstones, she felt at ease with this power, and she danced, spinning, leaping, arms sweeping through the air, as the hedgerow creatures came out to dance with her.

The faerie-lady sang. With words Curiosity didn't recognise, but in the familiar hissing, guttural tone that – to her ear – sounded as pleasant as the finest arietta. It settled in her mind as if meant to be there. By enchantment or her own doing, she couldn't tell and cared not a jot about it either. An instant later, the flowers around the pond erupted. Petals and pollen burst upwards in an explosion of colour, before showering back down as clouds of twinkling light.

Her heart soared. Her clodhopper feet reeled faster. Her legs twirled as if out of control, but still under the command of some unseen part of her mind. Not definite thoughts, but a passion to dance. The part of her that yearned for happiness, for the magic to deliver her from an unhappy home life and the misery of watching her parents backbite and bicker. Here with these creatures, in this enchanted place, her cares left her, and Curiosity knew true joy.

A mist began to billow up from the surrounding under-growth. It moved out slowly, and at ground level, winding over and though itself in ropes of swirling green haze that sprouted legs, advancing as if a million spiders had hatched from the hedges and were attached to the same bubbling, broiling, growing web.

As Curiosity watched it move closer, the urge to investigate was overpowering. She stopped dancing. She stepped towards the green fog.

A voice intruded.

'Curiosity,' it shouted. 'Are you in there?'

It was Mummy again, yelling from outside in the garden.

The fog shrank back and disappeared. The faerie-lady darted away. The host followed.

Her mother shouted again, and then once more.

The pristine hedges turned grey and, from within their foliage, thorny briars sprouted, snaked across the grass, and coiled around the pond. The walls collapsed, became a jumble of slime coated boulders. The faerie statue and its plinth crumbled. In its place, a rotting tree-stump stood, dappled with furry brown fungus, crawling with fat beetles and spiny centipedes. The flowers withered. They shed their petals and died, their fragrance now gone, the sparkling pond water they once embellished coated with a layer of sludge and mulch.

It stank like rotten cabbage and her gorge rose.

When the briars had choked everything within their range, they turned and slithered towards Curiosity. In seconds, they had reached her feet, and started to coil around her ankles.

She ran.

The briars pursued her.

She charged through the bushes.

They closed around her, rising up like cobras to stop her escape.

Recalling how they had trapped her before, she upped her pace. Her hands, feet, legs, and body peppered with barbs. Her flesh slashed and her pyjamas torn to shreds. Through will and painful tenacity, she forced her way through towards a glint of light that shone up ahead marking a passageway, narrow, sheathed in ragged foliage, but leading out from the dell and into the garden.

She burst onto the lawn.

Her mother stood, illuminated by twilight, rigid straight with her arms folded.

She looked angry, or perhaps concerned. Curiosity didn't stop to decipher which. She ran to the patio, dashed through the house, went upstairs, and into her bedroom. She slammed the door and pushed her desk across to bar her mother as well as anything else from getting inside and, jumping onto her bed, pulled her knees up to her chest for comfort. She was filthy. Her pyjamas were in tatters. Her whole body was scraped and splattered with blood. But she didn't care about her pain or the stains on Mummy's clean sheets. And she didn't care that her mother was coming up the stairs, entreating her to tell her 'what happened', in a voice that sounded piteous, pathetic even.

If Mummy didn't know by now, there was no hope for either of them.

Curiosity was scared. The dell had changed and wanted to hurt her.

Most of all, she had no one to console, protect, or love her.

TWENTY-THREE – Concerning speculation

Acacia Okeke had walked the whole three kilometres from Bingham Crescent to her flat in White City. It was a nice day and the journey took her forty minutes. She could have taken the bus or the Tube but, as with most of her enquiries, she liked to gather her thoughts after an interview, slowly, and with care to assess the whole picture. The people she investigated warranted at least that. They deserved to be given a thorough analysis before others, with greater powers, swept in and upturned their lives.

When she got home, she made a cup of tea and, without leaving her kitchenette, looked over the police report notes from the incident at Jeremy Portland's apartment.

Lauren Alcock had wounds conducive with self-harming. Only the police didn't find the expected blood-soaked razor-blade in the bathroom. Or anything else by which she could have inflicted her injuries for that matter. And there was also nothing in her medical records to support the theory she might hurt herself. She had no mental health issues that anyone knew of. In fact, she was in prime health and, when Acacia contacted the University of Greenwich student welfare service, they stated that they only knew of her much as they did any other student, by her registration number, and that she attended lectures and examinations.

No history of study difficulties or depression. No visits to the campus wellbeing advisor.

Acacia shifted her focus to the replies that Jeremy's daughter and ex-wife had given when she pressed them about his behaviour.

The mother was much like any other person living with the fallout of a divorce. And Acacia felt for her. Infidelity was a tough thing to handle, let alone come to terms with. There were obvious signs of alcohol addiction there too: a tremble in her hands and a tendency to be snippy and bad mannered. She had broken capillaries on her nose and a slight redness to her complexion. Never mind the stale, yeasty odour on her breath.

As for the girl, she seemed distressed but didn't show any of the usual hallmarks for mistreatment. At first glance, there were no signs of bruising or other injuries. Although, it would take a full examination by a medical professional to confirm it with any certainty. She did seem a tad withdrawn, and unwilling to answer questions, but there was nothing unusual in that either. Most children Acacia dealt with tended to shy away from strangers, especially ones making awkward queries about family members and their broken homes.

And, if the girl's last reaction was genuine, reluctance to speak her mind was a million miles away from being an issue for young Curiosity Portland.

She sure had a temper.

In Acacia's experience, however, there were defined markers to indicate whether a child was suffering abuse of one sort or another, which was why she had tried to press both the girl and her mother on a possible psychological aspect to Jeremy Portland's demeanour with his daughter.

Was he manipulative?

Had the supposed incident at the park been planned?

Acacia had seen it before. In her time, working first in social care and then with the police, abusive parents had connived all manner of horrific methods to *chastise* their children, and even more inventive ways to cover up their crimes.

But, on the face of it, that didn't look to be the case here.

Sure, Jeremy Portland was a blunt and forthright character but, in Acacia's professional opinion – and by what her gut reaction told her – he wasn't the violent or manipulating type, at least not with those closest to him. In her years working with the some of the worst parents that London had to offer, she had seen it all: cigarette burns, belt marks, broken bones, sexual abuse, and mental torture so severe the child in question need years of therapy to, in some cases, just hold a conversation with a stranger.

Yet, this didn't seem to be going on here.

And still, Acacia felt troubled.

She rang Lauren Alcock:

'Hello, my name is Acacia Okeke,' she said when the phone answered. 'I work with the police. We talked briefly at the hospital, but you were being treated at the time and I didn't want to trouble you too much.'

'Oh, yeah. I remember. You're the psychiatrist. What do you want?'

'Well, actually I am a psychologist, so nowhere nearly as

nosey.' She laughed. It was meant as a tension breaker but it sounded flat. 'How are you?'

'I'm fine. Why?'

'Have the doctors given you anything for your wounds?'

'They bandaged some of them, gave me cream. They told me to wash them regularly and take painkillers if they get too sore.'

'That sounds good. I'm glad there were no complications.'

'Look, what is this about. I'm very busy.'

Acacia paused then asked, 'I was wondering if I could ask you a few extra questions? I'll be quick. I promise. Most of the time, I don't have much of great value to say anyway.' She laughed again. Another tension breaker.

Lauren didn't seem amused. 'I suppose. But what can I add? I don't know what happened.'

'In what way?'

'In the *I don't know what happened* way. I told you before, I think I might've blacked out.'

Even though it was difficult to determine for sure over the phone, Acacia sensed an air of embarrassment in Lauren's words and got the impression she was holding something back.

'So, you don't remember how you came about your injuries?'

'Not really.'

Acacia took a second to think. Outside of a face-to-face interview, it was unprofessional to pose the question she was about to ask, some might deem it unethical, but she asked it anyway: 'Did you inflict these injuries to yourself?'

Lauren seemed shocked. 'No,' she said. 'Maybe. I don't know.'

'And where was Jeremy Portland at this time.'

'On the sofa in the living-room. Jeremy was a star. He came and saved me.'

'Saved you from what?'

'Nothing. I have to go.'

'You can tell me. I'm not really the police, just someone who wants to help.'

'I have to go.'

'Okay. Sorry. I will delay you no longer. But, can I ring you again when . . .?'

The phone went dead.

Acacia set her phone on the countertop, took a sip of tea, and bundled her papers into a neat pile. Lauren Alcock was definitely hiding something, and so were Jeremy Portland's ex-wife and daughter.

But what?

She decided the only way to know for certain, was if she paid another visit to Curiosity and her mother, after she had talked to the gardener.

Lauren set her phone onto the bedside table and continued putting on harem pants and the biggest t-shirt she could find. Her cuts hurt. Her clothes needed to be baggy so they didn't chafe. And she did so by the doorway leading to the living-room, fearful of going too far into the bedroom.

Behind her, Jeremy carried suitcases to the front door and sat on the arm of the couch.

'Who was that, Sweetie?' he asked.

'The psychology woman who works with the police.'

'What did she want?'

'Just to see if I remembered anything.'

'That's psychologists for you. They think they know everything.'

Lauren didn't answer. She found it difficult to admit to what had really occurred the night she was attacked. It was nonsense, fantasy, a story from a horrid fairy tale, and not something she wanted to reveal to Jeremy. Mostly because she doubted it herself, doubted her sanity.

'And do you remember anything?' Jeremy asked. There was genuine concern in his tone. He stood up, came to the bedroom door, and placed a hand on her shoulder.

She shrugged away.

He seemed to respect that, because he stepped back and put his hands in his pockets. 'Sorry. I didn't mean to . . .'

'It's okay,' Lauren said. 'It's just that the cuts are sore.'

Jeremy took another step back and smiled:

'Well, I've reserved a room at The Royal Kinnerton in Belgravia. The best they have to offer. Very plush. We can have a few nights of luxury until the holiday. I've booked that too. Portugal. Troia. You'll love it. There are Roman ruins there. We can spin it as a working trip.' He smiled. 'Anyway, all that remains now is for me to make the phone call from Hell. But I will wait until you're ready, and I've had a large shot of brandy.' He laughed.

So did Lauren. It hurt her face but felt good nonetheless.

Jeremy turned to walk back into the living-room.

Before he left, Lauren reached out and took his hand. She

moved closer. 'I am grateful, you know,' she said. 'For every-thing. Letting me live here. Helping me with my exams and assignments. And for comforting me when . . .' she pointed to the cuts on her face, upper chest, and arms '. . . well, when this happened. I don't know exactly what happened,' she lied, too embarrassed to admit to seeing the scary creatures. 'But you were here for me. When I needed you. And, after these have healed, I'll make it up to you in all the ways you like.'

She smiled.

Jeremy's eyes seemed to bulge in his head.

'Whatever you need,' he said. 'You know that?'

She nodded.

'And in your own time.'

She nodded again.

'Good. Anyway. I had better get that brandy. Before you get me all worked up.'

Watching him walk back into the living-room a sense of happiness rippled through Lauren's whole body. Maybe Jeremy wasn't like all the other men she had used to get ahead. He genuinely seemed to like her. After the incident, he had hurried her to the hospital, and put up with their accusative questions, also from the police and their psycholo-gist. And, when they had returned to his apartment, because she felt too frightened to enter the bedroom, he had piled the bed and the rest of the furniture against the wall so she could see the floor. He booked the hotel because she was too afraid to stay the night in his flat, as well as a month-long holiday. He helped her pack, and stood with her while she found clothes to wear to the hotel, changing the dressings on her cuts before she put them on, and all without asking a single question that might make her feel small or stupid.

All in all, Jeremy Portland was a nice guy. Too nice for his snarky ex-wife.

And too nice for Lauren Alcock.

His only problem was greed.

He liked money, so much so his other, nicer traits were smothered by it.

But there was nothing wrong with that. Lauren was just the same.

They would make a very good couple.

A half hour later, Acacia walked into a complex of four, six-storey-high blocks of flats, arranged around an open, hexagon-shaped grassy area. Before she left home, she called the station to request a person search, and had been issued with Brendan Cassidy's address taken from the electoral roll and some other personal information detailed in his medical records.

The man lived alone. He was sixty-nine years old, with no major health issues apart from recurring bouts of rheumatoid arthritis in his knees. He had no spouse or partner, and no children.

When she reached the central point of the grassy area, she turned down a short path to the second building on the left where a porch shaded a single, glass panelled entrance door. Sliding her forefinger down the names on the intercom, she pushed the button alongside a label marked *Flat 22* marked: *B. Cassidy.*

She pressed three times, waiting a minute or two between each buzz, and was about to give up when a crackled voice came over the speaker:

'Yes?'

'Oh. Hi. Is that Mr. Brendan Cassidy?'

'It is.'

'Terrific. I was wondering if I could speak to you for a few minutes.'

'What about?'

'Well, it's a bit sensitive and I don't want to talk where other people might hear.'

'I don't want anything. And I don't need saving.'

'It's not like that.'

'It's always like that. You bible bashers never give up. Look, I'm catholic and that won't be changing anytime in the future. So, go away.'

'I'm from the police,' she said, just before the intercom went dead. She pressed the button again and Brendan spoke instantly.

'The police? Why would the police be interested in me?'

'I'm sorry. I should have introduced myself sooner. My name is Acacia Okeke. I am a police appointed psychological investigator. I would like to ask you some questions about Jeremy Portland, and also about his ex-wife and daughter. I've been told you are the family's gardener?'

The front door clicked.

'Come up,' Brendan said. 'You'll need to give the door a good shove. It sticks in the changeable weather.'

Acacia gave the door a good shove, went inside, and

climbed the narrow, concrete stairwell to *Flat 22*. Although the paint was peeling in a few places, in general the building appeared well-kept, clean, litter free, and devoid of the graffiti she often saw on similar housing estates.

When she arrived at the door, it was ajar:

'Hello?' she called through the gap.

'It's open,' Brendan Cassidy shouted from somewhere inside. 'I'm in the sitting-room at the end of the hall.'

His place was much as she expected for an older person living on their own, with green and terracotta striped wallpaper dating back to the eighties, Persian patterned carpeting throughout – even up the stairs to the upper level – and the maximum amount of furniture that could be squeezed into a small, two-floor flat. Two bookcases, replete with well fingered paperbacks, lined the walls of the hall and ornaments dotted every flat surface of the sitting-room: inside and atop of three glass cabinets, on the window-ledge, and a row of porcelain ducks walking across the top of a broad mahogany sideboard much like a scene from a Beatrix Potter novel.

Brendan, wearing only a grey vest and blue striped pyjama bottoms, was sitting in a high-backed, tweed upholstered armchair gazing out through the window to the grassy area below. He seemed distracted, or vexed. His forehead creased below a mop of white hair. He was unshaven and his fingers worried a single bead on the rosary he held coiled around his hand.

Acacia walked into the room carefully, so as not to disturb any of his many bits and pieces.

He turned and pointed to a couch with the matching pattern to his armchair.

'Take a seat,' he said with a brief smile.

The cloth of the couch was threadbare, the cushions lumpy and, when she sat down, it felt as if she were sitting on rocks. Having had the luxury of Rosina Portland's epicurean sofa only a short while earlier, the contrast was glaring.

She set her briefcase on her lap.

'Do you want tea?' he asked.

'No. Thank you. I had a cup before I left home.'

'There's one in the pot. It's not a bother. My mother – God rest her soul – was a tea-aholic. The clock didn't pass twenty minutes but she was putting the kettle on again. She loved her brew she did. I think I might have caught her habit.'

'Thank you. But I am fine. I'll be peeing like a trooper if I drink anymore.' She laughed.

Brendan did too but unconvincingly.

'Anyway,' Acacia continued. 'As I said over the intercom, my name is Acacia Okeke and I am a psychological investigator working with the police. They call me in to look at the probability of abuse when a person is injured in a domestic setting, but claims normal factors, or decides to not press charges.'

'Press charges?'

'No. It's okay. No one has pressed charges on anyone. And not you, Mr. Cassidy. But there was an incident. At Jeremy Portland's flat involving his girlfriend. She is badly cut up but she won't tell us exactly what transpired.'

'You think Jeremy did it?'

'Not necessarily. But something happened and he claims

that he found her that way, slashed and bleeding in the bedroom. She is telling us – well *me* – absolutely zilch. She just hesitates and skirts around the question.'

Brendan frowned. 'How is she?'

'Shaken. As you might expect. But she will heal. I'm more concerned as to her mental state or if Jeremy has control issues.'

'I doubt it. He's a chancer – but not that kind of a chancer.'

'That's what his ex-wife said.'

'How is Rosina? And Curiosity?' He sounded worried.

'They're fine. Curiosity had a fright at the park but she seems fine now, albeit a bit ratty with her mother. Why do you ask?'

'A fright?' He sat up straighter in the armchair.

'Yes. She says she found a dead squirrel. It scared her. Her mother claims it's just her daughter making things up. My concern is if her father left it there to frighten her.'

'Rosina would say that. Did Curiosity say anything else? Did she *see* anything else?'

'She didn't mention anything. Like what?'

He sat back and gazed out the window again. 'Nothing.'

'Are you sure? Is there something you want to tell me?'

'No. Nothing.'

'If there is . . .' she began.

'I told you. There's nothing,' he snapped. 'At least not something that someone like you would understand.'

'Try me.'

He sat upright again and looked Acacia straight in the eyes. 'Are you a religious woman, Mrs. Okeke?'

'Miss,' she said. 'And call me Acacia.'

'Grand so. Well then, Acacia, would you call yourself religious?'

She glanced up to the wall and saw a crucifix there, alongside a large painting of Jesus as the Sacred Heart. 'I was born into and brought up Baptist,' she said, 'but gave up believing in such things a long time ago.'

'Well, my advice would be to start again. Prayer is the only protection.'

'Protection from what exactly?'

'If you have been poking around at Rosina Portland's house then they are already aware of you. They have eyes everywhere. They are everywhere. And, once they have their sights on you, there is no escape.'

Acacia was genuinely confused. 'Who are you talking about?'

'As I said, you wouldn't understand.'

'And, as I said, *try me.*'

For a few seconds, Brendan remained silent, seemed pensive, and then began, 'When I was a young lad, my mother told us a tale about a barrow that rose out of a hollow in the woodland at the back of our farm. It was an oak grove, beside a small lough, with patches of blackthorn. There was rowan there too. A complete tangled mess of branches, bushes, bracken, and just about anything else that had a mind to grow there.' He paused before continuing. 'I had two sisters. Both were older than me. None of us were allowed to go anywhere near the grove. Mam said it was haunted. Not by ghosts, mind you. But by the *aes sídhe.* The people of the mounds.

The *shee folk*. Faeries you would call them, but not the fluttery, smiley, friendly type you see in a child's storybook. I am talking about the oldest things that lived in Ireland. That lived anywhere. Long before people arrived, even the Celts, or anyone else who came afore them.'

He paused again and appeared distressed.

Acacia waited. It was her job to listen, no matter how outrageous the story might sound.

'Anyway, my mother said it was a cursed place. And she spoke of a girl she had gone to school with. Her name was Molly – Molly Mooney. Mam said she was a strange girl, withdrawn in a way but curious, adventurous, with a wont to go exploring places she shouldn't. She was an only child. Her mother died while giving birth to her and her father never re-married, just brought her up on his own. And, by all accounts, he was a good father, devoted but a busy man. In those days, running a farm took every moment God sends. Especially with little else but scrubland to work with. He spent most of his time in the fields. So, when not doing chores around the farmhouse or getting schooling, Molly was pretty much alone most of the time. Looney Mooney they called her, even the other parents, but not to her face. That's the thing with gossips, they never do anything upfront. They cower by their firesides, seeding division and malcontent then wash their hands of it when things go wrong. The Pontius Pilates in our midst, Mam called them. Those that have no good words to say about anyone. And Mam was no better at the time. She joined in with the jaw-wagging. She told us so herself. I think she felt guilty about what happened. Which meant, as I said before, Molly Mooney didn't get much chance to mix with the other kids. She was aloof, and Mam said she became as odd as a bull with teats. Forgive my crude mouth.'

Acacia smiled and nodded.

Brendan continued. 'Anyhow, as is with that type of youngster, word had it that she got to exploring the grove of trees at the barrow. She said she saw faeries there. She swore by it. Started acting stranger than usual. They would see her dancing all alone in the field like an eejit and taking herself off into the grove after school. Each day, when lessons were finished, they would see her heading out the back track, around the back of our farm, and disappearing into the undergrowth. She stayed there for hours. Sometimes until well after dark. And then, one day, she didn't come out.'

Brendan fell silent. He sighed, his head tilted forward slightly, his gaze fixed on some non-specific point on the floor.

'What happened to her?' Acacia asked.

'Some said she drowned in the lough. Pike can make short work of a carcass. I've seen it, when sheep have wandered too far and fell into the water. Others maintained that she just ran off. For a while, the Gardaí suspected that the father had killed her or something suchlike. Maybe because of money troubles. There was a big search of his farm and the outbuildings. They even got a helicopter up from Dublin to scour the countryside. But she was never found. It made the papers. And the national TV news: *Girl Missing in Monaghan Woodland*. The father became a total wreck, started drinking, which was bad for a confirmed *Pioneer* who'd never touched a drop in his life. Two weeks later, he was found floating in the slurry-pit. His death was deemed as suicide, but Mam always maintained that the wee-folk took her and then killed him too. She banned us from going near the barrow, and also the Mooney farm, which fell into ruin. She specifically forbade my two sisters. Something about young girls being more akin to the spirits of nature. I don't know for sure why she reckoned that, but I do know this . . . we didn't. We never went near either place. We knew better to leave such things alone. And so should you.'

Acacia took a moment. The silence felt heavy but she wanted to find the right words.

'But, Mr. Cassidy,' she then said, 'and forgive me for pointing this out, as you said at the beginning, that is just a tale. My own mother was the same. She had many stories. I grew up with old Nigerian folktales about bad juju and evil spirits. She even had one about the disobedient daughter who married a skull.' She smiled, hoping it might ease his tension. 'But that, like yours, was just a story.'

'Was it now? Just a story?'

'I would say so. Definitely. You see, I believe in science. For me, it's all about empirical evidence. I'm all about the facts. Hard, undeniable facts. Sure, there are many things we have yet to find explanations for, but nothing – and I've been at this a long time – can bring me to believe that weird spirits follow us around. As you said yourself, she probably drowned. Or maybe her father did kill her and concealed her body, so well the police couldn't find her. It would explain his suicide. Remorse is a strong emotion, especially after filicide. But who knows for sure? The only two people who were there are dead now. Or maybe she did run off and led a full and happy life somewhere else. What I am trying to say, is that there are numerous, logical explanations for what happened to your mother's school friend, and I know for certain that none of them will be because of fairies.' She laughed at the thought of it. She didn't mean to. It was unprofessional, but it just came.

Brendan huffed, raised his eyebrows as if he was about to say something but stayed silent.

'Oh, come on, Mr Cassidy. You don't really expect me to believe . . .'

He struck out and grabbed her wrist. 'Say your prayers, Miss Okeke. And keep your business to yourself. If I were you, I would have no more to do with the Portlands. Take it as a warning. That way brings only misery. Or death.'

She pulled her arm away. She stood and, deciding to sound more official, said, 'Look, if you think a crime has been committed or there is the threat of one, you must go immediately to the police. Better still, just tell me now.'

'You haven't listened to a word I said. The police can't help. And neither can you. Take my advice. Drop the case. Ask for the Lord's forgiveness and protection, and pray that they leave you alone.'

'Who, Brendan? Who are you talking about? Fairies?'

'You should go now,' he said. 'Go home. I will pray for you even if you won't.'

'Look, I will say this again. If you have . . .'

'Go. Get out. I have nothing more to say.' He turned and resumed gazing out through the window, his fingers finding a different bead on the rosary to rub.

In Acacia's experience, when a witness reached the point of belligerence, there was no point in questioning them further. She took a card from her briefcase and set it on the sofa.

'Okay. I apologise if I have upset you. May I call again? When you feel more settled?'

'That won't happen,' Brendan replied. 'Not if they have singled you out. Now, go. And may the Lord be with you.'

Acacia said nothing more and let herself out.

What had started as a possible domestic abuse issue had now become something more sinister. Lauren Alcock, Jeremy Portland's ex-wife, his daughter, and now the gardener were all acting or talking bizarrely. In fact, Jeremy himself, the whole focus of her investigation, seemed like the only sensible one in the bunch.

There was more to this case.

There was more to investigate, and maybe enough to involve her colleagues at *Social Services*. But not quite yet. Not until she had more to go on.

When she reached the porch outside, she thought about going back up to press Brendan Cassidy for more information. But she didn't. She would call by Rosina Portland and her daughter in a day or two. Let them settle for a couple of nights. Maybe then they might be ready to speak to her.

She walked up the path towards the central grassy area, passing a mangy black and white cat that looked an exact double for one she had seen back at Rosina Portland's house. She remembered that it had followed her all the way up Bingham Crescent, and as she walked down Westbourne

Grove, a journey that took her across Portobello Road and not far from where she was now.

Perhaps it was Brendan Cassidy's cat, moving back and forth between his flat and the places he worked?

She gave it no more thought.

Even when the cat arched its back, spiked its fur, hissed and bared its teeth.

TWENTY-FOUR – Concerning reflection

The phone rang. Mummy went to her bedroom and answered.

It was Daddy. And, listening to her mother's repetition of his words, Curiosity deduced that he wouldn't be picking her up for a while because he was taking his girlfriend to Portugal. Something about an archaeological dig and letting Lauren recover.

Mummy scoffed as she repeated the words, before letting loose at him down the phone. Which Curiosity reckoned he fully deserved. He was a bad husband – *ex*-husband – and a useless father.

His phone-call, however, did provide her with a certain convenience, if nothing else because her mother would seethe and bluster for a few hours, probably drink a whole bottle of wine and, in the main, leave her alone.

She might be confused and scared, but Mummy always made things worse. Maybe she had a point in hating Daddy, but she was no better, with her stupid rules and compulsion to make Curiosity some kind of normal girl. And she had danced ballet, but kept it quiet.

Curiosity was certain of it now. The photograph proved it.

If Mummy found the fountain in the dell, maybe she knew about the faerie-lady, the glitter-rain, and the other faerie creatures?

Maybe she wanted to keep them for herself, and why she always stopped her from exploring, or having fun, or being herself?

As these thoughts came to her, they firmed in Curiosity's mind. Daddy might treat her like a stranger, but Mummy always nagged. She was a manipulator. She wanted to keep the magic for herself, which was why she never went near the dell, in case Curiosity saw her and followed, found the secret place . . . *her secret place.*

She recalled how the dell changed when Mummy arrived. It was her fault. The dell didn't want Mummy. It wanted her. And, as for Daddy, he had been taught a lesson about not running out on his family, or abandoning his daughter for young girlfriends. Lauren had been hurt, because Curiosity hated her, and hated Daddy. She was certain of it. She knew she had only to hate someone and they would be punished.

Outside in the garden, the green light returned and shone through the oval window. The pulsing glow filled the room, a shaft of which illuminated something glossy lying on the floor.

Curiosity leaned down and picked up the photo of her mother, as a girl, wearing the same ballet tutu and wings that she now kept hidden in a plastic bag underneath her bed. The photo looked different, though, sharper, as though recently taken. And, on closer inspection, it wasn't Mummy dancing, but herself, poised on her tiptoes, her arms arched above her head, her body wrapped in an aura of glowing green light.

She set the photo on the bed. A second later, it disappeared.

Unbothered by this, Curiosity grabbed the plastic bag from beneath her bed, changed out of her ripped pyjamas, and put on the ballet costume. She ignored her wounds. From outside, hissing in her mind, the faerie-lady was calling, urging her to come out to the garden and down to the dell.

She pushed the desk away from the door.

She brushed the tutu into place, and straightened the wings on her shoulders. She walked across to the full-length mirror to check how well the costume looked on her. The scrapes and cuts on her face, arms, and legs looked sore. Blood oozed through the white tulle, but Curiosity smiled, happy she had danced with the faeries and would do so again.

The image shimmered. Curiosity yelped and stumbled back against the bed. Instead of her reflection, five hunched figures now stood, all of them wearing ballet costumes, the fabric tattered and blackened, clinging to their scorched skin like melted plastic. Their hair was burned away. The stench of charred flesh filled the room. Suddenly, in a synchronised pirouette, they spun around to face her.

They looked up.

They smiled, with eyes betraying their pain and their terror.

Curiosity ran out from her room. She crashed down the stairs, through the kitchen, and out to the garden.

Rosina crossed her bedroom to the window. She was still fuming with Jeremy and worried about Curiosity, but she didn't follow her this time. Maybe Faithe was right. Let the child be and she'd find her own way.

Below, Curiosity had stopped outside on the patio, a tiny

solitary figure in a sea of grey flagstones and grass. She peered up. There were tears on her cheeks and fear in her gaze. She looked lost, as if caught in the centre of something she didn't understand. Somewhere so frightening and lonely it caused her sadness. A good mother would comfort her child, would go to her, with assurances that all was well. She would wipe away her tears with her thumbs, hug her close to her chest and love her.

But Rosina didn't.

She stayed in her room.

Later that night, Acacia Okeke woke to mice scurrying around her bed, skittering along the wall behind the head-board, and insects, buzzing as if they were swarming beneath the mattress.

She had mice before. A lot of these old Victorian houses with too many flats squeezed into them had an infestation at some time or other. They came in through the gaps at the bottom of doors, or holes where the roof joists crossed into neighbouring properties. Mostly, they weren't a problem, and only showed their presence by the occasional chewed corner on a cereal box or by stripping paper towel from the roll on the kitchenette counter.

As for insects, she had a permanent colony of the buggers. Cockroaches. Black ones the size of fingernails. But such was the living standards for someone who was dependent on the gig economy. Contract, part-time work with the police and Social Services had a lower-than-average hourly wage as it was, and the work tended to be random. Most of all, compared to her mother who lived farther up the country in Leicester, her rent was extortionate. Even if the quality of dwelling left much to be desired. It was the downside of living in London and a symptom of having to leave home in search of work.

She sat up, reached out, and switched on her bedside light.

The room fell silent.

She leaned over the edge of the mattress and peered underneath.

Nothing moved. Her slippers were lying a half metre apart. Her socks stuffed into one of them. The suitcase where she stored her winter clothes sat, as usual, pushed up to the upper wall. And a pile of magazines lay, strewn over the floor at the opposite side of the bed where she left them.

She saw no mice.

Nor were there any cockroaches.

Only the hazy shadow, as if a cat was sitting on the lounge side of the open bedroom door.

Arching its back and baring its teeth at her.

TWENTY-FIVE – Concerning the restless night

The next morning, Rosina stumbled out of bed and staggered to the en-suite. She showered, dried her hair, tied it in a bun, put on underwear and stockings, before applying the customary amount of concealer, face-powder, mascara, and lip-gloss as was necessary for basic appearances.

Her hands shook. A couple of times, she dropped the mascara brush into the bathroom sink. The fallout from the quarter bottle of brandy she kept stashed in her bedside cabinet, and had downed before intoxication finally sent her to sleep. She huffed all the way through the procedure, then went to her walk-in wardrobe and selected one of her modest black dresses. Chanel of course. There had to be standards and Rosina Portland always made certain no one, not even the woman who delivered the post, ever encountered her in a non-presentable state. Fractured sleep and the want – no, *need* – for something strong in the middle of the night, might pose difficulties to maintaining those standards but, as with decorum and demeanour, outward presentation was fundamental.

The nightmares had returned.

The heavy ones for which she had been prescribed anti-depressants. Those she had assumed had gone forever and which, in turn, led her straight to the bottle. She wasn't proud of it. But, even now, she felt the call of a small glass.

Patting down the hems of her dress, she checked her reflection in the wardrobe mirror and phoned Faithe.

When Faithe picked-up, her, 'Yeah-ello,' sounded groggy.

'It's me.'

'Jesus, Rosina, it's like something stupid o'clock in the morning. And you know I never do mornings.'

'You sleep too much.'

'No, what I do is drink too much . . . and then sleep it off. Totally different. And fun. Anyway, what's up?'

'Nothing. I'm sorry. I'll leave you alone.'

'Just spit it out. I'm already awake now.'

'I'm scared.'

'Why? What's happened?' Rosina heard a scoff in the question.

'I've had a nightmare.'

'Nothing new there.'

'But this was a bad one.'

'How bad?'

Rosina hesitated then said, 'The burned girls are back.'

Curiosity woke on one of the circulation space sofas, roused by her mother clattering a bottle and glasses in the kitchen. It took her a few seconds to come around. She remembered running to the patio. She recalled crying and wanting nothing else but for Mummy to come and comfort her. For five full minutes, they had stared at each other through Mummy's bedroom window on the first floor. When she didn't come, Curiosity went back inside. She stayed all night on the sofa, away from her room and the mirror. Sometimes she slept. Mostly she stayed awake, feeling alone and terrified that the burned girls might return.

They didn't, but Curiosity sensed them watching her nonetheless.

The clock on the mantelpiece said seven twenty-two.

She sat up, wincing where the ballet dress stuck to the cuts on her body. She set her bare feet on the floor, rubbed the bleariness from her eyes with the balls of her hands, and panicked when the five hideous girls resurfaced, glaring down from the mirror on the wall above the clock.

She rushed upstairs, glancing across to her mother as she went.

Mummy didn't say a word. She was holding a glass of wine, her hand shaking as she attempted to light a cigarette. She seemed immersed in her thoughts, as lost as Curiosity, and just as frightened.

When she reached her bedroom door, without entering, Curiosity unclipped the fairy wings from her shoulders, threw them to the floor, and kicked them under her bed. She then dashed into the room, making sure to avoid eye contact with the mirror. She snatched her baseball boots, t-shirt, and shorts from a pile of dirty washing, darted back out to the landing, stripped out of the bloody ballet tutu and tossed it under the bed with the fairy wings. She put on her clothes as she ran downstairs, stopping twice to slip her baseball boots onto her feet. They hurt. The edges tore at her scabs and blood oozed through the rough canvas. She ignored the pain and dashed through the front door out to the front garden.

Behind her, Mummy was still in the kitchen, sipping wine and smoking.

The burned girls were still in the mirror.

As Faithe walked up the path to Rosina's house she remarked inwardly at its delightful vista. It truly was a gem. Built at a time when buildings harmonised with nature and didn't smother it. And she let her thoughts drift; imagining the countryside that once surrounded it: hills and meadows rolling over the horizon, the crimson touch of dawn's first light caressing the underside of a swatch of cotton clouds that bathed the scene in cooling shadows.

Indeed, at one time – as with all the places of the earth – no house stood here at all. This assemblage of red bricks, someday to become Rosina's triumph, was perhaps the first manmade object to occupy the woodland that had prevailed since tree and flower saw fit to set seed here. And the thought of that pleased her.

Curiosity was sitting on the grass in the front garden.

'Hi,' Faithe said. 'I'll let myself in as usual, shall I?'

The girl didn't reply. She sat gazing at her feet.

They were a moody pair, this mom and daughter combination. Especially the mother. A woman resolute in her refusal to cast away her burdens. She wore them like jewellery. Polishing and displaying them even when she wished to hide from the world.

When it came to the child, however, there was hope.

She had a spark.

Faithe sat down beside the girl, her knees cracking as she did so. Years and too much alcohol had taken their toll on her body. She longed for a new one with bones that weren't so creaky and didn't give out at the slightest strenuous movement. Setting her handbag on her lap, she rested her hands one on top of the other, and said, 'Do you know, we haven't spoken since your birthday,'

Curiosity looked up. 'Why would we?'

'Oh, I don't know, maybe we have some things in common.'

'Like what? You're big and I'm just a girl. You're Mummy's best friend.'

'We both like flowers.'

'You like flowers?'

'Yes. I like flowers. In fact, I adore flowers. My house is full of them. And my garden. I like to keep it so that wild things can live there. Like bees. Birds. My gardener, Nick, tells me that I have a hedgehog nesting underneath the compost heap.'

The girl stayed silent and appeared surprised.

'And, do you know what else we have in common?'

Curiosity shrugged and shook her head.

'We both know that your mother can be a right royal pain in the backside. In fact, she's can be a bit bonkers, as you Brits say. But never tell her I told you that.'

Curiosity sniggered.

'But it's only because she doesn't know how to deal with things. She can't cope, with your father being – well, the way your father is. And you. She doesn't know how to cope with you. But, you can leave her to me. Let me deal with her.' She looked up. The sky was clouding over. 'Anyway, you might want to come inside. It looks like it's going to chuck it down any minute now.'

Curiosity didn't answer.

'Suit yourself. I suppose a bit of rain never hurt anyone. It's just nature doing its thing.' Faithe got to her feet. She groaned as she did so, went to the front door, opened it with Rosina's spare key, but stopped just inside the vestibule. 'Those cuts on your arms and legs look sore. Did you get them searching for faerie paths?'

The girl looked up.

'Oh yes, faerie paths are everywhere, although they are not easy to see. But, there are ways to find them, if you're clever. Be careful, though. Curiosity can lead little girls on all sorts of adventures.' She paused then laughed. 'Sorry, Cupcake, I'm just yanking your chain. Everyone knows that faerie paths are only in storybooks. Are you sure you won't come inside?'

The girl looked confused, but stayed where she was and said nothing.

Faithe went into the house, still laughing.

A few moments later, Curiosity did follow Faithe into the house. Not because of the prospect of rain or even her confusion at what Mummy's friend had said about faerie paths – although it did seem strange. She went inside because of what always drove Curiosity to do anything: her tenacity and need to tackle things head on.

Until Faithe arrived, she had spent a good hour in the front garden watching the sunshine wither and clouds gather. An hour spent in contemplation, mustering the resolve to confront the things that threatened her. It was only when Faithe mentioned faerie paths and storybooks that it became clear to her. There were drawings of faeries in the sketchpad.

There was also writing. Maybe something she could use?

Once inside, she gritted her will and peered around. She checked the mirror above the clock.

The apparitions were gone.

The knot in her gut unravelled. She relaxed.

Maybe they were never there at all? Maybe she had lost her mind?

Daddy said Mummy had lost her mind and *imagined things*. Mostly when responding to her drunken accusations that his clothes stank of perfume. On those occasions, Curiosity agreed with her mother. Daddy was *up to his tricks*. It was plain as day in the way his kept shifting his eyes and his defensive accusations that Mummy had *lost her marbles* and maybe she should *lay off the wine, and start taking the pills again.*

Curiosity grew tired listening to her father's claims. Until now that was, these last few days, when the faeries became real, scary ghostly girls moved into the mirrors of her house, and she feared that she too had lost her marbles.

Regardless of her fears, however, and with the determination of *Alice*, she set forth upstairs to the attic room. Mad or not mad, the answers to her dilemma must be the sketchpad. All she needed to do was go and get it. She took the stairs two at a time. It was only when she arrived at the end of the corridor and the narrow stairwell that her apprehension returned. Shivers rippled down her spine. Her legs refused to move.

Downstairs, Mummy was telling Faithe something. She spoke loudly, but her words were so hurried and ill-defined Curiosity couldn't tell one from the other.

She did, however, hear her say, 'It was very distressing.'

Then again, when it came to Mummy, something as simple as the grocery delivery turning up at a non-appointed time was distressing. But, this time, there was a level of anxiety in her tone that Curiosity hadn't heard before. Her usual pretence and pomposity sounded ruffled and, for a few moments, Curiosity lingered in the distraction of eavesdropping, a respite from the prospect of what she planned to do next.

Her greater need won out, though.

She took her first step towards the attic room door, and then another, climbing each stair slowly, with only her shadow to keep her company, an extension of herself, yet strangely detached in its blackness. Her foot landed upon the final riser. It creaked, and Curiosity ran back out to the landing. Her hands were trembling. Her heart thumped in her chest. She realised it was a loose stair-board, and began to climb the stairs again. As before, she went slowly. She took deliberate steps, careful not to cause any more creaks. When she reached the small, panelled door, she placed her hand on the knob. Her dread pricked like needles, and she waited a moment before she turned, pushing the door open with the palm of her other hand.

Dulled by dust and the cloudy sky outside the skylight, it took a few seconds for her sight to adjust. She scanned the room for the sketchpad. It was lying where she had dropped it in the trunk, with its pages splayed open, revealing the sketch of the naked faerie girl with flowers in her hair and dragonfly wings on her back. Only a handful of days ago, the sketch intrigued her. Now it scared her and made her feel powerlessness.

She fought hard to summon her courage. Taking a step into the room seemed easy, but her thoughts swirled with the prospect of terrifying entities lurking somewhere back among the rafters. The doorbell rang downstairs. It made her jump. The subsequent cackle of Ophelia Heffington Jeffries shouting 'hello', along with the racket of Arabella Heffington Jeffries thundering up the stairs, prompted Curiosity to dash into the attic room, snatch the sketchpad, and charge back down the stairwell.

She slammed the door behind her.

When she reached the landing, she scurried along the corridor and into her bedroom. She tossed the sketchpad under her bed, a split second before Arabella burst into the room in a blaze of pink damask and lace, screeching a loud, 'Hiya,' followed by, 'what did you throw under the bed?'

'Nothing,' Curiosity said.

'Is it something good? Bet it's not as good as my new Karaoke machine. I wanted to bring it with me, but it's too big to carry and Mummy says it would damage the velour in the car, so I took my new phone. It's got a picture-warp app. If I take your photo, I can make your face look all wibbly. Why are you covered in cuts? Mummy says I must be careful with my dress because it's a David Charles. Do you want to watch me play Minions Paradise? I'm really, really good at it now. Do you want to see how good I am?' She pulled a phone from a pocket on her dress and shoved it into Curiosity's face.

Curiosity flinched, but didn't say anything. In her rush to leave the attic and hide the sketchpad, her first instinct was to run to her bedroom, which meant she was back with the mirror.

Arabella plonked down on the bed.

'I'm on level three now,' she continued. 'You should see how good I am.'

Curiosity let Arabella prattle on because, although she dared not look at it, her attention was fully focussed on the mirror. Before yesterday, it was a harmless piece of furniture. Now, like the one above the mantelpiece, it contained the threat of the burned girls. She dashed across to the wardrobe, grabbed her long winter coat from its hanger, closed her eyes, and tossed it over the mirror. She cracked an eyelid. A small triangle remained visible at the bottom, and she half expected to see a charred hand dart out and make a grab for her leg. That didn't happen. But, on the way back to sit with Arabella on the bed, she gave the mirror a wide berth nonetheless.

Throughout, Arabella sat with her tongue poking from the side of her mouth, tapping at her phone.

Curiosity listened to make sure Mummy, Ophelia, and Faithe were still downstairs.

'You look terrible, Rosina,' Ophelia said. 'Are you well?'

Mummy didn't answer.

Faithe said, 'I can't stay here for this. I'm off to the patio, rain or no rain.'

Confident she wouldn't be interrupted by the adults, Curiosity reached down and lifted the sketchpad out from underneath the bed.

'What's that?' Arabella asked. 'Can I see it?' She shoved the phone in her pocket.

'It's a faerie sketchpad.'

'What's a *fairy sketchpad*?'

Rain crashed against the window. Curiosity jumped. Arabella didn't, just sat with eyes wide, grinning and edging closer to the sketchpad on Curiosity's lap.

'It's a pad filled with sketches of faeries,' Curiosity said.

'Cool.'

'I think it holds all the secrets of the faerie world.'

'Super cool. Can it turn us into beautiful fairies? Is it like the wizard Merlin's book of spells? Can it do magic?'

'I don't know,' Curiosity said. 'I think it can.' She looked towards the covered mirror. 'But I want to make the magic stop.'

TWENTY-SIX – Concerning the unwanted task and a brave soul

Downstairs in the circulation space, Ophelia stood badgering Rosina about her obligations to the Westbourne Grove Ladies Forum. In the most how she was missing meetings and that 'Westbourne Grove needed everyone to do their best – for the community, of course'. She particularly focused on how only a week remained until the biennial election for Principal Lady. And, feeling it a duty, Ophelia was obligated to stand for another term. Making her, yet again, the only Principal Lady in the ten years since the forum came into existence.

Why she bothered to canvas for votes Rosina had no idea.

Nobody ever dared to stand against her. Perhaps she needed the justification.

Whatever the reason, Rosina had no time for Ophelia and her self-importance today. It was her act of rebellion, born from a desire to shed the frightening images that still lingered from her bad dream. Since Faithe arrived, she had been working up the courage, by way of two more glasses of wine, to tell her about the burned girls in her nightmare. Then, Ophelia charged in with her usual unscheduled and dominating manner.

'Can I get you a coffee?' Rosina asked, knowing full well that Ophelia hated coffee. She considered it the beverage of teenagers and tabloid journalists. She hoped the offer might shorten her stay.

'Good lord, no. Not at all,' Ophelia replied. 'Coffee is an atrocious drink. It's the beverage of teenagers and tabloid journalists. If, however, you have a nice *Earl Grey*, I would certainly be tempted by a cup. I know, I know. You will say that it is an afternoon tea. But what is life without whimsy. We should all live a little. *Earl Grey* it is then. Thank you.'

She sat down edgeways on of one of the sofas and adjusted the lilac, cashmere cardigan draped over her shoulders. Her posture was finishing-school perfect: spine erect, chest thrust forward, chin held with prominence, and hands – one resting atop the other on her lap – covering just enough knee to express modesty.

Ophelia had style. They were the same age, both thin. Too thin Faithe said, but Ophelia had aged well. Her skin was taut and flawless. Her A-line bob and caprice bandage dress made her look five years younger. Rosina couldn't help but feel untrendy in her little black dress, and she hated how Ophelia kept her figure just so.

'A skilful skin doctor can work miracles,' Faithe once said. If true, Ophelia hid her secret well.

Rosina nodded and smoothed the creases on her dress.

'I love your outfit,' Ophelia added. 'The *LBD* is a classic.' She emphasised the word *classic* in a way that made it sound like *unfashionable*.

'Thank you,' Rosina replied, brushing her waist and mid-riff with the palm of her hand. 'I like to think so.'

Standing by the patio doors at the other end of the kitchen – muffled by the rain but loud enough to carry the distance – Faithe scoffed and sniggered.

'Oh, I see your brash American friend is here,' Ophelia said. 'I didn't notice you standing all the way down there, Faithe. Why don't you come join us for tea, or have you already had a glass of your usual?'

'Not at the moment, my dear girl,' Faithe answered. 'I'm perfectly fine here, watching the rain. And yes, Rosina was kind enough to pour me a glass of *Merlot* when I arrived. I find that the day can get a little too bright without something to diminish the glare. Then again, we can't all have your talent to dull the sheen off things. We also aren't blessed with your absolute sense of self-worth. You must keep your-self the kindest company when in pursuit of whatever it is you pursue. Something I'm sure you do to the fullest of your ability.' She grinned, shooting a look of haughty derision.

Ophelia didn't reply.

Rosina felt glad for her surrender.

Prime narcissist or not, Ophelia was no match for Faithe's perfected sarcasm. She had the wit and cattiness of any society snob. What she lacked, however, was Faithe's Upper East Side breeding, the ability to hone putdowns into withering insults. Ophelia's derisions reinforced her sense of superiority. Faithe saw hers as an art-form, something to be celebrated. Not out of spitefulness but because the circles she moved in demanded that she performed her part. In the face of such aptitude, Ophelia didn't stand a chance. And Rosina reckoned she knew as much too.

Ophelia huffed and Faithe sniggered again.

Rosina went to the kitchen.

Her wine glass was still sitting where she left it on the counter-top when Ophelia had arrived. She slid it behind a basket of fruit and glanced across to Ophelia, who wasn't watching, just sitting, squinting, as if the room and its decor was an insult her eyes. But there was jealousy there too. Noticeable in the way she shuffled and huffed. Faithe was right. Ophelia envied her. Rosina smiled, and filled a teapot with tea leaves and water from the instant water faucet. She made sure to warm the teapot first, lest her efforts be found failing.

'Don't you have anyone to do that for you?' Ophelia asked. 'What about your Polish woman?'

'It's her day off,' Rosina lied. She suppressed the urge to clarify that Aurelija was Lithuanian, had resigned, and that she sounded scared when she did so.

'I see,' Ophelia said. 'And you have no other cover?' There was genuine perplexity in the woman's tone.

'No. Not at the moment.'

'Oh, I couldn't be doing with that. What an inconvenience. I'm much too busy to be bothered with household things. I'll ask around for you. See if we can get you a replacement.'

'Anyway, you were mentioning the Forum elections,' Rosina said. 'Of course, you can count on my vote. You've always been the stalwart of the group. Everyone knows that. Who would stand against you?'

'No one would, Rosina darling. And yet, we must be seen

to uphold our traditions. It's what English people do. It's why we have royalty. To do less, would make us no better than the French. Or, heaven forbid, Americans.' She glanced towards Faithe, who didn't respond.

Rosina arranged two china cups with saucers on a tray, along with the teapot, a companion sugar bowl, and some slices of lemon, before carrying the whole ensemble – with accompanying finger fancies – into the circulation space. She set the tray onto a glass coffee table between the two sofas.

'Thank you,' Ophelia said. Her tone sounded expectant and belittling. 'Anyway, the Westbourne Grove Ladies Forum needs its Principal Lady. And, as always, I am proud to undertake the duty. Now, tell me why have you stopped attending our meetings?'

Faithe sniggered again. 'The rain is dying off,' she said. 'So, as Robert Falcon Scott said to the other beardy guys in the tent, I'm going out to the patio to smoke a cigarette. Well, he didn't, but he would've if he had to listen to the bull going on in here. Care to join me Rosina, when you're finished sucking up to Frau Oberführer over there?' She pressed the button on the wall. The glass doors slid apart and she went outside.

Ophelia scoffed. She touched the edge of her cup, and Rosina took this as an instruction, and poured the tea, with a slice of lemon in each cup. She left the sugar for Ophelia to deal with herself.

'Americans can be so ill-bred,' Ophelia continued. 'It's because they have no proper culture to speak of. Money or no money, they would've fared better if they hadn't had their ugly rebellion. Look at the Canadians. They are a model of good manners and governance.'

'Oh, don't pay any attention to Faithe. As you say, they can be different to us in many ways. But she means well. Especially for me. I owe her so much.'

'Well, that is as may be, but she can be quite uncouth. Then again, money doesn't buy one class.' She dropped a cube of sugar into her cup, stirred, cradled the saucer in her palm, and took a sip of tea. 'So, as I was saying, the Ladies' Forum needs you Rosina.'

For what exactly? Rosina thought but didn't ask. *For someone to ridicule when her cake came last in the baking competition? Or, when her daughter embarrassed her by attending the church bazaar dressed as some sort of heavy-metal, punk-rocker freak?*

'I'm so pleased to hear you still have faith in me,' she said instead. 'Especially seeing how I've missed so many meetings.'

'And don't forget the Kensington Gardens Charity Run,' Ophelia interrupted. 'It is imperative you get involved with the organising committee. I need everyone to do their bit. The team must do better this year. It is for charity after all. Of course, I would love to be more involved, but my time is precious. Last week I attended a function with the Mayor of London. I don't approve of his politics, but he was very interested in what I do for the Ladies' Forum.'

'Yes, the *Kensington Gardens Charity Run.* I promise to be more proactive.'

Ophelia set her cup and saucer on the coffee table. 'Now, tell me, are you unwell? You look atrocious.'

'No, not at all. It's just that, since the divorce, I've been feeling somewhat out of sorts.'

'That's understandable. You never were one to take any

care. You have a tendency to make bad choices, and go charging around the place without weighing up the consequences.'

Rosina bristled. She sensed more than derision in Ophelia's words. There was an accusation there.

'But it's still no excuse to miss meetings. The work we do is very important. The mayor told me so himself.'

'Absolutely. And, now you say it and with such conviction, I feel quite ashamed. As soon as you leave, I will open my calendar and make sure I schedule the meetings into my routine.'

'Do that. We both know that tragedy can visit us at any time. Doing for others is how one atones for past actions.'

There it was again; an accusation. Many times before, Ophelia had made the same statement. Rosina had put it down to Ophelia being Ophelia. But now, since last night's nightmare, her words seemed more profound.

A memory had broken free.

TWENTY-SEVEN – Concerning Arabella

Ten minutes after it began, the rain stopped.

Sun-showers (Faithe called them). Although, lately, they were more downpour than shower, with very little in the way of sun. They became so after Curiosity stole the figurine from the toy shop, a metaphor for her moods, if she had the luxury of years to recognise the connection.

Yet, Curiosity knew enough to see how her moods mimicked reality. Her new, crazy reality, that began when she came across the ballerina figurine. An inanimate object that turned into a real live fairy – faerie - whatever the right spelling might be, she didn't care. The short and long of her situation was, through her discovery and fascination with the damned thing, she had unleashed something powerful: the ability to create magic, wondrous realms, and fantastical but scary creatures.

A power strong enough to manifest the ghostly woman and the burned girls.

The faeries were here to stay. She knew that. Her situation wouldn't change unless she did something about it. The same reasoning that prompted her go to the attic room for the sketchpad in the first place. Now, on one of the pages, she discovered a way to attack her problem head-on, to build a barrier against this power of nature, to bring normality back again.

The same normality she had strived so hard to be free of just a week earlier.

'We have to go to the back garden,' she told Arabella, who was watching Curiosity turn the pages of the sketchpad with an attentiveness she found unnerving. 'You can come if you want.'

'To do magic? Will I see fairies like in the drawings?'

'I hope not.'

'Ach.' She sulked. 'Then why go?'

'Because of this.' Curiosity pointed to a handwritten paragraph 'It says that faeries hate the ringing of bells.'

Arabella looked confused.

'Look, just come with me. You can help.'

Arabella brightened up.

Curiosity threw the sketchpad onto her bed, bounced across, dashed over to her desk drawer, lifted out an old shoebox and tucked it under her arm. On the way out of the door, she gestured for Arabella to follow her, lifting her index finger to her lips as she went.

Arabella smiled and followed, but with a little too much excitement.

'Shush.'

'Sorry.' Arabella placed her forefinger tight against her lips.

At the bottom of the stairs, Mummy and Ophelia Heffington Jeffries sat opposite each other on the circulation space sofas. Ophelia sipped tea. Mummy seemed distracted, and looked smaller, as if Ophelia had just chastised her. It bemused Curiosity how, one minute, her mother was a big bossy boots, and the next so boot-licky every time Ophelia stepped foot in the door.

Who cares anyway? Curiosity thought. *Let Mummy, Ophelia Heffington Jeffries, and all the other silly, old bats at the idiotic Ladies' Club do whatever they want.*

She had stumbled upon a reality that put all of their nonsense into perspective. Scary things existed in the dell that brought the dead to life.

How about that for a Ladies' Club?

How about that for cake bakes and church bazaars?

Only Faithe seemed down to earth enough to trust. But she was an adult, and Mummy's friend, and a bit weird. Somehow, she knew about faerie paths, but Curiosity reckoned it was better to keep her intentions to herself, and Arabella.

'Why have we stopped?' Arabella asked with a whisper. She looked disappointed. 'Aren't we going to see the fairies now?'

'Yes we are. I was going to leave by the patio, but your mummy is talking to my mummy and blocking the way.'

'Is it a secret?'

Good question, Curiosity thought. 'Yes it is. It's the biggest secret you'll ever have to keep. So, you have to be very quiet and not make a single sound.'

Arabella placed her forefinger back upon her lips.

'Let's go out the front door,' Curiosity said. 'We can sneak around by the side of the house and they won't see us. Faithe might, because she's out on the patio, but she doesn't bother too much about things. Sometimes I wish she was my mummy. She can be annoying, like all grown-ups, but she is really cool.'

Arabella looked confused, but didn't speak. She held her finger pressed hard against her lips so hard they were dimpled and white.

Curiosity guided Arabella by the arm, over to and out through the front door.

As a precaution, she clicked the snib open and rested the door to, gently, so as not to attract attention. She led Arabella around by the side of the house to the high wooden gate Mummy had fitted in response to a spate of burglaries in the area. Before her drinking sessions with Faithe became regular, Mummy bolted the gate every evening at dusk. Of late, however, it remained unlocked.

They went through and into the back garden.

Faithe shouted from the patio, 'I wouldn't go getting that nice pink dress too messy, Arabella Heffington Jeffries. I don't think your mother would approve of you making a pigsty out of all that fancy damask she's got you decked out in.' She laughed, took a smoke of her cigarette, and laughed again.

Arabella didn't answer. Neither did Curiosity.

When they reached the dell, Curiosity opened the shoe-box. Then, with a suddenness that made Arabella jump, she said, 'Wait here . . . and hold this.'

Arabella said, 'Okay.'

'I mean it. Wait right here. Don't move.'

'Okay.'

'It's important. Don't go any closer to the bushes.'

'Okay.'

Curiosity dumped the box into Arabella's hands, sprinted

back up the garden, ran around by the side gate, and in through the front door of the house. With quiet but speedy steps, she climbed the stairs. She went into her bedroom and, keeping one eye fixed on the mirror – glad to see her winter coat still draped there – she crossed the room to her desk drawer. She rummaged through an untidy mess of pens and stationery, picked out a ball of string and stuffed it into the pocket of her shorts. The ball was lumpy and made the cuts on her thighs sting. She ignored the pain and turned to leave, glancing up to the ledge below the oval window, expecting to see the figurine standing there. Not the faerie-lady who had revealed the enchanted fountain and now frightened her so, but the lifeless, alabaster statuette she took from *The Grotto Toy Shop*. Proof that the terrifying incidents were only her imagination playing tricks on her, or perhaps her insanity, and not evil entities that wished to baffle and ensnare her.

The ledge was empty. She'd expected as much.

She dashed from her room, downstairs, and out through the front door.

When she reached the dell, the shoebox was lying open on the ground. Her collection of tiny charm bells scattered over the grass.

Arabella was nowhere to be seen.

TWENTY-EIGHT – Concerning what had passed

By way of her broken free memory, Rosina recalled a cold Sunday in November, the images coming to her as sure as if they were a film playing before her eyes.

She had just turned eight.

The morning brought news that the six most gifted girls at Sophia Aleyev's ballet school had parts in the parish production of *The Nutcracker*. There were seven girls in the class and, at a special afternoon session she tried her best. But, while Sophia Aleyev wasn't looking, the other girls barraged her with nasty put-downs. Mostly, with no surprise, Ophelia Heffington and her twin sister Clarissa, who teased her about her *clown feet*, and told the other girls to point and laugh.

During an important arabesque, Clarissa pushed her and she stumbled. Sophia Aleyev glared, before she sent everyone away, telling them that a second audition would take place the following Sunday.

When Rosina arrived home, she ran to her bedroom, threw off her ballet costume and went out to the garden. She wanted to be alone. She wanted to think about the horrible thing that Clarissa had done. She wanted to hate her.

With her thoughts racing, she wandered all the way to the dell. It looked less sinister than usual. The leaves sparkled as though covered with silver raindrops, and the whole place glowed, as if the sun shone from someplace within. A black and white cat sat at the base of a hawthorn bush. Beside it something lay on the ground. A toy of some sort? A small doll? She moved closer for a better look. It was a figurine; of a fairy posed as a ballet-dancer.

The cat mewled and nudged the figurine towards her.

She picked it up and the dell grew brighter. Flowers sprouted, a passageway opened in the centre of the big oak tree, and hedgerows appeared, lining a path along which she danced and reeled, egged on by voices that spoke inside her mind:

Come in, they said. *Come in.*

And she did, she danced deeper into the dell. She followed the voices all the way to a clearing and the pond that she would call her 'enchanted pool'.

In her hand, the figurine trembled and became a real-life fairy-lady. It flew away. But not far, settling atop the fountain that stood in the middle of the pond. More tiny creatures came out. They peered down from the trees and emerged from the hedgerows. Dozens, maybe hundreds of them, with sniped noses and almond shaped eyes, all staring and smiling at her.

Rosina basked in the attention. She felt special.

In her thoughts, the fairy-lady spoke to her. She told her how to perform ballet steps as precise and graceful as any prima ballerina assoluta. And, in the days following – in the mornings before school and the evenings after homework – Rosina went to the dell and practiced with the fairies until her muscles ached. Aunt Lily said she was concerned about her obsession and the chill she might catch by wearing nothing more than a tutu. She insisted she took a coat; which Rosina wore to avoid arguments but removed when she got to the dell.

On Saturday afternoon, Rosina convinced her great aunt to come with her to the end of the garden and to watch her dance. Aunt Lily brought her *Polaroid* camera and took a photograph.

When she looked at it, her expression changed. Her brow creased. She grabbed Rosina by the hand and ran inside, slamming the back door behind her.

For the rest of the day, Aunt Lily commanded Rosina to remain indoors. She seemed agitated and worried. Rosina hadn't seen her like this before. It both unnerved and angered her, almost as much as being forbidden from going to the dell. So, she went to her bedroom and, with little else to interest her, practiced her ballet steps.

They felt lifeless without the fairies looking on.

Downstairs, Aunt Lily scribbled drawings in a sketchpad, kneeling on the floor with two books splayed open in front of her. One called: *The Magic in the Groves*, the other: *Ways of Seeing – a Treatise on Crossing to the Otherworld*.

Rosina knew this because, on more than one occasion, she tried to sneak past her to the back door. Each time, she was caught, scolded, and finally gave up.

As the day dimmed, Aunt Lily made a phone call and, half an hour later, Cassidy the gardener arrived. Rosina watched from the top of the stairs. He hugged Aunt Lily for quite a few seconds before, with his arm around her waist, they went to the sofa, sat, and looked through the two books together.

'I can't be long,' he said. 'I have to be up early in the morning. It's a work thing. But I'll call again tomorrow evening. Maybe I'll stay over. To make sure you are both okay.'

Aunt Lily nodded and smiled. It looked strained.

A short while later, Cassidy left, saying, 'Just don't let her out to the garden. We can deal with the rest when I get back tomorrow.'

Rosina went to bed and slept.

She dreamed of fairies and ballet dancing.

Sunday began with sunshine and the expectation of a better second audition. She had learned much. She felt confident and prepared. Again, Aunt Lily told her that she must stay indoors. She seemed more agitated than before, holding a page in her hand as though it was the most important document in the world. And Rosina was none too happy about being restricted for another day. She wanted to practice with the fairies and perfect her steps. The situation angered her, and she spent the morning in her bedroom, dressed in her pyjamas, sulking and peering out of the oval window, biding time before the second audition.

Around one o'clock, the phone rang. It was Sophia Aleyev.

Aunt Lily was shouting, 'What do you mean she can't dance? Of course, she can't dance. It's your job to teach her. This is because the Heffingtons own the lease to your studio isn't it? That whole family is a bunch of self-absorbed snobs. Including the kids.'

She slammed down the receiver and called Rosina down from the bedroom.

She said, 'Aleyev has cancelled your membership. Apparently, you're holding the Heffington twins back.' She called Sophia Aleyev *a talentless bat.* She said that she was better than them, but to not go sneaking out to the dell. 'It's dangerous there.'

Through her broken free memory, Rosina relived her disappointment, and rushing to her room to cry. On and off, she wept for a full hour, her heart in pieces. Then, from outside the window, the dell called to her.

She wiped her face and put on her ballet pumps and tutu; along with the fairy wings she had pestered Aunt Lily to buy for the second audition. She sneaked past her great aunt – who was sitting in the kitchen, occupied with her books and sketchpad – and went out through the back door. She ran to the dell. It opened up and led her to her enchanted pool. She needed the comfort of the fairies but, with her will to dance gone – crushed by Clarissa and Ophelia's spitefulness – her new friends didn't take too kindly to her melancholy mood and lack of commitment.

As she sat on ground, slumped against the walls of her enchanted pool, the fairy-lady fluttered close by, whispering in her ear, *Dance for us. Dance for us.*

Rosina ignored her demands, and the fairy-lady darted off into the undergrowth.

The sky grew dark. A shadow descended on the scene, and thorny plants emerged from the hedges, snaking across the path, coiling around the walls of the pond.

Rosina jumped to her feet. The white stones she had been leaning against turned grey and covered with slime. They fell away, some thumping onto the briar tangled path, others splashing into the water that was thick with black sludge and decaying leaf mulch.

The stink was foul.

At the centre of the pond, the fountain that, only seconds before, had been a resplendent statue, was now a rotted tree stump, coated with puffy, brown fungus and alive with a host of crawling insects. The clouds burst. In seconds, a downpour soaked her through. The briars coiled around her ankles yet, unlike Curiosity many years later, Rosina stayed put, her shattered heart feeling at home among the sodden raggedness unfolding around her. Her disappointment had turned to hatred as pure and potent as that now emanating from the fairy-lady, who had returned from the undergrowth as an ugly, gangly creature, and now hovered, like the devil of bad decisions at her shoulder.

The bushes rustled. An army of equally hideous and gangly creatures emerged. Creatures that, as the years progressed, Rosina forgot, encountering only in her nightmares, and now remembered for all their wickedness. Creatures which – in her hatred for the other girls at the ballet school – held no terror for the young Rosina Warren, because she welcomed the power they possessed.

The power bubbled up inside her. It heightened her anger.

In response, the tiny creatures shuffled around, as might children when craving the attention of their mother. Their hissing voices merging in a unified chant:

Dance for us, they said. *Kill for us.*

Rosina felt their rage like an encouraging friend. They

spoke to her thoughts and urged her to do wicked deeds. To take revenge. She threw her head back. She raised her arms and let the voices guide her. The thorns retracted. They slid away into the bushes. The creatures followed, but Rosina still felt them with her. They were connected now. Their power was inside her.

The fairy-lady lay at her feet. Not in the shape of the gangly creature, nor as the living fairy, but as the figurine. She picked it up, stuffed it in her waistband, ran out to the lawn and dashed up the garden.

Aunt Lily was standing by the back door, ushering her cats inside out of the rain.

'What the hell happened to you?' she said. 'Look at you. You're soaked to the skin, and scraped all over. I told you not to go to the dell. I told you it was dangerous. Why don't you ever listen? And why are you wearing your ballet costume?'

Rosina didn't answer. With a sideways movement, she slipped past her great aunt, ran along the side of the house, out onto Bingham Crescent, and down towards Westbourne Grove.

When she arrived at *The Grotto Toy Shop* she entered by a side door. She climbed the stairs to the first-floor landing outside Sophia Aleyev's ballet school. Her tutu was wet through. Her hair clung sodden and heavy to her cheeks. Violin music was rippling through the dance studio door; the calming, sweet tones of *The Dance of the Sugar Plum Fairy*. She recognised the melody because, all week, the fairies had played it while she practiced her steps.

She pushed the door open. All six of her classmates:

Evelyn Willoughby, Sarah Penthorpe, Hillary Downshire, Millie Beecher, and the twins: Ophelia and Clarissa Heffington were lined up along the wall mirror. They were dressed in full performance regalia, with their left hands resting upon the barre, crouched in a plié.

Clarissa Heffington looked across and snickered.

Ophelia joined in, followed by the other girls.

'Stop that sniggering right now,' Sophia Aleyev said. 'Ladies, especially ballet ladies, always know how to conduct themselves'.

The sniggering stopped but their smirks remained.

Rosina slammed the door hard against the wall, causing the candles to flicker. She marched inside, heading towards the other side of the room and a spot where the barre was vacant.

Sophia Aleyev followed her. 'What are you doing here? I called Lily to say your membership has been revoked. Did she not tell you?'

Rosina ignored the ballet teacher and, arriving at the barre, began practicing her plié.

The other girls stayed where they were but turned to watch.

'How rude,' Sophia Aleyev said. 'Come away from there.'

'It's *Little Miss Bumble*,' Clarissa said and laughed.

'Look at her,' Ophelia added. 'She's covered with blood. Yuck.'

All of the girls laughed, which became louder when the ballet teacher grabbed Rosina by the arm and dragged her, wet pumps squeaking across the polished floor, out to the landing.

Aunt Lily appeared on the stairs. 'Take your hands off of her.'

'Lily?' Sophia Aleyev said and stopped.

Rosina wrestled free from the ballet teacher's grip and ran back into the studio, over to the same spot at the barre. She continued with her poses. All the while, the other girls laughed. Only when a ballet pump hit her on the cheek did she snap out of it enough to notice that they were all gathered around her.

Clarissa moved out from the group. She pushed Rosina against the mirror, before turning to the others with her arms raised like a boxer having just floored an opponent. They laughed. When Rosina straightened up, Clarissa pushed her again and she stumbled. This time, only Ophelia laughed. The other girls, Evelyn, Sarah, Hillary, and Millie were glancing across to the doorway.

Out on the stairwell, Aunt Lily was shouting at Sophia Aleyev, 'Just who do you think you are?'

'I don't like your tone.'

'I don't like your face.'

'Look, Lily, I am only trying to respect the wishes of the families.'

'Who? The Heffingtons?'

'Yes. They were quite insistent, and the sad truth is, Rosina is no good at ballet.'

Rosina resumed practicing her poses. She wanted to dance. She wanted to show them what she had learned from the fairies. Clarissa shoved her. She teetered but, this time, she didn't stumble. She steeled her will and faced Clarissa.

The smirk fell from the girl's face. 'What's this? Are you challenging me?'

'Yes,' Rosina said. 'And I'm a better than you.'

Clarissa gritted her teeth. She punched Rosina in the stomach. Air burst from Rosina's lungs, nausea rolled through her gut, and she collapsed to the floor, pulling her knees to her chest.

She cried.

Clarissa snorted a laugh, spittle spraying from her mouth. She slapped Rosina on the cheek.

Her sister, Ophelia stopped laughing. She looked worried. 'Leave the cry-baby alone,' she said. 'Daddy might be angry if he found out.'

Clarissa seemed uninterested in her sister's warnings. 'Look at her,' she said. 'Look at the ginger freak.' She hit her again. Not a slap, but with a full force blow. 'Clown feet,' she said, punching Rosina hard on the side of her head. 'Weirdo. Ginger-nut.'

Pain shot through Rosina's skull. For a second or two, she went dizzy. When her vision cleared, all of the girls, except Clarissa, had backed away.

'Stop it, Clarissa,' Ophelia said. 'We'll get in trouble.'

But Clarissa didn't stop, and Rosina yelped when the next punch rattled her jaw.

Seeking comfort, she slipped her hand into the waistband of her tutu and gripped the figurine she had stashed there. It vibrated and grew warm, coming alive in her hand. Her fairy-lady had returned and, emboldened, Rosina raised her head and looked Clarissa straight in the eyes. She got to her feet. The other girls moved farther away. Even Clarissa took a step backwards.

'What?' she said, flexing her shoulders. 'What are you going to do, freak?'

Ophelia ran across the studio and out to the landing, shouting, 'Miss Aleyev, come quick. Rosina is doing stupid things again.'

She was drowned out by Aunt Lily yelling at Sophia Aleyev. 'You were always a stuck-up snoot. And a crap dancer.'

The ballet teacher answered with, 'Well, now I know where Rosina gets her rudeness from.'

'Out of my way,' Aunt Lily said and barged into the room. Sophia Aleyev followed her. Ophelia remained outside.

'Come on Rosina,' Aunt Lily said. 'We're going home'

'Yes, please do,' Sophia Aleyev added. 'And don't return.'

'Bite me,' Aunt Lily added.

Rosina ignored both of them. She stepped closer to Clarissa so they stood less than a metre apart.

'What are you going to do?' Clarissa asked. Her stance was defiant, but her voice quivered, as though the situation had taken a turn she hadn't expected or dealt with before.

'Nothing,' Rosina said.

Then there was a sound, like cockroaches skittering across the wooden floor. A gust of wind slammed the door shut, locking Ophelia outside on the landing, and all four candle-stands wobbled then steadied again. A second blast blew Aunt Lily backwards against the closed door. She slid spread-legged to the floor, her head drooping to one side. She was breathing but concussed.

By now, Evelyn, Sarah, Hillary, and Millie had dashed to the upper wall of the studio, and cowered together in a ball, whimpering like frightened puppies.

Sophia Aleyev stood in the centre of the room with a stunned look on her face.

The floor cracked. Fissures opened like multiple starbursts across the polished timbers.

Rosina glanced down at them. 'I'm not going to do anything at all,' she continued. She peered down at the tiny faces glaring up through the cracks in the floor. She smiled and said, 'But they are.'

A droning, hissing sound filled the room. From the clefts in the floorboards, briars sprouted, streaking up the walls and across the ceiling. They coiled around the skirting-boards, contracting until the wood splintered, before striking upwards, attacking the mirrored surface, until it too fractured, exploding in a spray of plaster and glass, the shards spraying out across the room and showering down upon the startled ballet teacher and the girls huddled by the opposite wall.

Clarissa stepped back. There was real fear in her eyes.

The briars continued their conquest of the ballet studio, spreading out across the walls in a latticework of tendrils, leaves, and barbs. When their dominance was complete, they paused for a second, as though assessing their next move, then struck out towards Sophia Aleyev. Rosina took delight in seeing the ballet teacher's terror. Aunt Lily was right. She was a stuck-up snoot. And Rosina willed the thorns to attack her, but not Aunt Lily, which they didn't, because she could do that now. She could control them. They were connected. Their magic was inside her.

She smiled when the Sophia Aleyev was pulled to the floor, her skinny body encased in briars. The ballet teacher screamed. The plants plunged down her throat. She convulsed and spluttered blood; one foot twitching, the other thumping like a jackhammer against the floor. The plants struck out again, this time, towards the four cowering girls who, if they had thought their teacher's plight to be their deliverance, they thought wrong. One by one they too were captured, struggling as the thorns tightened around their wrists and ankles, and then slithered into their mouths, muffling their screams.

Clarissa came next.

She had run off, and was crouching like a cornered rabbit in a recess closest to the door. The briars seized her. They wound around her arms and legs. They gripped her forehead and pulled her head back so she could look no other direction but straight at Rosina. Plant tendrils wormed down her cheeks and curled into her nostrils. She squeezed her eyes shut, but the thorns tore them open again. She whimpered but didn't say a word. Not a single putdown passed her lips.

Outside on the landing, Ophelia banged against the door. 'Clarissa,' she shouted.

But Clarissa didn't reply, just stared at Rosina.

Rosina sniggered. She approached and, for a second or two, loomed over Clarissa before she held out her hand to release the fairy-lady. At first, the tiny creature hovered, a centimetre or so above her palm, wings fluttering and arms swaying as though dancing on the air. Then, she changed, her face and body warping into the gangly grey creature she had been earlier in the dell. The creature skittered up Rosina's arm and stood upon her shoulder, as light as a leaf but Rosina felt it there nonetheless; bringing her comfort, anger, and a desire for revenge.

In a single bound, the creature leaped onto Clarissa's head.

It swiped downwards and cut a gash in her cheek. As the blood poured, it snickered, then unfurled its wings and took flight. It rose to the centre of the ceiling where it screeched, much louder than the droning, hissing sound still filling the room, and whereby the cracks in the floor split wider, and dozens of tiny hands reached up into the light. The hands became arms. Ovoid heads emerged. Heads with grotesque, grey faces and black, pin-like eyes, attached to wrinkly skinned bodies that were levered up by way of spindly legs and clawed feet, grappling their way up from beneath the floor and skittering out around the room, grinning, leering as though hungry for mischief and eager to do harm.

Rosina felt no fear of these creatures and, in her mind, she urged them to come forth and take revenge on those who mocked her and denied her the chance to dance. With a surge, the creatures fell upon Sophia Aleyev with such ferocity that Rosina had to glance away. When she looked back, they were crawling over the ballet teacher's body like maggots picking at a carcass. They bit her face and slashed her flesh with their claws. Sophia Aleyev twitched and gagged, her chest heaving, gasping for breath, or perhaps attempting to jerk the creatures away. It made no difference, her efforts were in vain, with a sudden spasm, blood spluttered from her mouth, and she became still.

Rosina knew the four girls would be next. Although they hadn't directly insulted her, they had condoned the abuse, egged Clarissa on, and never once came to help, or say it was wrong.

Out on the landing, Ophelia stopped banging the door. 'I'm going for help,' she shouted.

Not that it mattered because, although Rosina felt cheated that Ophelia was not in the room, she knew that everything transpiring in this side of the door was by her command, which was more than enough . . . for now. She had only to wish for something to happen and the creature hovering overhead would make the others obey. So, Rosina willed the creatures to lash out at the four girls cowering at the upper wall. Blood smeared their faces. There was fear in their eyes. And Rosina basked in it. It was her turn to laugh. It was her chance to demonstrate that people shouldn't insult others. Things happen. Situations change. People get stronger and acquire powers, and she would make them suffer for not helping her.

At her feet, Clarissa was crying.

Rosina chuckled.

The creatures detached from Sophia Aleyev. They attacked the girls, Evelyn, Sarah, Hillary, and Millie who thrashed beneath the mass of tiny bodies swarming over them. The creatures bit. They slashed. They ripped with their claws and tore away clumps of flesh with their teeth. Suddenly, because Rosina willed it so, the thorns retracted from the girls' faces. Blood dribbled down their chins. It pooled on their necks and stained their ballet costumes in blotches of crimson.

The girls screamed. The creatures stuffed their mouths with leaves. The girls wriggled, but the tendrils tightened around their wrists and ankles. Then, all except four of the creatures – one to each girl – scuttled to the floor. Some moved a few metres away, assembled like an audience waiting for a show to begin. Others grabbed the girls by the hair and yanked their heads backwards, forcing them to face the ceiling. The creatures that remained picked up thin strands of briar and went skipping, from one cheek to the other. With an air of playfulness, they bobbed and weaved like tiny circus acrobats, trailing the string-like briars behind them, threading them through the girls' lips, sewing their mouths shut with the leaves stuffed inside.

Again, the girls screamed. It was muffled.

They weren't laughing now. After today, they might never laugh again.

When their task was complete, the four creatures jumped down onto the floor. They did so with back-flips and cartwheels, as though performing a victory display for a job well done. They joined the others in the centre of the room and, en-masse, turned towards Clarissa.

The creatures attacked.

Rosina felt happy seeing them scamper over her tormentor's body. She took joy in watching them stab, bite, and slash with their claws. Clarissa writhed. She screamed. Whereby, as they had with the other girls, the creatures stuffed her mouth with leaves, and all but one of them scurried down to assemble a few metres away out on the floor. The thorns flexed, pulling Clarissa's head backwards. The barbs sunk into her forehead, blood streaming down her face to blend with the tears dribbling from the corners of her eyes. The remaining creature took up a strand of spindly briar, and hopping like a grasshopper, it skipped across Clarissa's face, sewing the strand through her lips, locking away her putdowns, sealing her nasty hateful words inside her mouth forever.

When it was done, the creature jumped down to join the others.

The flying creature, that had been Rosina's fairy-lady, circled the ceiling.

It came to a halt in the recess above Clarissa's head and hovered, stroking a knot of briars with its hand. One of the thicker strands disentangled, swung down and wrapped around Clarissa's upper body. It tightened and hoisted her upwards. She looked vulnerable hanging there, bound, her eyes swivelling, mewling through her sewn shut lips. The other girls couldn't help her now. Ophelia had left. There was no one to back her up or save her.

She was alone. She looked weak. Pee ran down her legs and Rosina laughed.

A sudden burst of flames flared by the door. The briars closest to it caught fire, and the creatures squealed, scattering across the room and disappearing down through the cracks in the floor. One of the candle-stands was lying on its side, with flaming wax oozing out towards the upper wall. Aunt Lily stood behind it, agitatedly gesturing for Rosina to come to her. She kicked another one over. It set alight to the clump of briars coiled around the barre. The creature that had been the fairy-lady shrieked. Like a trapped bird, it flitted from wall to wall, recoiling from the rising blaze, before it rolled on the air and darted down through a gap in the floor to join the others.

A sheet of flame shot across the ceiling. At the far wall, Evelyn, Hillary, and Millie started grappling with the binds on their ankles. Their efforts looked frantic and clumsy. Sarah wasn't with them. She was flopping across the floor, belly down like a landed fish, heading for the door. The latticework of briars behind them caught fire, shattering the plaster and setting fire to the skirting boards.

The wall cracked.

It fell, and all of the girls were engulfed.

While Rosina watched this happening, Aunt Lily had stumbled through the flames. She was only a few metres away, holding one arm in front of her face, with the other one outstretched towards Rosina. 'Take my hand,' she shouted, 'quickly.'

The fire flared and forced her back.

The ceiling above Clarissa ignited, causing Rosina to recoil at the sudden blast of heat. The room filled with smoke, the flames spreading to the strands that held Clarissa captive, crawling down them like fiery worms seeking refuge. Her ballet wings caught alight. Her hair followed, blazing like dry leaves. An instant later, she was a fireball, her skin crackling, blistering, and blackening. And, as Clarissa suffered, Rosina looked on. She was transfixed, watching as the tortured girl writhed in pain and tore apart her own lips to release the screams muffled behind them.

Rosina recalled little of what happened next.

Even within her broken free memory.

Aunt Lily shouted, 'We have to get out.' She was coughing. Her hair was scorched on one side and her face was covered in soot. She grabbed Rosina's hand, hauled her out through the door, ran downstairs and out into the fresh air.

Rosina remembered a considerate face. He smiled at her

and gave her oxygen. Lights flashed. People shouted. She was in an ambulance, followed by a hospital, followed by another, where she stayed for years.

Their drugs became her dependency.

She had been in rehab a long time before Faithe found her. But, even there, the screams of the dying girl always remained. They infected her dreams, accompanied by images of tiny terrifying creatures.

Mind-numbing, teeth-clenching screams.

Like the one she could hear now, coming from the dell, and Ophelia shouting out for her daughter:

'Arabella!'

TWENTY-NINE – Concerning the forgotten dead

Mummy and Ophelia Heffington Jeffries were charging down the garden.

Faithe was walking.

Arabella was in the dell, screaming.

Curiosity had to help her. It meant going into the under-growth, which she wasn't happy about, but she went anyway. She picked up one of the charm bells, gritted her teeth, and ran into the bushes. They instantly closed around her. Roots grabbed at her heels. Thorns spiralled around her legs and arms. Arabella was standing up ahead, wrapped in briars, smothered beneath a wriggling mass of ugly faeries but still unmistakable in her glaringly bright pink dress. Curiosity pressed on towards her. The thorns wound tighter, their barbs digging deeper, but she managed to push far enough to reach out with her fingers. 'Take my hand,' she shouted. 'Arabella, take my hand.'

The creatures turned and glared. The plants tightened around Arabella. She choked, her screams muffled by the strands coiling around her neck and inching into her mouth.

The girl stared, her face dotted with bloody bites and scratch marks.

'Quick, take my hand,' Curiosity shouted again and, with her thumb and forefinger, raised the charm bell and shook it.

The bell jingled.

The creatures scattered, the thorns around both her and Arabella retracting a few inches before they tightened again. She tinkled the charm bell again. The creatures moved farther away and the thorns recoiled. The paragraph in the sketchpad was right. Faeries hate the ringing of bells.

She jingled again, and again repeatedly. The creatures disappeared out of sight, and briars unwound fully, squirming off into the undergrowth. Curiosity ran forward. She grabbed Arabella's hand, dragged her through the bushes, and ran out to the garden where Mummy and Arabella's mother stood with worried looks on their faces. The faeries followed, crashing through the brush like a colony of angry rats. But, a few metres from the edge, they stopped, thousands of tiny eyes peering out:

Come to us, they whispered.

With tears streaming down her face, Arabella collapsed into her mother's outstretched arms. She cried loudly, her body shivering and with a frightened gaze flitting back and forth between Curiosity and the dell.

Ophelia Heffington Jeffries glared at Curiosity and yelled, 'I always knew there was something wrong with you.' She then turned to face Curiosity's mother. 'And you. Everything you touch turns to tragedy.' She stood up, took Arabella by the hand and marched her up to the house. Before she left, she shouted down the garden. 'Keep your freak away from my daughter.'

Mummy looked shocked. There was hurt there. Ophelia's words had rattled her. Or, more likely, in Curiosity's opinion, she was concerned about the negative influence that Ophelia might have on her image and standing. Curiosity disregarded this, and turned her attention to the task she had set out upon in the first place.

The tiny faces moved closer to the edge of the dell. Their voices hissed and filled her mind.

Don't do it, they said. *We will punish you. Like we punished the other girls.*

Curiosity assumed the girls to be the ghostly ones from the mirrors. She now knew that these faeries were no kindly beings, nor were they magical entities of allure and wonder. They were evil. They had come to torment her. For this reason alone, they must be stopped. She unravelled the string she took from her desk drawer and began threading the charm bells, one by one, along its length. They tinkled as she did so, and the creatures scuttled back into the shadows.

While she went about her task, her mother was shouting at her:

'What happened to Arabella?' she asked. 'What were you both doing in there?'

Curiosity ignored her. If Arabella had stayed put and waited, like she had told her to, everything would have been fine. She was always too nosey, totally daft, and never did what she was told. The faeries were mustering again. She felt them in her mind, confusing her thoughts, bringing up images of the burned girls. She had to be quick.

'What happened?' Mummy yelled. 'Speak to me now

young lady. Look at you, you're a mess. How did you get in such a state?'

Faithe arrived and said, 'Don't be so hard on the girl. Arabella always was an odd little miss. She's a nice girl – definitely nicer than her mother, but does tend to come across a bit daffy. My guess, she went wandering into those bushes there and got tangled up in the thorns. Seeing how she's been over-pampered since the second she plopped out of Ophelia's hoo-ha, the poor girl couldn't deal with it. She got a frightened, and went running off to find Mummikins.'

'Thorns didn't do that,' Mummy replied. 'Some of those were bite marks. Curiosity, tell me now. What happened in there?'

Curiosity continued threading the charm bells.

'Stop that. Answer me.' Mummy moved closer.

Curiosity carried on threading and, when she finished, secured one end of the string around a branch, before hanging the rest in a latticework across the front of the bushes. The charm bells jingled. The bushes rustled. It sounded like panicked rats, and she felt at ease.

'I said stop that,' Mummy shouted again. She snatched the chain of charm bells, gathered them into a ball, and threw the bundle into the bushes.

'Look what you've done.' Curiosity snapped. 'You're stupid. Now they'll get out.'

'I don't think I care for your tone.'

Curiosity started for the bushes. Mummy grabbed her arm and hauled her back:

'I want answers,' she yelled.

'You know the answers.'

'You're being rude. You'll spend the rest of the night in your room.'

Curiosity ignored that. 'Stop pretending. You knew about them and you didn't warn me.'

'What are you talking about? Knew about what? If this is some game to avoid telling me what happened to Arabella then it's not going to work.'

'Take it easy, Rosina,' Faithe said. 'Can't you see the girl's frightened?'

'Of course she's frightened. This is a serious matter. Tell me now, Curiosity, what happened to Arabella? If you're truthful, then you won't be punished. Tell me lies however and . . .'

'You would know about telling lies,' Curiosity interrupted. 'You've been telling lies all along. About how Daddy left us, when it was you who drove him away by being so moody. And the way you're always banging on about this house. That it's a triumph. That it's *oh so special*. Well, it is special. You knew the faeries were real and you never told me.'

Mummy looked shocked, as if a penny had dropped. 'What are you talking about? Don't talk nonsense. Just listen to yourself.' There was a note of guilt in her tone.

'Is it, Mummy? Is it nonsense?'

'Come on, Curiosity. Stop this now.'

Faithe sniggered. 'Nice imagination, kid.'

'I saw the photo' Curiosity said. 'I saw the photo of you when you were a little girl. You were dancing. They were watching you. You knew they were here but you never warned me.'

'I didn't warn you, Curiosity, because what you're saying is balderdash.' Mummy said the words but Curiosity sensed her lack of conviction. Her expression had changed when she mentioned the photo.

Curiosity seized the chance, 'Did you know about the burned girls too?'

Mummy's face went white. She stared at the dell and then backed away. She was clutching both hands over her mouth as though, should her words escape, they might attract something unpleasant:

'Good lord, you've seen them,' she said.

'What the hell,' Faithe said.

Mummy turned to face her. She looked frightened.

'Ah, come on, Rosina. Not this again . . . not the little-people and ghostly girls bull. They're just dreams. Nightmares.'

'Dreams?' Are they, Faithe? Just dreams? Just nightmares?'

'Of course, they're dreams, brought on by too much alcohol. Although I'm one to talk.' She laughed. 'Or maybe it's delusion. Or psychosis even. You were a very troubled child, remember? What else could they be?'

'Memories?'

'Really? Memories?'

'Yes. I've been there. I know it.'

'Been where?'

'In the dell. At the pond. I've been to the place where they live.'

'Where who live?'

'The fairies.'

'The fairies?' She rolled her eyes.

'Yes. It's all clear to me. It's like the memories came flooding back. I was there when they came to the dance studio, when the fire killed Evelyn Willoughby, and Sarah Penthorpe, and Hillary, and Millie, and Ophelia's sister Clarissa.'

'It's just some kind of post-traumatic flashback thing. Or maybe survivor guilt. Hell, I don't know. A shrink would have a thousand phrases for it, but I'll tell you what it definitely isn't . . . the little-people doing weird magic.'

'How do you know, Faithe? How can you be so sure?'

'Because, Sugarplum, fairies and magic don't exist.'

'They do exist,' Curiosity shouted. 'I've seen them.'

'Whatever you say, Cupcake.'

'I've seen them too,' Mummy said, 'in my mind.'

'Exactly. You've seen them in your mind.'

'No, not like that. I remember them. But as real as you and me standing here right now.'

'Damn it, Rosina. This is nuts. A moment ago, you were about to tear strips off your daughter for something tangible. Now it seems that you have regressed a couple of decades.'

'It's true. I know that now. If it wasn't true, how did Curiosity know about them?'

'Maybe it's a family hallucination.'

'But she knows about the burned girls.'

'And?'

'I've never told her about the fire.' Mummy then turned to Curiosity. 'I never told you about the girls.'

'You must have,' Faithe said. 'You just can't remember.'

'No, I always kept that from her. Mostly, because it was hazy for me too. I didn't want to think about it. How did you know about them, Curiosity? How did you know about the fire and the girls?'

'Because I've seen them too,' Curiosity replied.

'For Christ's sake, Rosina. Leave her alone,' Faithe said. 'Can't you see you're frightening the girl?'

'Where did you see them?' Mummy asked.

Curiosity didn't answer.

'Tell me now. How do you know? Where did you see them?'

'Everywhere,' Curiosity snapped. 'I see them everywhere. Is that good enough for you? Everywhere. And you didn't warn me. They're in the mirrors. They follow me around. Like the horrid faerie-lady and her creatures.'

The bushes rustled. The trees shook.

Mummy glanced once at the dell, scooped Curiosity into her arms, and rushed up the garden.

'What?' Faithe said. 'Now a gust of wind has you running for cover.' She laughed. 'I'm in the wrong business. With the right movie contract, I could make a fortune out of you guys.' She followed, walking.

Peering over her mother's shoulder, Curiosity kept her gaze on the dell. The whole place swayed as if a large invisible beast was moving through it. The hissing voices returned, but louder and angrier than before.

When they reached the patio, Mummy set Curiosity down and gripped both her arms.

'You mustn't go the dell again,' she said.

Curiosity didn't reply.

'Promise me. Promise you'll stay away from there.' She shook her, hard. It hurt. 'Please. You must promise me.'

'Okay. Okay. I promise. I won't go back to the dell.'

Mummy released her grip. She stood up straight and smiled, both at Curiosity, and Faithe, who had joined them on the patio.

'It's not safe,' she continued. 'They must never get out.'

'I promise,' Curiosity said.

Mummy patted her head.

Faithe winked, before she glanced at the dell. She smirked.

'But I think it's too late for that,' Curiosity added. 'They already have.'

THIRTY – Concerning the unheard prayer

Acacia Okeke had spent the morning, since just after dawn, in the park at the end of her street. Sitting on a bench, she occupied her time watching the sun move higher in a cloudless sky, before the rushed parents arrived, trundling pushchairs and other, calmer ones came to play with their brightly dressed toddlers in the soft surface play area. Joggers ran by. Some kids kicked a ball into the bushes behind her bench and fetched it out again. Cycle couriers cut through the grass at speed, as people in suits, ties, and nice dresses hurried past on their way to work or some special engagement that made them all but oblivious to the world going on around them.

Acacia made no input to the hubbub of city life. She remained sitting.

It rained. For no more than ten minutes.

She took shelter under a tree before returning to her bench where she stayed, struggling to come to terms with what she had seen the night before in her apartment. Which, now thinking about it, seemed the craziest thing she had ever contemplated.

A cat was a cat.

Mice were mice.

Insects buzzed at any time of the day, and none of them

were in any way sinister or threatening. But, the rub was, Acacia didn't see insects or mice. She saw something else: shadows, flitting around her bedroom like images from a child's shadow projector; a cat hissing as if about to attack and two tiny creatures sitting atop the bedposts at the bottom of her bed.

She screamed.

They sniggered and scurried off into the lounge.

She got up, switched on all the lights, crept into the kitchenette, fetched a knife from the drawer and, moving with stealth, searched both rooms and the bathroom. There were shadows everywhere, from the books piled up on her coffee table to the strings of the blinds, swaying in the breeze coming through the partially open window. In each room, she pulled the furniture away from the wall. She checked underneath her bed again, behind and inside the wardrobe, around the sofa, sideboard, the wash hand basin, behind the shower curtain, inside the toilet bowl, and stood with her knife at the ready, as she threw open all of the doors on the kitchenette cupboards. But her home was empty. Even Bertie her goldfish swam undisturbed in his bowl on top of the sideboard.

She sat on the floor, with her back against the wall and the lights on, until dawn's first light cracked the curtains.

The knife never left her hand.

She searched the flat another two times before she put on jeans, a t-shirt, and trainers. She set the knife on the counter, slipped her phone into her pocket, locked up and left, walking to the nearest place she knew that had open spaces and, more importantly, the prospect of people milling around.

In all honesty, she had no idea what she saw. The bafflement of which stayed with her until, hours later, still sitting on the park bench, she rang Brendan Cassidy on the number the police station had provided as backup for her original visit.

It took a few attempts before he answered.

'Hello?' he said. His tone was muted, hardly audible, and growly.

'Mr Cassidy. I'm sorry to bother you again. It's Acacia Okeke.'

He went quiet then asked, 'What do you want?'

'Well, that's hard to say really. I think I might be going mad. I'm seeing things.'

'What kind of things?'

She hesitated. 'I don't know.' She sniggered. It was meant to ease her tension but didn't. 'You will probably think I'm totally fruitcake nuts, but I woke last night and saw . . .'

'Saw what?' His tone amplified. He seemed interested, and angry, or concerned.

'Well, that's it. I don't really know what I saw.'

He remained silent.

'Oh. This is crazy. I'm sorry, Brendan. Sorry for bothering you. I'll go now and leave you in peace.'

She took the phone from her ear and was about to hang up.

'Stop!' he shouted. 'Don't go.'

She brought the phone back up to her ear.

'You've seen them,' he continued. 'But more importantly, they have seen you. I told you so. They are very dangerous, Miss Okeke. Not to be trifled with or taken for granted. As before, my advice is to pray that they leave you alone. If they wanted to hurt you, they would've already done so. Take it as a good sign.'

'A sign of what?'

'That they will let you live.'

Neither Acacia or Brendan said a word for the next few seconds.

'You've been given a reprieve,' Brendan then said. 'A warning not to meddle. Take it from me, such things cannot be bargained with. Leave them alone. Forget about the Portlands. And go on with your life. Remember, they will always be watching you. And pray. You might not believe in it, but it helps.' He paused again before finishing, 'Good bye, Miss Okeke. Keep safe.'

The phone went dead, and Acacia put it back into her pocket with a shaky hand.

This was nonsense. *What next? Daemons? Aliens? Shape-changing monsters?*

She stood. Her intention was to head back to her flat, make tea, eat a bowl of fruit porridge, and get back to the work she had left undone, or maybe the sleep she had missed when she went running off into the street.

Lauren Alcock, Jeremy and the Portlands weren't her only case.

She had a seven-year-old boy in Shepherds Bush with battery acid burns, a homeless man beaten up underneath the Westway by passing drunks, and a stressed mother caught by a keen-eyed busker seconds before she threw herself into the path of a *Circle Line* train at *Ladbroke Grove* station.

For a part-time, contract, gig-style job, there was no end

to the work she had to do, and to single out one case over another was just downright unprofessional. But – and this was the *big but* – those other cases didn't manifest tiny creatures or spectral cats in her bedroom at night.

Maybe it was a dream?

Maybe she was overworked and her mind had played tricks on her?

But, if that was the case, why did she feel so scared?

And, why were there two tiny faces watching her from the bushes behind her park bench?

THIRTY-ONE – Concerning the soothing salve of luxury

In their room at *The Royal Kinnerton*, Jeremy replaced the receiver on the hotel phone, moved across the room from the desk and sat on a seat by the open bathroom door. Lauren had asked him to watch over her, all but ordering him to stay with her while she took a bath.

The hotel room itself was huge. Two large sash windows overlooked Wellington Arch and Constitution Hill whereby, if there was a back gate into Buckingham Palace Gardens and they had the right clearance, within a matter of a few minutes they could nip across the street for afternoon tea with the King.

He chuckled inwardly at the thought.

In the middle of the room, a plump cushioned, beige couch faced two matching armchairs set either side of a large marble fireplace, where a fire once blazed but now a purple *Moorcroft* vase stacked with flowers filled the space. The flowers looked fresh and he assumed the hotel staff changed them daily. A small circular dining table occupied a spot in front of one of the windows. It had two accompanying chairs. One of which he had carried over to sit on by the bathroom door. A magnificent art nouveau wardrobe, with two wing-shaped mirrors rebated into the doors, commanded the whole space between the windows. A dressing screen stood close by, alongside the desk with a matching stool, both made from walnut, and a chest containing spare blankets stretched the full width of the end of the bed, which was a massive four poster, with twin rosettes atop the mahogany headboard, cluster columns with rose finials, and thick red damask curtains concealing the sumptuous mattress and pillows within.

At near on six hundred pounds a night, he didn't expect anything less. He was a man of expensive tastes and had the money to pay for them but, even with that, the room still amazed him. It was a cut above the rest, and exactly what Lauren needed to distract her from whatever she had done to herself back at his apartment.

Watching her sit motionless in the freestanding bathtub staring into the soapy water, she appeared small and fragile, the cuts on her face, neck, and chest marring her perfect skin, the stillness of her gaze betraying her fear of whatever hurts she had inflicted on herself.

If she had indeed inflicted them on herself.

It was the only explanation. A cry for attention.

Even still, Jeremy wasn't convinced. There was some weird shit going on. First, the branches and briars closing around him at Rosina's dell, followed by Curiosity and her insistence that she saw a dead squirrel at the park. Perhaps that too was a cry for attention, but it didn't explain away the branches. And it wasn't the first time it had happened. Maybe he was going crazy, like Rosina had in her childhood. It might explain what he had seen, or thought he'd seen.

But he wasn't going crazy.

And he felt certain that Lauren wasn't either. And neither was Curiosity.

He got up, walked into the bathroom and the sweet scent of Lauren's soap.

It was another large space; fitted and decorated in an Edwardian style, with a patterned stained glass walk-in shower, two white pedestal washbasins, a matching toilet and bidet, two wicker chairs for changing, and the bathtub at the centre of the light blue tiled floor, with Lauren sitting inside like the solitary passenger in a boat stranded out upon a lake.

She peered up and smiled. She still looked scared but with a hint of happiness, perhaps because he was there. He hoped it was the case. He liked Lauren. When she wasn't being difficult, she could be very nice. Better than nice. She could be charming, warm and affectionate.

'I've ordered lunch,' he said. 'Black truffle risotto, with fresh sour dough bread, and a magnum of bubbly to make our unscheduled stay a little more enjoyable.' He smiled and winked. 'I think we should spoil ourselves. More so than usual. I've asked them to deliver it to the room so you don't have to put up with the prying eyes and whispers of the other guests.'

'Thank you,' Lauren said. 'That sounds lovely.'

'How do you feel?'

'Okay, I suppose. The cuts are sore but it's good relaxing in this bath.'

'Do you need me to get you anything? A towel? A soft bathrobe?'

'You can, when I'm finished.' She paused for a second then added, 'You can also help me apply the ointment'

'Won't that hurt?'

'It will be fine. If you're careful. I trust you.'

'You trust me?'

'Yes. Why does that sound so weird?'

'I don't know. I always thought you were just in this for . . .'

'. . . the grades?'

'Well, yes. I was of the opinion, for you, our being together was merely transactional.'

After a pause, Lauren replied, 'Maybe. At one time. But it's different now. You're kind.'

'I didn't do anything that anyone else wouldn't have done.'

'You looked after me. You still are. Even when Rosina was laying it on thick about us going to Portugal and you not picking up Curiosity for a month.'

'They'll cope. They always do. Curiosity is a dreamer but she's also tough. She just got a fright is all. Probably something she made up in her own mind.' He said it but didn't quite believe his own words.

'But the point is, you thought about me.' She smiled. It was as stunning as always.

'I'll leave you alone,' Jeremy said, exiting the bathroom.

'Don't go far. I like to know you are near.'

'I won't. I'll be here when you need me.'

'Thank you,' were the words that followed him into the main hotel room and, letting them sink in, Jeremy saw the gentle side he had always known lay beneath the tough, inexorable exterior Lauren projected to the world. Somewhere in her life, she had taken a turn towards sternness, perhaps as a defence mechanism or as a means of survival. And who would deny her that. There were many manipulative people out there. A smart person guarded their innermost emotions with care.

And then, at other times, she really was pleasant.

Like now. Vulnerable. Fearful. Beautiful. Tender.

Nice.

Her only problem was greed.

She expected to be spoiled. Like this stay at one of London's best five-star hotels with its lavish furnishings, meals and champagne. For the months they had been together, she had all but demanded it. So much so her other, nicer traits became smothered by her lust for anything with a high price tag.

But there was nothing wrong with that.

He was just the same.

They might make a very good couple.

THIRTY-TWO – Concerning those who never leave

After the argument in the garden, Rosina had led Curiosity into the house and sat her down on one of the circulation space sofas. She sat with her for a while. The closeness seemed odd, awkward, but reassuring.

She stood, told Curiosity to remain seated and, moving to the kitchen, pulled up a saved number on her phone, pressed it and raised the phone to her ear.

'I hope you're not calling the loser,' Faithe said from just outside the patio doors. 'You know it's pointless.' She had been unusually quiet since they came inside, reserved, smoking cigarettes and, on occasion, glancing back with a look of derision.

Rosina interrupted her with a sharp, upward jerk of her forefinger.

'Pick up, you useless lump,' she said to the air and, when her ex-husband answered, 'Jeremy. I don't care what you are doing. Get over here now. Curiosity needs to spend the night at your apartment. No arguments. No selfish excuses. Right now. She has to go right now.'

'Hi to you too, Rosina,' Jeremy said. 'Been hitting the bottle heavy today?'

'No.'

'Drugs then?'

'No, nothing. Well, not much. Look, just get over here.'

Jeremy snickered. 'For what?'

'For your daughter. She needs you. She needs to go with you.'

'Look, Rosina . . .'

'Look, nothing, Jeremy. Just do it. For once in your life, try to be a father.'

'Is this about that thing at the park? She's a kid. She makes things up. And anyway, Lauren is still a bit jittery after her – well, her I don't know what. All I know is that she had some kind of episode and she needs me.'

'And your daughter can go to hell, is that what you're saying?'

'No, I'm not.'

'It sounds like it.'

'It's not. Honestly. But tonight's a bad time. Anyway, we are not staying at the apartment for a few days. We are at a hotel.'

'A hotel? How nice for you both. You can take her there then.'

'I only booked for two.'

'Well, book another room.' Rosina snapped, and then paused. She thought for a moment, before softening her tone. 'Look, I wouldn't usually ask, but whatever happened to Curiosity at the park scared her. She doesn't want to stay here.' If Rosina revealed the true circumstances behind her phonecall, Jeremy would think she was crazy. Crazier than he did already. She didn't quite believe it herself but, for expediency, and because he raised it already, the supposed incident at

Greenwich Park was as good a reason as any. 'She needs you,' she continued. 'You are her father. Perhaps you can look after both of them. They might be good for each other.'

'I don't think Lauren has much time for children. Most of all she needs rest.'

Rosina's anger surged again. She tamed it and continued, 'You never know, they might share something in common. Seeing how they're both feeling a bit vulnerable?'

For many seconds, Jeremy said nothing.

Rosina waited. She felt sure she'd convinced him. Even now, while on the phone, horrific memories from her childhood continued to re-emerge. The fairies. The fire. Her burning classmates. She had to get Curiosity away from this house, away from the dell. In her daughter she saw something of her younger self. She too had been wilful. She too had attracted those wicked things. And they smothered her. They brought tragedy. She should've seen them coming. Instead, she put societal acceptance above caring for her child. Now, she must put that right. As sure as she reclaimed this house, she must reclaim her daughter. Or at least send her as far away from the dell as possible.

'I'm sorry, Rosina,' Jeremy said. 'You know I would, any other time. But I have to think about Lauren. Right now, she needs as little distraction as possible.'

'Well, you do that,' Rosina snapped back. 'You have your precious girlfriend.' She closed the call and tossed her phone onto the kitchen counter.

'I take it he was as accommodating as ever.' Faithe said, stubbing out her cigarette with her foot before walking inside.

'What do you think?'

Rosina went to the sofa and sat beside Curiosity. She hugged her to her chest, felt she ought to do. And Curiosity didn't pull away. She responded by snuggling closer. She seemed to enjoy the affection.

Rosina hugged her tighter. 'It will be okay. I believe you. I know the fairies are real. And we'll face them together.'

'God damn it, girl, have you gone nuts?' Faithe said. 'I've a good mind to get some of those drugs they used to give you. I can see now why they did. Do you really believe you saw fairies at the bottom of the garden? Are you nuts?' Faithe took a cigarette and lit it. 'And I don't care about your *not smoking in the house* rule. The circumstances call for it. I need nicotine. Actually, I need a drink. You need a drink. And Curiosity needs to work through this on her own.'

Rosina looked up at her friend, her only friend, the one person who helped her turn her life around. 'They are real,' she said. 'They follow me. They lured me back here to Aunt Lily's house, and they made me stay. I know this now. And, when Curiosity said she saw them too, I knew they would never leave me alone. Not in my dreams. And not in reality.'

'Have you heard yourself? Christ, Rosina, get a grip . . . *fairies?* Come on.' She laughed and drew on her cigarette.

'Aunt Lily knew all about them. She tried to warn me but I wouldn't listen. I just wanted to dance. And they helped me.'

'Dance? You danced?'

'Yes. I danced ballet. In the dell. With the fairies.'

'Jesus. Are you listening to yourself?'

'I thought they were only dreams and nightmares.'

'And now you think they are real and you can see them?'

Rosina paused a few seconds then said, 'Yes. I do.'

Faithe took a long puff at her cigarette. She went to the kitchen and stubbed it out in the sink. When she returned, she sat on the arm of the sofa.

'Listen here, Rosina dear. Fairies aren't real. They've never been real. And I'm beginning to think the doctors should've kept you dosed-up on drugs.'

Rosina didn't reply. Faithe's statement hurt.

Curiosity spoke up. 'You know about them too,' she said to Faithe. 'You told me outside. You told me that there are faerie paths.'

Faithe appeared stunned. No, not so much stunned as guilty. She shrugged. 'That was just me being talkative. I was playing with you.'

'Fairy paths?' Rosina asked.

'Yes. I met Curiosity at the front door. I was only making small talk. I didn't think it would cause all this. I should've known to be more careful around you two.'

'So, you do believe in fairies?'

'No. I don't. Nobody could. It's nonsense.'

'I can show you them, if you like,' Curiosity said. 'There are drawings. In the sketchpad.'

'What sketchpad?' Rosina asked.

'The one I found in the attic.'

'I thought I told you not to play up there. It's grubby and . . .' Rosina stopped there. 'I'm sorry. Tell me about this sketchpad.' She couldn't remember seeing one, even during the renovations. But, then again, she didn't make any changes to the attic. She kept it as her great aunt had left it when she died. Neither she nor the builders went there. She did recall, however, Aunt Lily making sketches. It was the day before the second audition for *The Nutcracker*. The day before the fire.

The thought chilled her.

'It was in a big wooden chest,' Curiosity continued. 'It has drawings of faeries. And writing. That's why I used the button charm bells. It said that faeries hate the sound of them ringing. But you tore them down and ruined everything.'

Rosina caressed her daughter's cheek. 'I know. I was angry. But I will put it right.'

'There was photo of you attached to the back cover. You were a little girl. You were dancing. And it changed. At first, it was you. Then it became me. Probably the faeries doing magic.'

'Where is this sketchpad now?'

'It's in my bedroom,' Curiosity said. 'I don't know where the photo is. It just disappeared. I'm not going up there. The burned girls are in the mirror. I covered it with my coat but it doesn't stop them getting out. They follow me around.' She shrunk back on the sofa. 'This morning, they were in that mirror above the clock. I haven't seen them since Arabella came. And I don't want to. Am I going mad?'

Rosina saw tears well in her daughter's eyes and hugged her close.

'No, you're not, Curiosity, and neither am I. What you saw is scary, and very dangerous. But you have me now. And Faithe,' Rosina looked up to her friend. 'If she'll help us?'

'This is ridiculous,' Faithe said.

'Whereabouts in your bedroom did you leave the sketch-pad?' Rosina asked Curiosity.

'On my bed.'

Rosina stood up and moved towards the stairs. 'You stay here. Don't worry. I'll be back before you know it.'

Curiosity didn't protest any further and Rosina noticed – maybe for the first time – the resolve she spent years trying to crush. She turned to Faithe, 'Are you coming?'

Faithe huffed, said, 'Jesus, why do I bother.' She joined Rosina at the bottom of the stairs. 'Let's go then.'

THIRTY-THREE – Concerning a friend indeed

The sketchpad wasn't on the bed as Curiosity had stated. So, Rosina searched around the floor. She checked around the back of the door and over by the desk, avoiding the mirror that was still hidden beneath Curiosity's winter coat.

Faithe helped. Well, she helped with the same lackadaisical attitude she went about anything, by pointing out areas to investigate, and Rosina didn't ask for more. It was enough that her friend had come with her, if only to sit on the bed and tap her knee.

'She did say it was on her bed?' Rosina asked.

'She did,' Faithe answered. 'And, now I have you up here away from Curiosity, are you honestly going to tell me that you believe this bull?'

'I thought you were here to help.'

'I am helping. I'm helping you to come to your senses.'

'Yes, I do. I believe it because it's true. How many times do I have to tell you? I've seen them. They exist. So, are you going to keep grilling me, or help me find the sketchpad? Aunt Lily was a clever woman. She knew how to sort things out.'

'Clever enough to make a crazy woman out of you,' Faithe mumbled.

Rosina let it lie. She opened the desk drawer and rummaged

through Curiosity's pens, pencils, and other stationery bits and pieces. The sketchpad wasn't there. She crossed to the wardrobe.

'You never did tell me what happened to Aunt Lily,' Faithe said. 'I fully understand why you wouldn't want to. And I didn't ask before, because I didn't want to cause a regression. But, now, seeing how you're verging on doolally as it is, maybe reliving the memory will bring you back down to earth.'

'My god, Faithe, would you give it a rest.' She opened the wardrobe and scoured through Curiosity's clothes. 'If you must know, she drowned. A week or so after the fire. But nobody told me. Apparently, I was in too much of a sensitive state to receive such bad news. It was Cassidy who told me. When I took over the house. I had assumed that she just didn't want to visit her messed-up great niece. He's a good man, Cassidy. I never appreciate the good ones enough.'

'She drowned? How?'

'She died here at home. Cassidy found her.' A lump formed in Rosina's throat. She swallowed it. 'He said that, after the fire, she began acting strange, became detached. So, he would stay overnight to keep an eye on her. One evening, he saw her go down the garden and into the dell. It was dusk. He said he couldn't see too well but felt pretty sure she was carrying something with her. After a while, when she hadn't come out, he became concerned and went to look for her. He found her face down in the pool. She was dead.' Rosina came away from the wardrobe. 'Well, there's no sketchpad in there. Have you checked under the pillow?'

'I have,' Faithe said. 'And there's no magic book. No flying pixies or dancing leprechauns either.' She snickered.

Rosina ignored her.

'Did Cassidy say what she was carrying?'

Rosina hesitated then said, 'It was an old sack.' She kneeled down and looked underneath the bed.

'A sack of what?'

'Good lord. Would you look at this? It's my old tutu and wings.' She reached the ballet costume out and sat beside Faithe. 'Aunt Lily must have taken them home with her from the hospital. I didn't remember about the dancing until Curiosity mentioned it.' She laid the costume on her lap and caressed the torn fabric. 'It's a bit worse for wear. I loved ballet. I remember now. It was the only thing I wanted to do.'

In her mind's eye, the years stripped away. She was eight again, dancing in the dell. Her thoughts moved to the dance studio. Her resentment grew, for the teacher who excluded her, for the girls who mocked her. For the first time in years, the whispered voices spoke to her. They weaved through her mind, planting memories there. She pushed them away. She folded the tutu into a bundle with the wings and set them to one side on the bed.

'I'll destroy these later,' she said. 'I was obsessed. And that obsession caused all this.' She stood up.

'My god, you are all over the place today,' Faithe said. 'I was asking about the sack.'

'I know,' Rosina replied. She rummaged through Curiosity's pile of washing. 'Gracious, that girl is a mess. If I've told her once, I've told her a thousand times to put her clothes in the wash-basket. The child doesn't listen.'

'You're avoiding me,' Faithe said. 'You're not answering the question. No wonder you're having bad dreams. You've suppressed everything, about the fire, about your great aunt's death.'

'Maybe. But Cassidy told me about Aunt Lily years ago. If finding out that she was dead can cause a relapse, why didn't it happen when he first told me?'

'The mind is a complex thing. I'm no psychiatrist, but I know it builds walls around sorrow. Perhaps it took this long for the news to sink in. Curiosity told you about her fantasies and that was enough to bring those walls down. It's a logical explanation. And a far better one than nymphs and pixies dancing at the end of the garden.'

'You could be right,' Rosina said.

'Damn right I'm right. So, what was in the sack?'

'Cat heads. Aunt Lily killed her cats.'

'Christ on a bike.'

'All thirteen of them. She hacked off their heads, put them in a sack, and took them to the dell. When Cassidy found her lying in the water, they had spilled out over the ground. *Like a pile of bloodied tennis balls*, he said.' She paused for a second before continuing. 'That's why I thought the sketchpad, if there is one, might be important. I need to know why she would do such a horrible thing. She adored those cats. They were her companions. So why cut off their heads?'

A shadow flashed past the open door.

Faithe shrugged. Rosina dashed out to the landing.

A grey mist, shaped like a woman, was hovering at the base of the stairwell leading to the attic, the wall at the end of the corridor visible through the wispiness of its body. It quivered, and Rosina took a step back. It began to solidify, and a chill gripped her heart.

THIRTY-FOUR – Concerning the courageous plan

Curiosity waited until Mummy and Faithe had reached her bedroom. She had a job to finish. Whether Mummy regretted it or not, she had destroyed the chain of charm bells that Curiosity had draped across the bushes at the dell, and they must be put back. It was the only way to stop the creatures getting out.

She gazed out through the patio doors to the garden. The disturbance in the dell had grown. A grubby, green fog had risen up, broiling across the surface of the bushes, reaching out across the lawn like fingers clawing through the dirt. In her mind, the whispering voices increased in intensity. The oak tree shook, its leaves falling to the ground. The bushes rustled.

The creatures were mustering. They were calling to her.

She went to the patio, but no farther.

A little way out on the lawn, a black and white tomcat lay, belly up, on the grass. The same cat she'd seen at *The Grotto Toy Shop* on a day she regretted more than any other. It was licking its front paw, with its gaze fixed on her. She thought she saw persuasion in its stare. As though the cat was urging her to set out and drive the creatures back into the dell.

But her courage wasn't quite there yet.

The tumult in the dell settled. The green fog retracted into the brush. In her mind's eye she saw the creatures waiting, biding time for her to come to them. She glanced behind her, and thought of fleeing back inside. But, in the glass of the patio doors, the spectres of five charred girls glared at her. There was only one way to go now. There was only one thing she could do: gather up the charm bells, lay them out, and imprison the creatures in their dell for good.

She went out, and had reached only halfway down the garden when the beautiful version of her faerie-lady flew out from the bushes. With slender fingers, she beckoned Curiosity to come closer. The golden door reappeared in the oak tree. The pathway opened up. Tiny eyes peered out from the hedgerows and, at the end of the path, the circular pond with the fountain at its apex re-emerged, its water trickling with the sweetest music that, if not determined to her task, she might've succumbed to its enchantment and forgotten what terrors these creatures truly were. She hummed a song. One from her favourite punk band. She hummed loudly, to drown out the voices and the hypnotic music.

The string and charm bells were dangling from the holly bush where Mummy had thrown them. It wasn't far, just a few metres to the side of the oak tree but, to Curiosity, it was a few metres into the one place she dreaded to go. So, she took a deep breath. She flexed her shoulders, raised her arms above her head, and set off through the bushes. The faerie-lady swooped down. The creatures moved out from the hedges and advanced towards her. In a matter of seconds, there were dozens of them. They were the nice ones that she had danced with. They swung from the branches. They came up from the earth beneath her feet. Not with menace, but with fondness. They smiled. They sang. But she was wise to them now. They were not what they seem.

When she got close enough to the charm bells, she reached out. She touched them with her fingertips and they tinkled. With great disturbance, the creatures mutated and skittered away. The path, hedgerows, pond, and fountain flickered, became indistinct before growing firm again. The faerie-lady also changed and darted up into the branches of the oak tree. Curiosity pressed forward. Straining against the brush, she looped her finger over a free strand of string. She shook it. The bells jingled again, and she kept shaking.

The creatures shrieked. The pretty vista disappeared, melting away like a watercolour painting soaked by the rain. Dozens of ugly creatures then dashed out from the undergrowth. They swarmed over her body, scurried down her arms, onto her hand, and into the holly bush. They twisted her fingers, yanked the bundle from her grasp before they jumped away, taking the charm bells and string with them, screeching as if the tinkling caused them physical pain.

The charm bells fell silent.

The green fog returned and enveloped her, clouding her vision and stealing her breath. She coughed, blindly reaching out for something to give her bearings. Her fingers found only bushes, bracken, sharp thorns, which disappeared beneath her touch and only mist remained.

With a sudden gust, the fog cleared.

Instead of the undergrowth, where the dell had been, there now stood a great forest. It was dense and lofty, with trees much taller than those from the dell. On all sides, it reached back hundreds of metres, perhaps kilometres into the distance. Shadows moved across the trunks like black spiders. The boughs creaked. This place was old, and animated, each tree stretching its gnarled limbs as if it had conscious thoughts and feelings, and every nook harbouring some unknown thing. A hidden shadow, just like the enchanted forests of her storybooks, poised to pounce, grab, and drag her down.

Up ahead, a muddy pathway stretched over humps and hollows. Its surface layered with decaying leaves, bordered by tangles of briars, nettles, and all manner of other unpleasant, stinging plants. Some were green. Most had withered, mottled with mould and boil-like blisters, creating a barren barrier in case an unwary girl strayed from the path and found themselves lost amid the trees.

But a path to where?

Overhead, the tree trunks rose like giants, their foliage dappled in browns, greys, murky greens, and blood reds. Moonlight battled to get through, but only managed a handful of silver shards that were, in turn, quickly smothered by the canopy. The ground was soft. Gooey brown muck oozed up from beneath her feet. It pooled around her toes and released a foul odour that stung her nostrils. In this place of shifting shapes and shadows, she was as far from Bingham Crescent as any nightmare might take her. The silence was oppressive. It was punctuated only by the familiar whispered voices, unseen in the fading light, but close enough to be terrifying.

THIRTY-FIVE – Concerning disbelief and resignation

Rosina's instincts told her to flee back along the corridor and down the stairs. But she was rooted to the spot, immobilised by the vision of Aunt Lily shimmering before her. The air was cold, her breath misty. Struck by a blend of panic and disbelief, she stared at the ghostly figure, a strange paralysation brought on by a compulsion to run away but also to discover.

Was Aunt Lily really standing there? Or had the neuroses returned?

Taking care to keep the vision, delusion, whatever it might be, within eyeshot, Rosina checked if Faithe had joined her on the landing. She hadn't. She was alone. The thought of this heightened her anxiety. The apparition began to solidify, took on a more substantial form. A dull, grey entity with puckered flesh, lifeless eyes, and strings of dank hair melding with the pond weed that hung about its shoulders. And yet, it was unmistakeably Aunt Lily, standing with a single finger pointing up the stairs to the attic.

Rosina blinked her eyes in the hope that, when she opened them again, the apparition might be gone. It was still there, however, slowly climbing the stairs. The urge to follow was strong. It spoke to her mind with Aunt Lily's voice:

You must come with me, it said, *for Curiosity.*

Apprehension prickled her gut. Sanity dictated that she should go with her first impulse and flee down the stairs but, instead, she stayed where she was, peering up to the small panelled door leading to the attic. It was ajar. A few metres inside, a wooden trunk sat with its lid open. Aunt Lily's apparition stood behind the trunk, gesturing for Rosina to come to her, her voice still murmuring through Rosina's thoughts:

You must come, now. To save Curiosity.

Rosina climbed the stairs. A moment later, she was standing inside the door, her gaze darting from apparition to trunk, trunk to apparition, and back to the trunk again. Within it, an A4 sized sketchpad sat atop a bundle of patterned kaftans. The kaftans sparked a memory, and then sorrow. The sketchpad she recognised as the one Aunt Lily had been drawing in, all those years ago, on the day of the fire. She also assumed it to be the one that Curiosity had spoken of.

She picked it up. Curiosity said she'd left it in her bedroom. If she was telling the truth, it had been moved here, *but by whom?* Something skittered, followed by many things moving across the floor and rafters. The apparition backed away, became indistinct. The air grew warmer.

Rosina stayed put. She leafed through the pages. There were drawings of weird little creatures, and one of a slender girl with skin as pale as plaster. She wore flowers in her hair and had multicoloured dragonfly wings on her back. At the top of the page the words *tylwyth teg* and *aes sídhe* were written in Aunt Lily's handwriting, with the word *faerie* written below, the whole image embellished and bordered with coils of bright, green ivy. A theme repeated on other pages of the sketchpad.

A photograph was clipped to the back cover, of a girl wearing a ballet tutu and fairy wings.

Gazing down at her younger self, Rosina's mind raced with the desire to both relive the past and to run from this room, leaving her memories where they should be: locked away where she couldn't consider them. Her sanity would thank her for it.

Whatever stalked her daughter, however, was not defined by sanity. It was both supernatural and real. It was sorcerous and manipulative. It was enticing her from within the photograph.

Rosina tossed the sketchpad and photo down. Somewhere at the back of the room the skittering things scurried around, as if in dissatisfaction.

There was a single page inside the trunk. Not from the sketchpad but from a book. She picked it up. In her mind, she sensed Aunt Lily's approval, and also the skittering things' displeasure. The page had a title: *Ways of Seeing – a Treatise on Crossing to the Otherworld*, below which another line – a chapter title – said: *Breaking the Spell*.

The page began with:

To live in harmony with the spirits of nature, one must adhere to the simple principle: the paths of fae and men can only converge on the rarest of occasions, and then expressly on their terms.
They are the masters of attraction. They deem humankind to be their plaything.

*Should their attention be drawn, you belong to them. And, to
break the spell, a token must be paid. Or a soul taken.*

*To the ancient Britons and Celtic tribes of Europe, this token
came through offerings of the severed heads of their enemies. To
do otherwise, meant invoking the spirits' wrath, which might
require a greater sacrifice, perhaps the giving of a loved one.*

The page went on to talk about ancient rituals where rings
of wooden poles were built atop high mounds, with severed
heads impaled upon them.

It finished with:

*Remember, the fae-folk hold to no reason and are not swayed by
logic or petition. Only sacrifice will appease them. It must be something personal. Something loved and preferably familial.*

With this last line, Rosina finally knew why Aunt Lily had
killed her cherished cats. In an attempt to appease the fae-
folk's attraction to Rosina, she had sacrificed her only other
loves. But it didn't work. The fairies weren't in the dell. The
fire had trapped them in the dance studio until Curiosity set
them free. This realisation flared in her mind as sure as if she
had gone back in time and was looking through Aunt Lily's
eyes. She felt her dashed hope. She experienced her despair
and the moment she plunged into the water and drowned
herself.

She also sensed the fairy-lady in her mind, battling with
Aunt Lily for command of her thoughts, enticing her to pick

up and look at the photograph. While they commanded her to stay in the attic, Aunt Lily urged her to leave, now, to use the knowledge and put an end to their enchantments once and for all.

A sudden noise made her jump. She spun around.

Faithe was standing in the doorway.

THIRTY-SIX – Concerning the glamorous friend

Rosina's heart leaped to see Faithe standing there. Like a beacon of hope, she shone out. She had wisdom, a defined good sense wrought from years spent in full participation in life and all its intrigues, from grabbing challenges by the scruff of the neck and dominating them.

Faithe always knew what to do.

'I know why Aunt Lily killed her cats,' Rosina said. 'She did it to protect me. And I know how to stop them. It's written here.' She held out the page. Her hand was trembling.

Faithe didn't respond. She didn't do anything except stare.

'Please. You must believe me.'

'You just couldn't leave it alone, could you?' Faithe said.

'Read it,' Rosina said. 'Please. See for yourself. I need to know what you think.'

Faithe glanced down to the page and back at Rosina. 'I don't need to read it. I already know.' She took a step closer. She leered. It reminded Rosina of the fairies from her nightmare. 'Why couldn't you just be content with being a messed-up drunk? If you had just ignored your child and left it there, then everything would've been fine.'

'I don't understand.'

'Sure, you might've cried a few tears, and might have even

meant them too. As long as the wine was flowing, that is. Anyway, I had to put up with your crap for far too long to let you interfere now. My job was simple, keep you occupied while your daughter grew, then steer her in the right direction when she came of age.'

'Faithe, we don't have time for this. Curiosity needs me.'

'As if you care about Curiosity.'

'What are you talking about?'

'You see, it's a magical number, the number eight. It's the number of resurrection. The Bible mentions it. The Chinese go absolutely nuts for it. It's also the age when a child passes from infancy. When they possess a spirit so strong it attracts all sorts of natural forces. If crazy old Aunt Lily hadn't interfered it would've been you. But she did. So here we are. And, as for her pitiful attempts at lifting the enchantment, well that was butchery at its worst. Cats are precious. We like to think of them as our window to the world. Spies, if you like . . . familiars.' Faithe scowled. 'If she hadn't gone and killed herself, we would've made sure her death was slow, and painful.'

Rosina took a step forward. 'I don't have time for this,' she said. 'Curiosity needs me.'

Faithe blocked her path. 'You're going nowhere, Sugar-plum. You and your issues are the last thing Curiosity needs right now. She needs us. We are her true family.'

Rosina huffed. 'I know you don't believe me about the fairies. But this is just ridiculous. Get out of my way.' She went to push past.

Faithe grabbed her by the arm and threw her back against the trunk.

Rosina stumbled but straightened up again. She was too shocked to speak. Her arm hurt.

'Stay there,' Faithe said. 'Do as you're told.'

Rosina felt her tears well. 'Why?' she asked. 'Why are you doing this?'

'Look. It's simple. My duty was to make sure you came back to this house. To build you up so that Jeremy could take you down. We needed you so self-absorbed that you would neglect your daughter. We needed Curiosity alone and un-loved. You were good at that. Who did you think let slip to the Portlands about this place? Or that you were in the market for a husband? Of course, I knew he would do the dirty on you from the get go. Cue one carefully placed party, some harsh words, and whammy, you fled down the garden and into the arms of any old tomcat waiting for a chance rendezvous. But it wasn't chance. None of it. It was a masterful connivance. One of my best, if I say so myself. Curiosity is truly a wonderful child. Of both worlds.'

'I don't understand. I'm leaving.' She pushed past Faithe again.

Faithe caught her and flung her back. 'I said, stay. Jesus, you really are stupid. It was me. I did all this. I had to free my folk. Curiosity was a nice by-product. She will be a useful addition to our world.'

'It was you?' Rosina said. 'You did this to us?'

'Well, I can't take all of the credit. You being a bundle of neuroses helped things along nicely. I just had to make sure Curiosity was in the right place on her eighth birthday. Your laughable parenting skills and her inquisitiveness took care of the rest.'

'Why?'

'Because, by starting the fire at the dance studio, your bone-headed great aunt trapped our kindred folk there. Fire does that. It destroys. Even magic. We all suffered. We are like that. We are connected. We needed our queen.'

Rosina was lost for words. Everything was false. Faithe was false.

'Woh! You look like someone just smashed your favourite dolly.'

'Did you ever care for me? I gave you my spare key. I shared my life with you. How could you be so . . . well, creepy?'

'Oh, that hurts,' Faithe replied. She took a step forward. Rosina stepped back, clipping the trunk with her heel. 'But I suppose I've been called worse. And, as for the sharing, I was only keeping you distracted and mentally messed-up. It's why I cast the charm. Through that magazine I gave you years ago. That glamour magazine you read all the time? Get it? *Glamour*? As in *enchant*?'

Rosina said nothing.

'Oh. Never mind. You never could take a joke. Anyway, I cast a spell of confusion so you would feel your guilt but never see it.'

'What guilt?'

'*The* guilt. The *big* guilt. Why, did you honestly think someone like me would be interested in a saggy old wino like you? Stupid woman. It wasn't friendship. It was part of the plan. You're so emotionally unstable you couldn't see you were being played. And, if you had shown even the slightest affection for your daughter, I don't think we would have gotten close. Anyway. Enough of this chit-chat. It's time to get down to business. We have our queen back. And we have Curiosity. So, we don't need you anymore.'

'What do you mean *have Curiosity*?'

'Do I really have to spell it out? We have Curiosity. She is with us. Now, all that's left is to deal with you. Once that unsavoury job is done, a few malign charms, some well-placed rumours about this place being haunted, and we should be left alone for years.'

'Who are you?'

'Isn't it obvious, dumbass? I'm one of them. The *little-folk*, as the Irish so eloquently call us. Clever people the Irish. They always maintain a healthy wariness for our kind.'

Rosina moved to the other side of the trunk.

'I know. Who would have thought? We come in all shapes and sizes. There are some weird looking ones too. There's this troll, in Norway, with long ears all the way to his waist.' She sniggered. 'He's a really funny looking guy. Some of us can fly too. But you know that already. Others, like me, can take on pretty much any form they choose. I think you are already acquainted with a certain tall, dark, gentlemanly chap. A very attractive chap I hear. Especially when encountered down among the bushes at the end of the garden.' She laughed.

Rosina recoiled. The penny fully dropped. The stranger, Robin Goodfellow, was Curiosity's father.

'There it is. I must say your face is an absolute picture. And, the fact that you're only seeing it now puts another feather in my cap of abilities. Anyway, time's a wasting. I have to get out of this ridiculous human-suit. I want to go home

. . . to the forests. I need greenery and lots of it. We have to save it before you self-obsessed jabber-monkeys destroy what's left.'

The colour drained from Faithe's face.

Her skin turned grey and shrivelled.

Her body contorted, creaking with nauseating, dull snaps. She hunched over, retaining the same height, but bent forward, her flesh shrinking like vacuum-wrap to her bones. Draped in her elegant but now oversized garments, she appeared creepily clown-like. Even her coiffured hairstyle held no immunity to the transformation. It receded inwards. The remaining few threads hanging limp and greasy from her skull. Her nails grew longer, bursting talon-like from elongated fingers. Her eyeballs sank into their sockets, the pupils bleeding outwards to become oily black orbs. The skin on her face withered. Her nose folded inwards, and her mouth stretched in an extended grin, above and below which knots of jagged teeth erupted through the flesh at crooked angles.

When Faithe stripped out of her clothes, Rosina felt physically ill to see what her friend had become. The haggish thing standing naked before her had been her confidante, and her only true friend. Now she was this creature, a shrivelled sack of skin and bones, grinning, dribbling spit, advancing towards her with arms outstretched and claws grasping for her face.

She jumped back.

The creature lunged forward, leaping over the trunk, grabbed Rosina by the throat, whereby Rosina staggered backwards, punching, kicking, pushing, grappling with both hands to wrench its grip from around her neck. It held fast.

Its breath smelled foul. Her stomach rolled and vomit rose, lumping beneath the creature's tightening fingers. In seconds, her sight dimmed. Her legs weakened and, seen through the fog of her withering consciousness, a grey mist moved up to envelop them both.

The air chilled. The mist coalesced.

It became Aunt Lily, in her vaporous, spectral form but with a solid arm locked around the creature's neck, which shrieked, squirming like an eel touched by boiling water. Aunt Lily hauled the creature backwards. Its grip relaxed. A rush of air filled Rosina's lungs, her sight and strength returning enough to wrestle its fingers free from her throat. It shrieked again. So loudly Rosina's eardrums thrummed. She staggered and tripped over the trunk, twisting her ankle. Pain shot up her leg. She yelped but carried on, crawling towards the door.

Clasped in Aunt Lily's arm, the creature stopped struggling. It went limp and, for a few optimistic seconds, looked beaten. Then whispered voices rose up from the gloom. The skittering, that had stopped since Faithe arrived, started up again. Dozens of tiny eyes came into view, spread out across the rafters like pinholes in a black sheet. A slew of small, emaciated bodies emerged. They moved out into the half-light, massing like a miniature army on the brink of battle. For a few seconds, the multitude stood, in silence, their bodies partially in shadow. Then they attacked. As a single entity, they leaped from the rafters and hacked at Aunt Lily's spectre with terrible violence. Her arm dropped from around the creature's neck. She fell back. Her ghostly frame sliced to swirls of mist that merged with the dust before it drifted away like smoke on a breeze.

When Aunt Lily was gone, Rosina felt her loss as deeply as when Cassidy first told her about her death. The melancholy returned. And so, did her worry, for Curiosity and how she might save her. She attempted to get up. A spasm shot up her leg and she fell. She tried again, biting down the pain, struggled to her feet, steeled her will, sidestepped the trunk, and rushed for the door.

The creature stood and blocked her way. It grinned, and struck out, slashing a gash in her cheek. In seconds, the army of tiny things were clambering over Rosina's body, stabbing with their claws, as she tore them from her flesh, tossing those she captured smashed and squealing into the shadows. The more she crushed, the more came. Some hacked at her legs. Others scrambled onto her head, yanking out clumps of hair like a gardener ripping weeds from a flowerbed. The creature she had known as Faithe Henning laughed then moved closer. It snarled and lurched for her.

Rosina stood firm.

The creature stopped. It seemed bemused by her boldness.

Rosina gathered her strength and, although weakened by the onslaught and her ankle injury, she lashed out, shoving it out the door and down the stairs, where it crashed onto the landing with a crunch that made her stomach churn.

The horde shrieked, jumped away, and scampered back into the shadows. Seconds later, they regrouped. But Rosina took her chance. She threw off the last few still clinging to her shoulders and hobbled down the stairs. At the bottom, the creature lay on its back, staring up at her. Two spikes of shattered shinbone poked through the flesh of both legs. Its right arm hung limply at its side. The centre of its face was crushed, a messy pulp of puckered skin and jagged teeth. And still it sniggered, spitting blood.

'You can't have her,' it said. 'She is ours.'

Rosina gave the creature a wide berth as she slipped past. It made a laboured grab for her legs but failed. Then it hissed and, like a wounded dog, staggered back up the stairs to the attic. The door slammed. Rosina limped along the landing and down to the kitchen. She felt weak. Her ankle ached.

When she reached the dell, it seemed calm. Sunlight dappled the foliage. Leaves rustled in the breeze. The trees and bushes looked as ordinary as might be expected by any-one who knew nothing of the otherworldly things that lived there.

She shouted out, 'Curiosity.' Her throat felt raw. The words had no vigour but she shouted again anyway.

The only reply was the buzz of many voices talking to her mind:

She is with us, they said and, as if to prove the point, the branches parted.

Curiosity was standing amid the bushes. She was tangled in briars, facing away, and reaching out for the bundle of string and charm bells that Rosina had earlier cast into the bushes. Above her, high in the oak tree, a little flying creature hovered.

Rosina recognised it as the fairy-lady, but in its grotesque form. The charm bells tinkled. The flying creature hissed and the deafening shrieks of many others echoed through the undergrowth.

A green fog billowed up and engulfed everything.

When it cleared, Curiosity was gone.

THIRTY-SEVEN – Concerning the lost and the unloved

Something moved in the bracken. It leaped from one bush to another then scampered away. Another small thing ran across her path and disappeared into the trees. A few more followed, tiny shapes flickering in the dim light. By their unpleasant whispers, Curiosity determined they were close. Maybe behind her. Perhaps at her shoulder or on the branches that hung only centimetres from her face.

She ran. Not with a destination in mind. She just ran. A dream-like flight, where her pace felt sluggish, and each step covered a distance much less than her panic required. As if to aid the sluggishness, plants tugged at her ankles and briars scratched her skin, adding yet more wounds to her growing tally of injuries. Ploughing through the puddles and potholes, globs of fetid slime splashed up and showered her skin. It slid down her arms. Some splattered onto her face and into her mouth, her chest heaving under the exertion of scaling up-turned trees, their decaying trunks crumbling in her hands as if with the deliberate intention to disgust her and slow her pace. But she stayed the course. To where, she didn't know. She was too scared to stop or to look behind.

Something leaped into her path, backlit by a shaft of

silver moonlight. A small spindly creature stared up at her. It hissed. More creatures came out and congregated around it. They glared at her then swarmed.

She was hauled backwards to the ground. She struggled to get up but the creatures held her down, pressing her body deeper into the mud. Hands burst from the clay around her. They were children's hands, grimy with muck, flaked with charred skin, and crackling as though still aflame. Curiosity screamed but, in the vastness of the forest, it just petered out and was lost to the trees. She screamed again. The hands seized her. She tried to wriggle free, but they gripped tighter and the creatures pressed harder. Sticky mud welled up around her face. It spilled into her mouth, filled her nostrils, and she spluttered, gasping breaths, terrified that a single creature had jumped onto and now crouched on her chin. It sneered. Perhaps it smiled. In her panic Curiosity found it difficult to distinguish which.

A metre above the creature, the faerie-lady hovered in her beautiful form, glowing, smiling as might a kindly friend or something come to show her wonder.

Then she changed, became the ugly creature that Curiosity now knew as her true form.

You belong to us, she – *it* – said.

And the hands dragged her down.

Not for the first time in her life, Rosina felt useless. Attitudes shaped from denial and the choices she made for showiness, but which now seemed pointless in face of her current, terrifying predicament. Curiosity had been taken, abducted by the same creatures that had sought to take Rosina all those years ago. To where, she had no idea. For what purpose, she knew even less. Speculation was pointless. All she knew for certain was that a cruel force had connived – from the beginning – to both create and claim her daughter.

If she had only listened to Curiosity on occasion.

If she had only behaved as a mother should.

She ran at the bushes. Instantly, the briars intertwined and created a wall of barbs. She tried to push past them, but the brushwood thickened and barred her way. Three more times, she rushed the undergrowth and, each time, the foliage grew dense and thorns entangled and halted her progress.

She gave up. She sat on the grass and stared into the dell hoping to see her Curiosity's face rise up and smile at her.

It didn't happen.

Apart from her triumph home, persistence had never been a major part of Rosina's make-up. The ability to find efficient solutions was a faculty more attributable to the daughter than the mother. She was a self-confessed surrenderer. When life got tough, she gave up, usually blaming someone or something else for her misfortunes.

The sky dimmed. It started to rain. Rosina got up, wiped her face, and limped back to the house. A lonely soul, with no one to call family or friend.

When she reached the patio, she glanced back at the dell.

Nothing stirred except for the percussion of the rain splattering the leaves.

She sighed and went inside.

Jeremy was sitting at the kitchen counter.

'I came,' he said. 'Lauren insisted I should. Now, how can help my little girl?'

Rosina smiled.

THIRTY-EIGHT – Concerning into the fold

It was pitch black. Her backside felt wet. The air smelled damp and earthy like wet clay. Curiosity was sitting on dirt. She leaned back, her spine met with a hard and soily surface. She laid one hand on the ground and her fingers sank into mud. She also smelled charred flesh. It was faint but potent, coming from somewhere back within the darkness. There were things there too. They whispered to each other. They moved around.

For a few hopeful seconds, she thought this might be no more than another one of her creations. Like the delightful meadows and valleys, perhaps she had merely manifested this place, which meant the illusion could be undone. But that was just wishful thinking. This was no dream.

The hands had dragged her here. She knew that now.

She reached out to her side. Her fingers touched something dry. She snapped her hand back and tittering voices rose up. She waited. The voices died off. She reached out again and picked up a bundle of twigs. Turning it in her fingers, she worked out that the twigs were weaved together and shaped like an angel or perhaps a faerie, and she recalled what Daddy had said as they drove through Piccadilly Circus.

The bundle flew from her hands.

A light flashed, then dwindled, but remained shining. Shading her eyes, Curiosity blinked, and kept doing so until her sight cleared. Her floral dress was dirty. As were her hands, her arms, legs, and feet. But she felt no pain. Her wounds were gone. No scrapes, no cuts, not even streaks of blood.

Overhead, plant roots hung down from the ceiling. To either side, clay walls stretched far into the distance. She was in a cavern, reaching back into blackness, where she suspected a horde of tiny creatures lurked, unseen for now, but bustling with excitement.

The faerie-lady, the source of the light, was hovering overhead. She was beautiful and, for a second, Curiosity forgot how she had conspired to steal her away. Perhaps this was a test. A trick to gauge if she was worthy of the magic. Which was a fair explanation for why she was here, and indeed for all the incidents that had happened since finding the figurine in the old toy shop. Perhaps this was the last time they would frighten her. And, then again, perhaps not.

The faerie-lady floated down, morphing into her true ugly form as she descended.

A huge shadow moved out from the back of the cavern, the unseen creatures humming like a choir as if to urge it forward. It crept across the muddy floor, oozing like ink spilled across a desktop and, upon reaching Curiosity's feet, rose up, undulating, taking shape from black liquid, to black sludge, to black form. Figures emerged. Five girls with misshapen bodies, dressed in scorched tutus and fairy wings. They stood hunched and facing away.

Unlike Curiosity, these stricken girls hadn't healed. They

suffered, still burning, their skin crackling beneath an invisible yet ferocious flame. In unison, they pirouetted. And they danced. Their steps stiff. Their faces streaked with the oil-like tears.

A mass of tiny creatures came forward.

Above, another host of the flying ones swarmed out to fill the spaces overhead.

Two red squirrels hopped into view. One was chewing on a cobnut. The other was twitching, bloody and headless.

Terrified, Curiosity squeezed herself into a ball. 'Please,' she whimpered. 'Please, let me go.'

She knew, however, there was no reasoning with the creatures. By surrendering to temptation, she had sought their attention. Through a lapse of will she became theirs.

And, maybe she had always been theirs.

With this realisation, she peered up to watch both of the squirrels, even the one without a head, transform into tiny creatures. After which, they blinked, smiled, and scurried back to join their fellow folk with eyes glistening like stars breaking through a cloudy night or dewdrops on the early morning grass.

The incident at the park had been an illusion; a faerie glamour.

She knew this now. A scenario planted in her mind so she might be fearful, crave comfort, and seek a place to feel safe. Faeries defended animals. They protected nature. They never killed it. People killed nature. People like Daddy, Lauren, and Mummy, who were more concerned with destroying the planet so they could buy a fancy sports car, or sweat-shop-made clothes, or whatever it took to impress the snooty women at the Westbourne Grove Ladies' Forum.

The humming grew louder.

At the front of the assembly of creatures, the charred girls skipped and spun, and, with every step, the voices grew more excited. More tiny creatures came out from the shadows. Some approached and gathered around the girls. The rest bunched to each side of Curiosity, their shrivelled bodies swaying in time with the dance. She sensed no malice in their actions. They seemed calm and friendly, like brothers and sisters welcoming a lost sibling back to their fold.

Unlike these tortured girls, she was one of them.

She belonged here.

In this underground place she had found her true and eternal home.

THIRTY-NINE – Concerning they who do little but see much

Later that night, having seen a report on the television news, Brendan Cassidy put on his raincoat and rushed to Rosina Portland's house. For years he had kept an eye on this ragged, little bunch. He reckoned himself as more of a guardian than keeper of the garden. The person who watched over the family's wellbeing as much as he did the lawns, the flower-beds, or even the desolate dell with a history older than any occupant of the house had family to remember.

Given the present circumstances, however, he now felt wanting in the title, weighed down by the burden of having been less than diligent at his post.

His prayers had been unheard, or ignored. Maybe the Lord did that. Ignore prayers that were made because the petitioner was too cowardly to do the right thing.

Either way, he had failed Rosina and her daughter. He should have come back and insisted harder that she take Curiosity and run from this place. He should have dragged them both out and set a torch to that accursed dell.

Now it was too late and, as he looked upon the smouldering, burned out husk of Lily Warren and Rosina Portland's once magnificent home, the burden of his guilt weighed even heavier. Its ruddy brick was blackened with soot. The floors and woodwork hunched like defeated soldiers standing destitute amid the rainy haze of a lost battle.

Curiosity's *witch's hat roof* had collapsed inwards. Where the front door and bay windows had been, a large fissure had opened up. Only the chimney-stacks at each end of the roof remained intact, like lofty bureaucrats glowering down on the results of all the bad choices that Lily and Rosina had made. Even the peaked turret to the rear had foundered, leaving a direct sightline all the way to the great oak and dell at the end of the garden.

The fire crews were still present; gathering their hoses and equipment. White suited personnel combed through the charred wood and collapsed brickwork. Acacia Okeke was there too. She seemed daunted to see him and shied away as if, like him, she carried guilt or was fearful to go too close to the house.

He walked across to where she stood by the open front gates.

'So, you saw the news as well then?' he asked.

'I have to be here,' she replied. 'The station called me. Rosina Portland and her daughter's names were in my profile reports. They want me to be here in case they turn up – hopefully alive – whereby I can find out what exactly happened. I don't hold out much hope, though.'

'Are you okay?'

'No.'

'Did you see them again?'

She didn't answer.

'Did you pray?' he asked.

She didn't answer that either.

'Did you pray?' he asked again but with greater insistence.

'I did pray,' she said. 'I prayed a lot. It wasn't enough.'

'No. It wasn't,' he said soulfully.

'Anyway, I have to go. They need me to interview the neighbours.' She turned and walked off, before stopping and glancing back. 'I won't bother you again, Brendan,' she said. 'And there was nothing either of us could have done.'

He offered her weak smile. In his heart he knew she was wrong.

She walked away, with a hunch to her shoulders that looked to be the start of something permanent. Brendan gazed up at the fallen down house and, plucking up the courage, went through the gate. A metre into the front garden, a policeman stopped him and escorted him back out to the street.

'You can't come here,' the policeman said. 'It's a crime scene.'

'I'm the family gardener,' Brendan said, and the policeman asked him questions:

How much petrol was there in the shed?

Who had the key?

And did he know anything about the mental state of Mrs Portland?

He answered as best he could. There were three containers of petrol for the lawnmower. The shed was always kept unlocked. And, it was beyond his responsibilities as gardener to speculate on anything else.

He lied about the last one.

Brendan Cassidy speculated on a lot of things with regard to Rosina Portland, so much so that, if only to quell a nagging sense of dread, while the fire crews loaded equipment onto their vehicles and the policeman joined Acacia Okeke to interview neighbours, he slipped through the gate, around to the back garden, and walked through the rain to the dell.

He didn't run. Partly to avoid attracting attention, but mostly because he feared what he might find.

Had he waited too long for Rosina to remember?

When he'd called on Sunday, should he have stayed with them instead of going to Mass?

The questions rumbled through his mind like boulders rolling down a mountain of remorse, growing in urgency and increasing his panic as he reached and pushed his way through the undergrowth.

At the spot where his beloved Lily had breathed her last he saw grey smoke, wispy like those rising from the ruined house at the top of the garden. The wisps coalesced, became humanlike with an arm, hand, and finger pointing downwards to the pool. Floating on the murky water there was a lump of sorts, much like a football, almost unperceivable in the dim light, caked with dead leaves, and crawling with insects.

He touched it with his foot.

The lump bobbed, turned over and, revealed by a shaft of silver moonlight, Jeremy Portland's face stared up at him.

FORTY – Concerning the full circle

So, dear reader, we have reached the concluding pages of this remorseful tale.

The story has been told. The lessons maybe learned. And I heartily wish you only good fortune as you contemplate the myriad of living things that call this ball of rock, earth, and verdure home.

Yet, as I send you out perhaps a wiser, more curious individual, I think it fair to apprise you of the final occurrence to befall this unfortunate family.

You see, as I walked up Westbourne Grove, I saw her sitting against the derelict building that was once called The Grotto Toy Shop. Her clothes were soaking wet and she, a dejected looking soul squeezed into an undersized white ballet tutu and fairy wings, her eyes fixed upon some imaginary spot burrowed deep beneath the rain-soaked pavement.

People passed. Most turned their heads in alarm. Some good sorts even stopped to enquire about her wellbeing.

Overhead the clouds gathered, a thunderclap shook the sky, and the rain became a downpour.

The onlookers scattered, and I intervened.

I'm like that.

I have a big heart.

The passers-by left me to my undertaking. Humankind can be such a trusting breed. And, through it all, Rosina just sat, seemingly unaware of the attention drawn to her, the hollow shell of the old toy shop and dance studio a painful reminder of the horrific, fantastical events she once witnessed there.

And believe me, that building was indeed fantastical.

How else did it remain all these years in its derelict state, below the radar of the diligent councillor, hidden from the glare of an avaricious estate-agent?

Like the dell, this spot had history, a legacy born in a time when the creatures mentioned in this tale held sway over all. They were and are a capable bunch, these orphic entities of the forest, with the power to create, to change, to conceal, to hide, to wait, and apt to pop up anywhere should the eye not discern them, or the mind wander such as they manifest in some dark corner of a room.

As for poor Rosina – who lost everything to their influence – I think, in forlorn hope, she came to this place to play out the final chapter by her terms. By donning the ballet costume, she hoped to confront the place where her childhood ended and her nightmares began. But, as with all things in nature, lives and loves are bound by the eternal triplets: cause, effect, and balance, each of which, if not monitored and nurtured, are apt to invite disaster.

Most maintain these with dedication, and face up to life's duties with vigour and responsibility. Others, however – those of weaker will – fudge their obligations in an attempt to discover some effortless solution in order to shirk the challenges that life throws at them.

They don't indulge in the lesson.

Earlier that evening, when Rosina entered her home and noticed her ex-husband sitting at the kitchen counter, one might think they saw affection in her surprise.

Her eyes lit up.

She smiled.

I now know, however, that her affection was excitement, bolstered by malicious intent because, in her hand, she still clutched the page from the attic, its heinous yet hopeful suggestions rolling and maturing within her mind. Jeremy was to be her effortless solution. His unexpected gesture to familial duty rebuffed, severed, along with his head, on the edge of one of her Japanese steel carving knives.

Sadly, her efforts were in vain.

Her offering was rejected. Curiosity didn't return.

A few hours later, with her triumph home destroyed in the blaze started by her own hand, here she sat on Westbourne Grove, drenched with rain, and watching blood stream down her arms from the self-inflicted wound her neck. Yet, even in this final sacrifice she failed to show true commitment. Her attempt at suicide had resulted in little more than a superficial scratch.

I approached her.

For this task, I chose the appealing form of Robin Goodfellow. A chap I utilised at length in the medieval and Victorian periods, and someone I thought she might recognise from one salacious encounter nine odd years before.

At other times, I favour the form of a black tomcat.

You might be familiar with me. I have a white patch on my chest and can be seen with one leg drooping over the edge of an old shed, or atop a fence post, or mewling at your patio door begging for a scrap or to curl up by a warm fire.

For the most, however, I am simply the púca or Puck.

The teller of tales. The story weaver and father to those select few who have delusions that they are fully of this world but are really the lost ones, the different ones, the indigo, crystal, and star children . . . my offspring of the fae.

When I reached Rosina, I bent down and lifted the bloodied knife from her lap.

As I did so, I offered her a look of reassurance.

Her eyes widened. She smiled and took my hand.

With the rain-soaked spectators looking on, I escorted Rosina Portland, nee-Warren, back up Bingham Crescent to her ruined home, past the fire people and police officers to the end of the garden, and onward, unseen by Brendan Cassidy, into the bushes where she would spend as long as we deemed necessary in repentance for how she treated her daughter, together with us . . . deep inside the dell.

EPILOGUE – Concerning the never-ending tale

Today was Francesca Purview's birthday. She was eight years old, and sat on the garden swing scraping holes in the ground with the heels of her shoes. It was supposed to be a special day. It was supposed to be *her* day, with a cake, candles, chocolate milk, and maybe even caramel swirl ice-cream in a bowl with wafers, hundreds and thousands, and thick, sticky strawberry sauce. But, both Daddy and Mummy had emergency meetings at work, and Janice the housekeeper didn't have time to play because of too much washing, ironing, and many other duties that meant Francesca was all alone.

Everything was quiet in the garden, with no breeze. A squirrel, struggling to carry a large chestnut, scrambled up the trunk of a tree and a pigeon did a poo down the wall of the garden summer house but, other than that, nothing stirred. Not even the leaves piled by the swimming-pool pump house.

She was bored.

Her parents hadn't bought her any presents either, saying – before they left – that they would work something out when they returned home from their jobs.

'Maybe we can go out for a meal,' Daddy had said, 'if I can get away early enough.'

Mummy nodded agreement, and smiled, before she looked at her watch and said, 'Good Lord, is that the time? See you later, Sweetie. Be good for Janice.'

Daddy winked and they both hurried out the front door and into their cars.

Usually, on Francesca's birthday, her friend Beatrice called by, but, two months ago, Beatrice's parents moved to Surrey, which was far, far away from Notting Hill and, apart from one video-chat, she hadn't talked to her since.

Maybe she had forgotten. Or had a new friend and didn't like her anymore.

The garden gate swung open and a girl wearing red baseball boots, a ballet tutu and fairy wings came through. She had freckles and curly red hair. A scruffy, black and white cat walked by her side.

Approaching the swing, the girl suddenly spun a full circle and skipped for a few steps.

She stopped. The cat stopped too, sat down, thrust a back leg into the air and began licking its behind.

Francesca chuckled.

The girl laughed too, and asked, 'So, do you believe in fairies?'

Take care sweet child, don't wander near,

To darkened groves through freak or fear,

For deep within that ragged ground,

Some awful fate mayhap be found.

Acknowledgements

Thank you to my wife, Lynsey, who is my first and constant reader, to my family and friends, who are always there for me, and to my daughter and son-in-law, Emma and Niall, for their unending encouragement.

A special thanks goes to the guys at *Fire Hornet Codex*, without whom this book would never have made it to print:
Marg, who – as always – gave the final go-ahead for publication.
Brett and Sandra, for their keen eyes and editorial insights.

To my teachers (from many many moons ago) who introduced me to Celtic folklore and laid the foundations for what transpired in this book.

And, finally, to my late, dear friend, Sal Nensi, who pushed me forward. You are missed.

About the Author

Martin Treanor enjoys all things historical, archaeological and metaphysical, with a strong interest in quantum physics which he likes to introduce into his books and stories. He has a fondness for the dark and macabre.

Over the years Martin has worked as a university technician, trade union representative, engineering tutor, lift installer, labourer, bar manager, bookseller, and a writer.

Other works include his conspiracy mystery, *The Logos Prophecy (Fall of Ancients Book 1)*, his illustrated, political satire series, *The Tales of Trumplethinskin*, his urban fantasy novel, *Hellmaw: Dark Creed*, released as part of *DnD Forgotten Realms* creator Ed Greenwood's *Hellmaw* series, and his Amazon best-selling in metaphysical fiction, debut novel, *The Silver Mist*.

From Ireland, Martin now lives in Lisbon, Portugal with his wife Lynsey and their overdramatic but insanely adorable cat, Kitty.

MartinTreanor.Com

www.ingramcontent.com/pod-product-compliance
Ingram Content Group UK Ltd.
Pitfield, Milton Keynes, MK11 3LW, UK
UKHW041445161224
3696UKWH00034B/192